DK small business guides

starting
your
business

small business *guides*

starting your business

PETER HINGSTON

A Dorling Kindersley Book

Dorling **DK** Kindersley

LONDON, NEW YORK, SYDNEY, DELHI, PARIS,
MUNiCH, and JOHANNESBURG

Project Editor Mark Wallace
Senior Art Editor Jamie Hanson
DTP Designer Julian Dams
US Editors Gary Werner, Margaret Parrish
US Consultant John Woods
Production Controller Michelle Thomas

Senior Managing Editor Stephanie Jackson
Managing Editor Adèle Hayward
Senior Managing Art Editor Nigel Duffield

Produced for Dorling Kindersley by
Grant Laing Partnership
48 Brockwell Park Gardens,
London SE24 9BJ

Managing Editor Jane Laing
Project Editor Jane Simmonds
Project Art Editor Christine Lacey
Picture Researcher Jo Walton

First American Edition, 2001

00 01 02 03 04 05 10 9 8 7 6 5 4 3 2 1

Published in the United States by
Dorling Kindersley Publishing, Inc.
95 Madison Avenue
New York, New York 10016

Library of Congress Cataloging-in-Publication Data

Hingston, Peter.
Starting your business / Peter Hingston.
p. cm. -- (Small business guides)
Includes index.
ISBN 0-7894-7199-X (alk. paper)
1. New business enterprises--Management. I. Title. II. Series.
HD62.5 .H56 2001
658.1'1--dc21

00-053105

Colour reproduction in Italy by GRB Editrice
Printed and bound by Mondadori in Verona, Italy

see our complete catalog at

www.dk.com

CONTENTS

INTRODUCTION

S tarting your own business is a huge step to take, and is likely to herald a major change in the direction of your life. This book is a comprehensive and, above all, practical guide to planning, starting, and running your own business.

A large part of the process is learning the hard way; *Starting Your Business* will prepare you for some of the possible pitfalls ahead. But becoming an entrepreneur can also be fun: you will learn a broad range of skills and deal with people and situations you have never encountered before. Finally, starting and running a successful business can be a uniquely fulfilling experience: you may be putting your dreams into action, providing employment for others, and creating a life for yourself where you make the decisions.

This book takes you through the process – from getting to know how your own skills and abilities equip you for running your business, and developing your initial business idea, to making your plans more concrete and raising the money you will need. Finding premises and staff are covered, along with

ways of selling and marketing, both at home and abroad. Financial aspects of running your business are discussed in detail, including day-to-day preparing of financial statements and dealing with financial problems. Long-term plans are also dealt with – whether you want your business to keep expanding into new areas or simply to provide a means for your retirement. The final section of the book is an up-to-date guide to all the legal and financial matters likely to affect a small business. There are suggestions for useful contacts and further reading, plus a glossary.

Starting Your Business is suitable for the self-employed (sole proprietors), those in partnerships, and incorporated companies, and for all types of businesspeople, including caterers, consultants, contractors, designers, exporters, hotel owners, internet firms, manufacturers, mechanics, those providing office services, and retailers. Time is precious when you are starting a business: this book can be read from cover to cover, or you can dip into the relevant sections as you need to. Due to the many complexities involved when starting or running a business, you would benefit from taking sound professional advice before making any important decisions.

BEFORE
you start

Some of the most important decisions concerning your new business need to be made long before you have your first customer. The key to building a sound, viable business is to combine thorough research with careful, detailed planning, covering every aspect of the business – from developing your initial idea, to finding the financing, to locating new premises.

DOING THE GROUNDWORK

Starting your own business, be it a modest part-time undertaking or a major enterprise, can be one of life's important milestones. Before you set out on such a great adventure, it is important to establish whether starting a business is likely to be the right step for you. Being your own boss, and maybe that of other people, does not suit everybody, but if it suits you you are unlikely to want to work for anyone else again. This chapter includes three self-assessments to help you understand your motivation, your personal attributes, and your business skills and knowledge.

Most people's life experiences do not equip them fully to understand the implications of being self-employed. The main exceptions are those people born into families that run their own businesses and, to some degree, those who have been involved in sales. Working in a large organization gives you little idea of what it will be like to be your own boss, and working in the public sector helps even less. Starting your own business is not like changing your job – the differences are more profound and far-reaching. It is vital, therefore, to take the time to think about the reality and the consequences of starting your own business, and to assess and define exactly what you hope to achieve on a number of levels – including the personal, professional, and financial.

Be realistic about your strengths and weaknesses, and try to remedy the weaknesses

Ask yourself why you want to start your own business. Is it because you have always wanted to be your own boss? Is it because a friend suggested it? Is it because you are unhappy in your current job? Do you feel that you have something to prove? Whatever the reason for wanting to start your own business, be completely honest with yourself because, once you have set the wheels in motion, it will become increasingly difficult to back out without loss of capital, loss of face, and possibly the loss of any paid employment.

Having clear goals and ambitions that you are eager to fulfill is a great first step on the road to starting your own business. Work through the questions in the self-assessment exercise opposite to explore and analyze your own personal goals and motivations further.

CASE STUDY: Making the Most of Experience

ALISON WAS laid off after the branch of the bank where she was employed closed down. She enjoyed working on her own and found the idea of being her own boss very appealing; starting a business with her severance pay seemed a natural option. In her banking work, Alison had been involved in introducing internet banking for customers and latterly had been responsible for liaising with the branch's business clients. As she enjoyed these aspects of her work, she decided to set up as a business consultant specializing in e-commerce. She could operate from home, and the low start-up costs and flexibility suited her. Although her existing skills and knowledge formed a good starting point, she signed up for a course in selling to brush up on her sales technique.

ASSESSING YOUR GOALS

Completing this questionnaire will help you to determine whether starting your own business is the right move for you. It is not a test that you either pass or fail; the questions instead prompt you to assess your life goals. Take your time and think about each one before answering "Yes" or "No," then read the comment that follows. By the end of the questionnaire, you should have a clearer idea of what motivates you, and how this equips you to run your own business.

Have you always wanted to run your own business? ☐ Y ☐ N

Having a long-held ambition to run your own business will help you get through difficult patches, and you are more likely to succeed in the end.

Do you know what work you would like to be doing in five or 10 years? ☐ Y ☐ N

You need to take a long-term view, since it will take several years for the business to become established.

Do you want to work on your own? ☐ Y ☐ N

Starting a business can be a lonely experience, and it does not suit everyone. There tends to be less social contact than when working as an employee.

Do you want to be the boss? ☐ Y ☐ N

You will probably answer "Yes" to this question, but have you ever held a position of responsibility in a business or a club? Would you be happier working as a team member?

Is a career of less importance to you than other ambitions? ☐ Y ☐ N

If you are career-orientated, then self-employment is probably not for you.

Do you want to realize your full potential? ☐ Y ☐ N

Self-employment requires far more skills than many people realize. It will stretch you to the fullest, since you will probably have to do all the work associated with your business, especially in the early years.

Do you think you will have a better quality of life running your own business? ☐ Y ☐ N

Although you will undoubtedly work longer hours, particularly at the outset, most self-employed people feel their quality of life improves.

Do you expect to earn a lot of money? ☐ Y ☐ N

You will probably answer "Yes" to this question. Although some people start a business with the sole intention of making money, most seek independence and a better quality of life. This is just as well, since it usually takes several lean years of business before a successful business becomes established and adequately profitable.

Would you like a greater degree of financial security? ☐ Y ☐ N

Although you will probably answer "Yes" to this question, you may believe that being self-employed will give you less financial security. At first this is usually the case but in the long term it is possible that you will have more security working for yourself as you will have greater control over your own destiny.

Do you have a specific business idea you would like to see become a reality? ☐ Y ☐ N

Some people just want "to start a business", while others want to see their pet idea – a new product or business concept – become a reality. Experience shows the latter tend to be more motivated and likely to succeed.

RESULTS

If most of your answers to this questionnaire are "Yes," then it is a good indicator that starting a business might be the right step for you. If the majority of your answers are "No," think again about exactly what you hope to gain from starting your own business.

What is it Really Like?

Do you know what it is really like to own and run a small business? If not, take a methodical approach and find out as much as you can about the pros and cons. You may feel that you want to get started right away, but, as any experienced entrepreneur will tell you, it is better to proceed with caution, taking small steps to avoid any major missteps.

STUDYING EXISTING BUSINESSES

First, you could talk to anyone you know who is already self-employed. The best people to approach are family or friends, since they will take the time to talk to you, be candid about their own experiences, discuss your project, and give advice. Do not just focus on the good points – note and ask more about any downsides or pitfalls. Individual relatives or friends may even be prepared to act as mentors to guide you through the whole process.

Every day you will come into contact with people who run their own businesses, such as your local bookseller, nursery owner, taxi driver, hairdresser, and so on. They may not have time to sit and chat with you but are often happy to answer a few questions and generally give their opinions on self-employment. Later, note down what you learned from them. Bear in mind, though, that you may have to read between the lines: you are their customer, and they might feel they should provide a positive view, or want to give the impression that their business is a great success. They may even quote their turnover to you (if it is impressive), but they are likely to be more reticent about their actual profits, which are much more relevant to you.

To get a sense of what running your business might be like, try to visit a similar sort of establishment. This is easiest if you are thinking of starting a business with open access to the public, such as a shop, café, or small hotel. Walk in and look around. Look at the staff, the customers, the decor, and any stock. Can you imagine yourself running all this? If so, is there anything you would do differently? Would you enjoy the responsibility and the work on a daily basis? Try also to imagine the work that will be needed behind the scenes. If your proposed business is office-based or requires an industrial unit, it will be more difficult to experience. Some offices and industrial units may have open days or outer offices to which you can gain access, or you may be able to visit a friend who is employed in a similar workplace to get a feel for actually owning the business.

READING UP

Autobiographies or biographies of successful entrepreneurs can also provide valuable insights. Most started from nothing and ran small businesses to begin with, and it is revealing to learn which personal characteristics helped their businesses to survive and prosper. Many of their initial trials and mistakes are common to all businesses. Luck often plays a part, but is usually combined with qualities such as an ability to spot an opportunity, a dogged determination to succeed, and, in some cases, the use of clever or innovative ideas. Look at the assessment opposite to see which of the relevant attributes you possess.

LOOKING AT MISCONCEPTIONS

MYTH	REALITY
You will make lots of money.	Some do, some do not; most just manage.
You will have fewer work problems.	There will be a greater variety of problems – some serious.
You will have more spare time.	Most work longer hours and have fewer vacations than they would if they were not self-employed.

Assessing Your Personal Attributes

Read each of the following questions and then decide which of the answers best describes yourself. The questions are not in any order of importance. Score 4 points for each A answer, 2 points for each B answer, and 0 points for each C answer. Add up your scores then look at the assessments in the Results panel at the bottom.

Are you able to concentrate?
A I can concentrate on one thing for long periods. ☐
B I am able to concentrate for some time. ☐
C I am not too good at concentrating. ☐

Are you enthusiastic?
A I get quite excited about things. ☐
B I am guardedly enthusiastic. ☐
C I rarely get excited about things. ☐

Are you a risk taker?
A I like to minimize my risks. ☐
B I am happy taking risks – personal or financial. ☐
C I do not like taking any risks. ☐

Are you creative?
A I enjoy thinking up new ideas. ☐
B I find new things interesting. ☐
C I do not think creativity is one of my attributes. ☐

Are you decisive?
A I like to make decisions. ☐
B I make decisions only if I have to. ☐
C I hesitate because I am not sure what is right. ☐

Are you determined?
A Once I start something, I like to see it through. ☐
B I try hard but eventually stop if things are not working. ☐
C I really cannot see the point of trying too hard. ☐

Are you good at math?
A I enjoy making calculations, some without a calculator. ☐
B I will work things out if I have to. ☐
C I am not very confident at math. ☐

Are you happy working long hours?
A I am used to working evenings and some weekends. ☐
B I do not mind working some evenings or weekends. ☐
C I prefer not to work evenings or weekends. ☐

Are you self-confident?
A I am happy to talk to new people in a business context. ☐
B I have to force myself to approach new people. ☐
C I do not really know – previously, I have rarely needed to approach new people. ☐

Are you well organized?
A I usually have lists to work through, and I set deadlines. ☐
B I do not like to be disorganized. ☐
C I sometimes forget to do things, or I do them late. ☐

Results

0–10 points
Are you really sure you are ready to run your own business? Think again about whether you are likely to be happy working for yourself.

12–20 points
You have strengths and weaknesses. You might consider involving someone else who has complementary attributes.

22–30 points
Although you have many attributes that make you suited to running your own business, you have a few weaknesses. Think about and improve upon the areas where you scored the lowest.

32–40 points
Your personal attributes seem well suited to running your own business.

ECONOMIC CONSIDERATIONS

When considering what it is like to start your own business, an immediate and significant aspect is the economic one. When you start a business there is no regular pay check, and you will probably have to plunder your savings to fund the new venture. On the day you start up you may be rich in enthusiasm and ideas, but if you were previously an employee you are likely to be poorer financially than you have been for a long time.

Make sure that your plans include an escape route

Ideally, where there are two people involved in starting a business, try to arrange matters so that one remains in relatively secure paid employment while the other works to set up the business. In this way there is continuing and predictable income to support domestic and other regular expenditures. At some future date the two people can decide when the new business is ready to support them both. This is a common start-up strategy. For more information on starting a new business as a sole proprietor, in a partnership, or as a corporation, see pp. 162–4.

INVOLVING OTHERS

As part of your pre-start preparations, you should discuss your ideas with all those who might be affected. This may not be relevant if you are single. If you have a partner and/or dependants, you need to discuss the ramifications of your decision to go it alone at some length and on several different occasions. They need to understand exactly what you are planning to do, the risks you will be taking, and how this could affect them should things get difficult. You need to assess whether you have their full support, which is vital. If your business is going to be home-based, either temporarily or permanently, this can introduce a whole new range of problems and strains. For more information about working from home, or choosing other premises, such as shops, offices, industrial units, or workshops, see pp. 68–75.

LIFESTYLE ASPECTS

A related issue is the lifestyle that you (and your family) are prepared to accept. This should be taken into account at a very early stage. Depending on the type of business you are intending to operate, your new lifestyle may involve financial anxiety and long or erratic working hours.

■ **SHOPS** These often have large stock, onerous leases (if rented), and may suffer from staffing problems. On the other hand, retail is a cash business – your customers do not expect any credit. Opening hours are set, but you have to be there to open up, whatever happens. Hours can also be very long – a shop or newsstand, for example, demands a seven-day week with a very early start to the day, and possibly a late finish too. If you want to take a vacation, you may need either to close down while you are away or arrange for someone else to run the shop.

■ **MANUFACTURERS** These businesses may suffer from customers who take many months to pay (or never do). Some firms supply only one or two large companies and as such are vulnerable if they lose a major customer, and most have to operate on small margins. However, at least you can close the door and go home on a Friday evening (even if you take some paperwork with you).

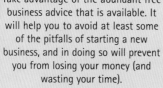

MONEY SAVER

Take advantage of the abundant free business advice that is available. It will help you to avoid at least some of the pitfalls of starting a new business, and in doing so will prevent you from losing your money (and wasting your time).

BALANCING WORK AND HOME LIFE

Whether you are working from home, or bringing work home, starting a small business is likely to have an impact on all aspects of your life, and demand large amounts of your time, at least until the venture is up and running.

■ **SERVICE BUSINESSES** Some have the advantages of requiring little stock and low overheads and are quick to start up. These are also frequently the type of business that have fierce competition or are readily copied by competitors. Customers may expect the phone to be answered when they have a problem, even at 9 p.m. or on the weekend – or you may choose to offer this service to gain the edge over competitors.

These lifestyle aspects need full consideration, as they will be with you for the lifetime of your business. Since your waking hours will be spent predominantly working in your new business, then you need to get it right. Once you have started a business you will be fully committed, and it is not easy to escape if you suddenly realize that you are unhappy and this is not what you had planned on doing.

THE APPEAL OF INDEPENDENCE

Everyone who starts a business thinks they will succeed, but in fact around one in three will close their business within a few years. Although some will give up without much distress, for others it will involve a great deal of pain and disillusionment. There is no sense in thinking "it will not happen to me": you should always plan a course of action for damage minimization should things not work out as hoped.

On the other hand, ask anyone who runs their own business if they made the right decision and their reply will usually be "yes." Many of those who fail try again at a later date. More surprisingly, even those people who work longer hours for less financial reward than they would have as an employee usually choose to remain their own boss. Many say it is the independence that self-employment provides that holds the essential appeal.

Business Skills and Knowledge

When you start your own business you need to have not only the right personal qualities, but also sufficient business skills and knowledge. Many people think that all they need is the technical or trade skills and experience to succeed in business, but in fact it is probably more important to have general business skills and knowledge. Why is this the case? The reasons are many but experience has shown that small businesses thrive or fail principally due to general business reasons rather than to the technical or trade skills of the proprietors. This assumes that your technical or trade abilities are at least adequate for your proposed business – only you will know if this is true. Although your skills are central to the success of your business, there is plenty of help on hand from other quarters, some in the form of free advice, and some from paid experts.

LEARNING NEW SKILLS
Before you start, and once your business is underway, take the time to update and supplement your knowledge by undertaking courses and training.

KEY SKILLS

Although a multitude of skills are needed to run a business, there are two that seem to lie at the core of business success:

■ **THE ABILITY TO SELL** Whether you are in a service, retail, or manufacturing business, this is essential. From the start you will need to sell your business and business plan to potential backers, and, once you are up and running, selling will bring in and maintain the revenues. Selling also incorporates negotiating skills, which are essential for giving you a financial edge, but also help generally in dealings with people.

■ **AN UNDERSTANDING OF MONEY** This has implications in all aspects of a business, from how to price your goods or services, to recognizing a good deal from a bad one, and being able to keep the finances of the business in good shape.

The actual breadth and depth of knowledge required to survive in business is quite surprising to the uninitiated. Have a look at the self-assessment exercise opposite and test yourself to see how you rate. The good news about business knowledge is that it can be learned. Although a natural talent is an advantage, all of us can learn to do a good job if we are interested and motivated by the need to succeed in business. Many colleges provide training courses for small businesses, which are often run as evening classes. Subjects covered in these classes include bookkeeping, computer skills, marketing, and sales.

ASKING THE EXPERTS

In addition to strengthening your own skills, there are many other organizations and people you can call upon. These include:

■ **ACCOUNTANTS** Consult an accountant when setting up a business and to help with your tax returns. Accountants can help enormously with your business plan and in setting up good accounting systems. Choose carefully to find an accountant you are happy with who charges a reasonable fee.

■ **BANK MANAGERS** Banks have a good range of business knowledge and are willing to advise small businesses. Keep them abreast of any developments.

■ **BUSINESS DEVELOPMENT ORGANIZATIONS** Most of these organizations can answer your questions or put you in touch with the right person. Their advice is usually free.

■ **GOVERNMENT TAX OFFICES** Many of your straightforward tax questions can be answered by the appropriate tax office.

■ **LOCAL GOVERNMENT** Government offices often run workshops and have experts who can advise on planning and licensing.

■ **LAWYERS** Consult a lawyer before you start up, before you take over new premises, and on other legal questions.

ASSESSING YOUR BUSINESS SKILLS AND KNOWLEDGE

Read each of the following questions and select the answer that best describes yourself. Score 4 points for each A answer, 2 points for each B answer, and 0 points for each C. Add up your scores then read the Results panel at the bottom.

Do you understand your market?
A I have worked in this market for a long time. ☐
B I have some experience in this market. ☐
C I have no experience in this particular market. ☐

Do you know about marketing?
A I have a lot of experience in marketing, advertising, etc. ☐
B I have some experience in marketing. ☐
C I do not really know about marketing. ☐

Do you have sales skills?
A I am an experienced sales professional. ☐
B I have done some selling in the past. ☐
C I have never sold anything before.* ☐
   (Score 1 point if you have negotiated a good sale price for your own car.)*

Do you have experience dealing with customers?
A I have had to deal with customers for several years. ☐
B I have had to deal with customers on occasion. ☐
C I have never had to deal directly with customers. ☐

Do you have knowledge of business taxes?
A I have a good working knowledge of the relevant taxes. ☐
B I have some idea as to what taxes apply. ☐
C I do not know what taxes there are. ☐

Do you have bookkeeping knowledge?
A I understand double-entry bookkeeping. ☐
B I know a bit about single-entry bookkeeping. ☐
C I do not know how to do bookkeeping. ☐

Do you have knowledge of business budgets?
A I have been responsible for budgets and costings. ☐
B I have helped with budgets and/ or costings. ☐
C I do not know how to do budgets and costings.* ☐
   (Score 1 point if you have done domestic budgets satisfactorily.)*

Do you have knowledge of business laws?
A I know the laws that apply to my business. ☐
B I know about some of the laws. ☐
C I really do not know which laws apply. ☐

Do you have experience of managing staff?
A I have been a manager for many years. ☐
B I have had to supervise staff for several years. ☐
C I have little or no experience in managing staff.* ☐
   *(*Score 1 point if you have led a sports team or club.)*

Do you have computer skills?
A I have good computer skills and knowledge of e-commerce. ☐
B I have some computer skills. ☐
C I have few or no computer skills.* ☐
   *(*Score 1 point if you have access to a computer at home.)*

RESULTS

0–10 points
You have a lot to learn even before you start your own business.

11–20 points
Although you have some skills and knowledge, you still have much to learn.

21–30 points
Your skills and knowledge may be reasonable, but find ways of filling the gaps.

31–40 points
Your business skills and knowledge appear to be satisfactory, but don't be complacent.

GETTING INTO THE RIGHT BUSINESS

Once you have decided that starting your own business suits your abilities and is what you really want to do, then you need to consider what sort of business you are going to run. In fact you may have thought initially of the business you wanted to start and then considered if it was the right step for you. This chapter looks at ways of finding a good business idea if you are starting from scratch, then covers some options for going into business using an existing framework: by direct sales, investing in a franchise, or buying a business that is already up and running.

The basis of your business is a business idea – one that is likely to be viable and, when put into practice, will give you a good quality of life in more than just financial terms. You might think that coming up with such an idea is purely a matter of inspiration, with the lucky entrepreneur waking up in the middle of the night with the plan fully formed that will make him or her into a millionaire. That happens on the odd occasion, but it is the exception rather than the rule. Often chance throws out a business opportunity, but the real skill is in recognizing it when it happens and then having the courage to do something about it.

Keep your focus on finding a product or service for which there is a market

Deciding what your business is going to do usually requires a good deal of hard thought and careful research. When you have come up with a business idea, subject it to broad and detailed scrutiny; develop the idea as far as you can to get a feel of its essential viability. The importance of finding a business for which there is a market need cannot be stressed too highly. Anyone can start up a business, but if there is not a sufficient need for its products or services then that business will fail – all too many businesses go under simply because there are too few customers. Your business idea will have a better chance of succeeding if you can

CASE STUDY: Starting to Form a Plan

HELEN AND JAMES had wanted to start a business together for some time. Helen had worked at management level with a major department store, and James had done a number of jobs using his accounting degree. They both thought there was scope to open a quality gift shop in their town because it was a major tourist destination; with their respective training they felt they had the expertise to make it work. Although they considered the possibility of acquiring a franchise or buying an existing business, neither was available, so they had to start from scratch. This would be more risky but would allow them to plan and do things their own way, which they found appealing. Finding the right site would be one of their biggest challenges.

develop a "unique selling proposition" (or USP) – a product or service that customers cannot obtain elsewhere. The whole business does not need to be unique, but you must offer something that is different, such as the style or speed of your service, or the manner in which you package your products. If your business idea passes this basic test, then you can undertake more detailed market research (see pp. 28–39) to help quantify and remove some of the risk of starting a business.

Think also at this stage about your business status: will you work alone, in a partnership, or as a corporation (see pp. 162–4)?

Starting from Nothing

If you are thinking of setting up in business but have not yet thought of what to do, there are a number of means that you can use to come up with a business idea.

COPYING AN EXISTING IDEA

This is probably the most common way a business idea is conceived. You might see a product or service that is not available locally, and decide that you could fill the gap by introducing it to your area. Almost every shop is an example of this, but there are many other possibilities such as leisure activities, local magazines, and so on. To gain inspiration, you could visit another area or city, or even travel abroad. Towns and cities abroad can be a rich source of business ideas, trends, and products. Take time to walk around the streets, look in the shops, watch the TV commercials, and read the papers and magazines. Of course, not everything that is a success elsewhere will be a success in your area. That is where market research is essential.

One form of copying that is not usually recommended is to mimic an established local business and set up in direct competition. This will work only if you are convinced that the

other business has serious weaknesses and that you can do it much better. You need to be sure that potential customers will back you by changing their allegiance, or that there is room for two such businesses.

SPIN-OFFS FROM WORK

Many new businesses are started by ex-employees who set up to do on their own as consultants or outsourcers what they were doing as employees. Frequently their ex-employer is one of their first customers. Other employees notice a business opportunity in the course of their work. For example, a salesperson might find a need among their customers for something that is not currently being sold. Or a designer working on one product may realize that a variant of that product has quite a different use and so set up a new business to exploit that. Alternatively, he or she might think of a significant improvement to an existing product which, if it were to go

---

DEVELOPING YOUR BASIC BUSINESS IDEA

1 Describe your product or service in as much detail as you can.

2 Be clear about what you are offering that is different from others.

3 Think of your intended market; try to define its limits both geographically and in terms of the types of customers.

4 Look at options for selling your product or service – via a shop, distributors, by telephone, over the internet, and so on.

5 If your business is based on selling a product, will you manufacture it, or find someone else to do so?

6 Think what you may need to start in terms of premises, staff, equipment, finances, and expertise.

7 Be critical of your idea; try to spot and resolve potential flaws.

into production, would take a good share of the market. (Legal advice may be required to avoid infringing on any patents.) Their position gives them inside information, they have the appropriate trade knowledge, and can choose their timing, so the chances of success are good. In some cases the spin-off may benefit their original employer by providing them with a service or product that they need.

Building on Personal Experience

This is often a good way to stumble on to business ideas, a personal experience having revealed a market gap. For example, a pregnant woman might find it hard to buy interesting maternity clothes, and so decide to set up a mail-order clothes business to meet the needs of that market.

Arts and Crafts

Trying to start a profitable business based on your artistic talents is difficult for a number of reasons, including finding enough outlets to distribute your products widely. You will need to allocate enough time for (and, if necessary, develop skills in) selling and distribution in addition to the time needed to produce your creative work. Often an artist or craftsperson may be selling works part-time; it is a big leap to transform this into a full-time livelihood. On the other hand, starting on a part-time basis allows you to develop contacts and assess the potential market.

Inventions

There is a widespread belief that coming up with an original invention will lead to success in business. The fact is that few

Intellectual Property Rights

If you have come up with an invention or new design on which to found your business, it is well worth trying to protect it with a patent or by other legal means. Note that you can only protect something physical; it is not possible to protect an idea.

■ **Patent** A patent gives an inventor the right, for a limited period, to stop others from copying the idea without the inventor's permission. Patents generally relate to products, processes, mechanisms, materials, and so on that contain new functional or technical aspects. To be patentable, an invention must be new, involve an inventive step, be capable of industrial application, and not be on the exclusion list (discoveries, aesthetic creations, and computer programs are all on the list). Meeting these criteria can be difficult and the whole process of taking out a patent

can be costly and complex, particularly the necessary searches to ensure no one has patented a similar invention before. It is advisable to contact a patent attorney at an early stage; look in the Yellow Pages to find your nearest patent agent. Note that patents are territorial, so you have to apply for one in each country where you wish to have your invention protected. Registering a patent discloses your invention publicly to others.

■ **Registered Design** The term "registered design" relates to the outward appearance of an article or a set of articles of manufacture.

An Early Vacuum Cleaner

This Hoover is an example of a patented invention whose name has become synonymous with vacuum cleaners. It is vital to patent such innovations to protect against illegal copying.

businesses start this way, and although some have been hugely successful, it is not an easy path to tread. If you have come up with and designed a new device, this is only the first hurdle. You then need either to find an enthusiastic manufacturer or to raise the funds to manufacture the device yourself, and start to carve out a niche in the marketplace among customers, many of whom are naturally conservative and wary of new things. To launch an innovative product requires substantial promotional or advertising budgets.

BUILDING ON HOBBIES AND SPORTS

Sometimes business opportunities arise from a hobby or sport. In this situation, success requires the entrepreneur to have a fair amount of experience in the sport or activity to know what is required. For example, a model aircraft competition winner might open a model shop. In particular, many good sportsmen and sportswomen use their talents to make money outside of their sport but related to it. Golf professionals, for instance, may open golf shops. Their experience allows them to know what products to stock, their reputation can be used to publicize the enterprise, and their

To be registrable, the design must have significant eye appeal, be new, and not be excluded (for example, a work of sculpture would be on the exclusion list). Again, it is best to contact a patent agent for further information.

■ **TRADEMARK** A trademark can be applied to words, logos, or three-dimensional shapes that can distinguish the products (or services) of a particular business and can be represented graphically. Trademarks provide protection for the goodwill and reputation of a firm. Applications are usually handled by either a patent agent or trademark attorney.

■ **COPYRIGHT** The concept of copyright relates to original literary, dramatic, musical, and artistic works (including paintings, photos, sculptures, works of architecture, technical drawings, maps, and logos), films and sound recordings, computer programs, and material on the internet. Often no registration is required to receive protection of copyright, but it is vital to have proof of the date of origination. Protection is automatic and immediate, but it may be advisable to use the copyright symbol © together with the date the work was first created.

■ **DESIGN RIGHT** Although registering a design gives you the strongest protection, there is automatic "design right" for certain designs, which does not require registration. Unlike copyright, the protection afforded by design right is effective only in the UK. Design right applies to original, noncommonplace designs of the shape or configuration of articles, so two-dimensional designs such as textiles will not qualify, although they would qualify for copyright protection.

advice will be appreciated by customers. There is a risk with this approach that a business is started more for the love of the sport or hobby than to meet a clear market need, and will never earn more than pin money. Bear in mind, too, that some people who have turned their hobby or sport into a business find that, though it works financially, it eventually spoils their love of the activity.

Consider direct sales only if you are self-motivated and gregarious

Starting Up in Direct Sales

One way to start your own business within an existing structure is by direct sales. The process of direct selling is where a manufacturer bypasses the retailer by selling directly to the consumer. These sales are usually made by self-employed people, who are generally home-based and often work part-time. The manufacturers give their salespeople various titles, such as "distributors," "associates," "consultants," or "demonstrators," and these titles are sometimes prefixed by the word "independent." Many products are sold in this way, including clothes, cosmetics, household goods, jewellery, books, and dietary and nutritional products. Almost 90 percent of the sales are made on a person-to-person basis, with the balance being by party plan. Ideally, to enter direct sales, you need to know a lot of people who can be your initial sales contacts.

WARNING SIGNS IN A DIRECT SALES FIRM

1 The company promises that you will "get rich quick."

2 Products are unsellable, unattractive, overpriced, or of poor quality.

3 You would not choose to use their products yourself.

4 It is not clear exactly what you will be getting from the company until you have made an initial payment.

5 Earnings are primarily made by recruitment of new distributors rather than by selling actual products.

6 The company asks you for fixed, regular payments.

7 The company has not been in business for very long.

ADVANTAGES OF DIRECT SELLING

Being involved with a direct sales company has many advantages over setting up a business on your own. Doing the market research, developing and testing new products, planning, pricing, and working out sales techniques are all done by the company. All you need do is to absorb their sales training and sometimes to purchase a starter pack of goods to sell. The sales procedure has been written by experts, so if you follow the training you should, in theory, be able to make sales.

PITFALLS TO AVOID

There are a number of reasons why people have difficulties in making a living from direct sales – that is, they don't make sufficient sales:

■ Not following the company's instructions.

■ Not allowing enough time (you need to commit yourself for as long as 12 months to give it a chance).

■ Becoming disenchanted with the cycle of selling and absorbing the company hype.

■ Working for a company that does not have a code of ethics – this implies an unprofessional attitude and, if goods are shoddy or fail to arrive as promised, end-users become disgruntled.

■ Working for a company that has unsellable goods (a not uncommon problem).

CHOOSING A COMPANY

Joining a direct sales company is usually very easy. The relevant trade associations can give you the names of their member companies, or you may already know a distributor. It is important that you like what the company has to sell and will use the products yourself, rather than just selling them to others.

NETWORK MARKETING

Some, though not all, direct sales companies operate a multilevel system of sales where a salesperson can recruit other salespeople and will then receive bonuses depending on how well their recruits perform. This way of selling is called network marketing (networking) or multilevel marketing (MLM for short), and it

---

HOW IS DIRECT SELLING DONE?

Before getting involved in direct selling, it is important to know the main types of selling and how each one of them works.

■ **DOOR TO DOOR** This type of selling tends to operate by the salesperson leaving a catalog and then returning a few days later hoping to take an order and pick up the catalog. Success tends to rely on repeat business. Typically the salesperson gets about 20 percent commission on each sale.

■ **SELLING TO CONTACTS** This is also known as "personal referral." You find the people who are interested in obtaining the product, visit them, and try to make a sale. The idea is that by making contact before you visit you know they are interested in the product, so it is not "cold calling," and you have a reasonable chance of making a sale. The key is to know a lot of people and be prepared to approach them all. You might contact neighbors, friends, relatives, people who are in clubs that you belong to, people in a religious group of which you are a member, parents of children with yours at school, and (where applicable) contact lists that you receive from your company. Be warned, though, that not everyone likes to be on the receiving end of this form of selling, so choose who you approach carefully.

■ **PARTY PLAN** This form of selling is still sometimes referred to as "Tupperware parties," after the company that first popularized it. A host – the salesperson or a friend of theirs – invites a group of friends and relatives to his or her home. The salesperson (or "demonstrator") brings samples of the items for sale, demonstrates them, and encourages the guests to place orders. Some people who sell in this way prefer to hold stock so the customers can take away their goods. Others take orders and then supply the goods later, collecting the money when the goods are handed over. Party-plan selling relies on good demonstration rather than a hard sell.

DOOR-TO-DOOR SELLING
Some of the most successful door-to-door selling is done when a salesperson has built up a foundation of regular customers to visit.

ASSESSING A FRANCHISE

WHAT TO LOOK FOR

A proven business format that is viable, with advertising support and an operations manual.

The use of a business name and/or trademark.

Training in both trade and business skills.

A contract that clearly defines the rights and obligations of both parties.

Long-term market research to ensure that the business keeps up with marketplace changes.

An exclusive territory large enough to generate sufficient income.

Full support before, during, and after start-up, including ongoing advice and troubleshooting.

WHAT TO AVOID

Only one outlet in the country (the franchise is not fully proven).

Sales pitch based on the success of the franchise in another country.

The franchisor does a hard sell on you.

Huge projected profits from a small setup fee.

Large initial fee.

Claims that there is little selling to do (unlikely).

Territories mapped out, without researching the different areas of the country and their very differing markets.

A dismissive attitude toward competitors.

accounts for about a quarter of total direct sales. It works like this: you sell the products to friends and contacts. One or two of them might think they can sell it to their friends and so agree to become distributors. By recruiting them, you earn bonuses that are dependent on their sales. If those new distributors recruit more people you get a share of their sales bonuses, too. This continues as the network expands. The people who recruit you are called your "uplines," and the people you recruit are your "downlines."

For achieving high sales levels, most direct sales companies have prizes such as holidays, appliances, even cars. This is usually related to recruitment success as well as individual sales. Some people (a small minority) do achieve high incomes from this type of selling, and the companies they work with are huge multi-billion-turnover concerns. Network marketing, along with other aspects of direct selling, is regulated by law (see p. 172).

Investing in a Franchise

In franchising, you copy someone else's business, with their full approval and support, under a license agreement called a franchise. In this the franchise-giver (the franchisor) allows you to use their trade name, provides training and backup, and gives their expertise with all its benefits. In exchange, you as the franchisee have to pay the franchisor an initial fee, then ongoing royalties. The major advantage of this method is that you get into business more quickly and possibly with less risk.

The franchise you take on should be a well-proven business idea; unfortunately, the success of franchising has attracted many unscrupulous businesspeople who are offering franchises of dubious value. There is therefore a need for caution and independent professional advice. Franchising was developed in the US in the 1950s, and many of the well-known franchise names are still American.

HOW DOES FRANCHISING WORK?

Setting up any business takes money, but with a franchise operation it costs you more, because you are also paying for the business experience and proven product or service of the franchisor. In return, they may set up the whole business for you, including taking care of all the legal work, training you and any partners and staff, and helping you to select stock and/or tools. In some cases this handholding is very complete, but you need to decide if the extra cost of a franchise is worthwhile.

The franchisor provides an operations manual, which lays down the whole format of how to run the business. There is also a contract, which forms the basis of the close association between yourself and the franchisor. Check this document very carefully, no matter how well-known the franchisor. Read all of it and ensure you understand it. Ask questions about any part you do not understand. Before you sign it, consult a lawyer – some contracts have hostile clauses that, should you have a problem running the business, are likely to work in favor of the franchisor rather than you.

HOW TO ASSESS A FRANCHISE

Many franchisors are members of a national association, which you can contact for information, and there are a number of franchising magazines available. To meet franchisors, there are various franchise exhibitions held annually. When you have found several franchises that interest you, get their free information packs (also called prospectuses). Each should describe the franchise in detail. If your bank has a franchise unit, get their advice. The next step is to visit the franchisor's head office.

If satisfied so far, ask to see a specimen contract and take it away to read carefully and show it to your attorney. After the meeting, visit at least two of their franchisees (of your own choice) and get their viewpoint. Now do your own market research (see pp. 28–39). You need to find out just how strong the market demand

is for such products or services, what customers think of the franchise, and the strength of the competition in your area.

A common complaint is that franchisors understate the necessary capital to start the business. They sometimes entirely omit your living costs prior to the business making a profit, they may quote a low figure to purchase a secondhand van or other piece of essential equipment, and omit your own legal and accounting fees.

Taking on a franchise does not guarantee success. Some franchises fail altogether, while others do not meet projected turnover figures. A franchisor's membership in a national franchise association does not lessen the need

---

QUESTIONS TO ASK A FRANCHISOR

When you visit a franchisor, ask probing questions – even if some are answered in the prospectus – and note down the answers.

- When was the business established?
- Are they members of the national franchise association? And, if not, why?
- How many outlets are there in the country?
- How many outlets have closed, and why?
- What are the credentials of the people behind the franchise?
- How good is the company's financial performance?
- What is the initial capital required?
- What are the addresses of franchisees you can visit?
- How is the royalty calculated?
- What do you get for your money?
- What ongoing support do they give?
- Are there other charges, e.g. advertising?
- What are the long-term prospects for the franchise?
- What is the length of the agreement and how can it be terminated?
- Who is the competition?

A FRANCHISE
*Pizza Hut is an example of an international franchise.
Many international franchises originate in North
America. Other franchises are on a smaller scale and are
confined to a particular country.*

for careful checking on your part. Even if you
join a good, well-managed, ethical franchise,
your own business could still have problems
due to local competition and business
circumstances. Franchising works for many
thousands of people, but it is essential to
choose your franchise very carefully. Even if it
is successful, the business will require plenty of
hard work and some considerable time to
become established.

Buying an Existing Business

This is a popular way to get into business and
can be highly successful, as it shortcuts
much of the difficult start-up process.
Businesses are sold by word of mouth, and
advertised in local newspapers and trade
publications. Shop sales are also handled by
business transfer agents.

To buy a viable existing business you need to
do your homework thoroughly and to maintain
an open, yet cynical mind. Why cynical?
Because one must examine why a good small
business is being sold. If the business is doing
even reasonably well, it is more likely to be
taken over by a close friend or a member of the
proprietor's family, or the proprietor could
employ a manager. That is not to say that good
or potentially good businesses do not come on
to the market, but you need be fully aware of
what you are taking on and why it is being sold.

First, ensure you are well informed about the
industry and the type of business you are
contemplating taking over. Contact your local
business development office for their advice
and ask if they can put you in touch with a
similar business far enough away so as not to
be in direct competition. Consult books and
trade publications. If you are still interested, the
next step is to value the business for sale.

DOING YOUR RESEARCH

Obtain good advice from an accountant, who
should go through the last few years' financial
statements of the business and explain to you
all the salient features. Be sure you also
understand any tax implications of the purchase.

By buying an existing business you have
access to their real trading figures, so you can
make better cash flow and profit predictions
than if you were starting from scratch. But
business conditions vary constantly and you
must still do thorough market research to
ensure that market conditions are not likely to

vary adversely for the foreseeable future. If there is any existing staff, look carefully at their terms, conditions, and rates of pay as you will have to observe these. If you plan to reduce the number of staff, you could be liable for severance pay.

Inquire fully into the situation regarding the premises. Are the premises owned by the business or rented? If rented, then check the lease carefully (see pp. 69–70). It is essential for a structural survey to be done and to find out if you would be responsible for the repairs and insurance of the building. The surveyor can also comment on the lease prior to you consulting your attorney.

If the business you are buying is a corporation, you will need to obtain excellent legal advice, because when you take on a company (usually by the purchase of a majority of its shares) you take on not only the assets, but also all of its liabilities, which might be substantial. Ideally, and wherever possible, you should aim to acquire the assets rather than the company itself.

VALUING A BUSINESS

Every business has its strengths and weaknesses. In general terms, however, the value of a business (what you have to pay) is the sum of the following four factors:

■ **STOCK** This is best valued independently (not by the seller). All businesses suffer from dead stock – stock that is unlikely to be sold as it is either out of date, damaged, or was never sellable in the first place. The valuation should therefore be the depreciated cost price (not retail price) of the sellable goods.

■ **FIXTURES AND FITTINGS** Again these should be valued independently, taking into account their value after depreciation.

■ **MACHINERY AND EQUIPMENT** This is valued like fixtures and fittings.

■ **GOODWILL** Whereas the above categories can be valued precisely (though may still be subject to disputes), goodwill is the gray area of valuation and is highly negotiable. Goodwill equals the value of the business less the tangible business assets. It is a measure of the momentum of profitability that the business has built up. It should therefore be based on the proven profit of the business, looking at the last few years (since the business may be growing rapidly or declining). If a typical net profit (before-tax) figure can be agreed upon, then the goodwill for a small business can usually be valued at between one and five times the profit figure. The actual multiplier chosen is dependent upon all the other factors involved in the sale, such as the perceived growth potential of the business, any patents or designs owned by the business, the quality and training of staff, and the size of the existing customer base. The larger the business, the greater the multiplier used when calculating the goodwill. If it relates closely to the personality and reputation of the former owner, then part will be lost when he or she leaves, and so the business will be worth less. Note that in simple terms if the goodwill is, for instance, three times the net profit of the business, it will take you three years just to recoup that money, and that assumes the business continues to generate the same profits.

FACT FILE

Depreciation is the amount by which equipment is diminished each year. If depreciation is 25 percent, the depreciated "book value" of a $100 asset will be $75 after one year, $56.25 after two years, and so on. The depreciated value of an item is often less than it might be worth to a buyer, so a balance needs to be struck when valuing a business.

DOING THE MARKET RESEARCH

Armed with your business idea, you need to answer the fundamental questions: "Is there a market for my product (or service), and is it big enough to support me and my business?" Finding the answers takes market research to define the size of the market and its area, and to develop a customer profile. You can then assess whether you will be able to make enough sales to make even a modest living. Other key elements to consider are who the competition is, and why people will come to you instead of your competitors.

Frequently would-be entrepreneurs say "I'm not trying to make a lot of money, just enough to live on." What they may not realize is that just to make enough money to survive might require more sales and success than they had anticipated. For example, assume you want to manufacture a car accessory called a SAYIT device, which you plan to sell through car accessory shops. This particular product attaches to the rear of a vehicle, and when the driver wants to flash a message to the vehicle behind, he or she operates a switch on the dashboard, and the SAYIT lights up the word "Thanks" or "Sorry" as appropriate. The material cost in the device is approximately $10, and if it is wholesaled to the car accessory shops for $12 then the gross profit per unit will be $2. To make the equivalent of a $16,000 wage, you need to sell 8,000 units to make the wage itself, plus probably half again as many to

DETAILED RESEARCH
Market research takes commitment and a methodical approach. Libraries are a good starting place; here you will find magazines, reports, and plenty of background information.

CASE STUDY: Learning from Research

RAY HAD TAUGHT shop for many years, but wanted to leave teaching so that he could develop his real passion, which was woodcarving. First, he had to be sure there would be a sufficient market for his work. He spoke to other craftworkers and visited a number of national trade shows to see what others were selling and to get a feel for the market. He also made trips to a number of shops with samples of his work, to get their reaction and to discuss pricing. Ray discovered that many of the retailers had very precise requirements and that it was vital to speak to them in advance about new products to get the details right. He also realized that pricing was crucial, and that he would have to produce sufficient quantities to keep his unit costs low.

cover overhead, such as workshop rent, telephone calls, postage, travel, and so on. The questions your market research needs to answer are: first, is the market interested in such a device; second, is the price right; and, finally, are you likely to sell 12,000 SAYITs per year? Another point to consider is whether 12,000 SAYITs are likely to swamp the market; if so, you are likely to do little trade in your second year.

Basic market research falls into two broad areas: analysis of the market, and analysis of competitors. You may also decide to test the market before collating the results of your research. It is a good idea to start to look at your prices at this point. This is a highly involved issue relating not only to covering your own costs and matching the prices of your competitors, but also to how you want your business to be perceived by its customers. For more detailed information, see pp. 84–8. Keep pricing considerations in mind throughout your market research.

Follow up leads you found during your market research when you start in business

Analyzing the Market

The "market" is those people or businesses who might be your customers. Analysis gives you an inside picture of the industry you are thinking of entering, the trends both nationally and locally, and an understanding of the needs of your potential customers. The international situation will also be relevant if you are considering exporting (see pp. 114–21).

First, look at the national situation. Many industries are described fully in market research studies, and copies of such reports are available at large public libraries. The internet is a rich source of information – try government websites as a starting point. Other sources of market research information are relevant trade magazines, trade associations, and their shows and exhibitions. Your local library should be able to give you the names of relevant trade magazines and the addresses of the appropriate trade associations. From these you can find out details of exhibitions.

BEING AWARE OF TRENDS

Keep up to date with the business pages in newspapers, and read relevant current affairs magazines. Copy, print out, or cut out useful information and start to compile a file. Keep adding to it even after you have started in business – it will help you to keep abreast of how trends change over time. Beware, however, of excessive media coverage given to a temporary trend. In such cases dozens of firms will pop up in response to the media signals, but it is unlikely that the actual market size is large enough, or that the demand (if it existed in the first place) will be sustained for long periods. Rely on an overview of your own market research to guide you.

Even if your proposed business does not need a national-sized market to sustain it, national trends can have a significant effect at the local level. You need to know if the market you are entering is expanding, contracting, stable, or very dependent upon another market, which itself is changing rapidly. Markets tend to start slowly, expand rapidly, then plateau, or sometimes decline. Businesses that offer a new product or service early on when the market is expanding often do much better than those that come along later in the life of the market, but the early entrepreneurs are exposed to greater risk. The way to find out which stage your market is at is through desk research.

Write down the questions you need to ask before a meeting

There may also be legislation in the pipeline that could have a major effect on your plans. If in doubt, contact the relevant trade association for information.

LOCAL RESEARCH

Once you have built up some knowledge of the national situation and relevant trends, you need to find out much more about the industry on a local level. To this end there is no better source of information than the industry itself. Speak to the sales representatives of your likely suppliers – they can provide good information if asked the correct questions. Try to find out from them about consistent long-term sellers as well as what is popular right now. Contact your local business development office, and ask if they can put you in touch with someone who is

PITFALLS TO AVOID WHEN DOING MARKET RESEARCH

PITFALL	HOW TO AVOID IT
OVERCONFIDENCE Being convinced that your product or service will work	Take any warning signs or negative feedback seriously. If potential customers display no interest as you do your research, ask them why, and try to accommodate their suggestions. Above all, keep an open mind.
IMPRECISION Failing to define your target market	Usually 20 percent of the customers provide 80 percent of the turnover. Plan to identify and focus on the few key customers.
PRICE CUTTING Assuming that cutting prices will allow you to compete successfully	The buying decision is a complex one – look at all the alternatives. Factors such as quality, guarantees, and speed of service influence the sale as much as price.
SHORT-TERM THINKING Underestimating how long it will take to enter a market and obtain a reasonable market share	Obtaining a market share takes years not months. It is hard to estimate the reactions of competitors, but the only safe strategy is to assume that they will react aggressively, and to plan accordingly.
COMPLACENCY Being too reliant on contacts who promise to supply work when you start	Ask yourself how they manage without you now. Ask your contacts for more details of their needs, and for estimates of orders to test their genuineness.

working in the same business but located in a different part of the country (so that you would not be in direct competition).

YOUR TARGET MARKET

Next you need to consider the "target market" – the section of the population that could potentially use your product or service. Aim to define in detail who your customers are, their needs, and what benefit they will derive from using your product or service. They are obviously surviving without you at present so why will they want to use your business in the future? Also, are there enough potential customers within reach of your business?

At this point, you need to be clear about whether your customers will be other businesses (trade), or whether you will sell directly to the general public, or both. Business customers generally have larger budgets and different requirements, such as the precise date by which a service must be completed, or specific details relating to the design of the packaging. They also expect credit, whereas a private customer is usually prepared to pay immediately, which can have a significant effect on your cash flow.

Talk directly to potential buyers – there is no substitute

If your target market is business customers, first prepare a list of some or all of the businesses that may be interested in your product or service. Get their names from the Yellow Pages, or a similar local business directory, then find out the name of the best person in the firm to approach. Contact them and find out their views on what you have to offer.

In contrast, if your target market is private customers, trying to find out who will buy what from you is much more difficult. In this case, start by asking people already in the same business (where they are not direct competitors) for their views and advice. The next step is to speak directly to likely customers and the most thorough way of doing that with the public is with a questionnaire.

Using Questionnaires

A questionnaire is the best way to find out about the needs, views, and habits of local customers in a structured manner. There are five golden rules to follow to compile effective questionnaires:

1 **KEEP IT SHORT AND SIMPLE** Ask yourself what it is you are really trying to find out. Concentrate on the most important questions and avoid any fringe issues. There should be no more than five to 10 questions. A multiple-choice or Yes/No format is best as it is both easier to answer and quicker to analyze.

2 **AVOID LOADED QUESTIONS** This is best illustrated with an example. If you were considering opening a mail-order business, then you might ask potential customers their views, to assess if the business would be viable. A question such as "Do you regularly buy products from mail-order companies?" would be reasonable. Asking "Would you buy from a mail-order company if it were cheaper than your local store?" is a loaded question, and invites a positive reply. It is very easy to fall into the trap of asking such questions. Also, try to avoid emotive or exaggerated phrases in the question. Be aware that, out of politeness, people often give the reply that they think you want to hear.

3 **MINIMIZE OPEN QUESTIONS** The purpose of the questionnaire is to pose specific questions that you have thought out carefully so that the answers allow you to draw firm conclusions. The danger of an open question (such as "Do you think mobile shops are a good idea?") is that it could lead to a long debate. There is, of course, value in open questions: the responses can reveal useful and relevant factors of which you are unaware. The best plan is to start with questions that have straightforward answers and to make one (perhaps the very last question) an open one.

■ **Approach the Right People** Finding the right people might involve door-to-door interviews, phone interviews, or, if you are doing the survey in the street, stopping only those people who you think might use your product or service (such as those who seem to be within a certain age group). There is little to be gained from asking someone who is unlikely to be a customer. If you plan to mail the questionnaire to people, include a stamped, self-addressed envelope, and give them some incentive to complete the form – such as a coupon – or you are likely to receive few replies. If possible, try to choose places where your likely customers congregate. For example, if you were planning to set up a business selling personal sports equipment, you could visit local gyms, sports centers, and athletic clubs

Compiling a Questionnaire

It takes time and careful thought to put together a questionnaire that will provide you with enough of the right sort of information in the right form – data that you can use as part of your market research.

You do not need to know the name of the person you are asking, but it may be useful to include data on their age and sex. When you have compiled your questionnaire, try it out on a couple of friends to check that there are no ambiguities or loopholes.

Sample Questionnaire: Poor Example

This questionnaire is from a newspaper wanting to increase the number of local retailers who use its classified advertisements. As some of the questions are unclear, the results are likely to be inconclusive.

Two questions are asked, and the first one is too open; there is no question about how often the shop advertises

Two questions are asked, and there is scope for an ambiguous answer

This question is imprecise: does it mean window displays, interior displays, or display advertisements?

Although this is a rather nosy question, which people might not answer, it may provide useful information for the newspaper's advertising salespeople

Questionnaire for Retailers

Q1 What is your attitude to advertising, and where do you advertise? ....
....
....
....
....

Q2 Do you use classified or display advertisements?
....

Q3 What emphasis do you place on displays?
....
....
....

Q4 How do you try to compete with the big department stores and discount stores?
....
....
....
....

(with permission from the owners).

5 APPROACH ENOUGH PEOPLE The more people you ask, the more accurate your survey results will be. Try to ask at least 50 to 100 people – more if possible. To make analysis of the data easier, use a fresh questionnaire for each person.

Once you have gathered a reasonable amount of useful and representative data from your questionnaires, you need to analyze it. Try to quantify the data into percentages where possible, although do not assume that your results are totally reliable or not subject to change. The data you produce from a questionnaire can form an important part of the market research section of your business plan (see pp. 44–5). If you have included any open questions, look out for and note down any themes and suggestions that emerge from the answers – they can often lead you in a direction you had not previously thought of.

The introduction stresses benefits to the reader

This question defines precisely what is meant by "regularly"

This request allows for the compilation of a precise list of the competition

This question, along with the next one, will provide clear data on the percentage of people who use each type of advertisement

Open question enables advertisers to add the aspects that are most important to them

This question will provide information about the motivation of advertisers

QUESTIONNAIRE FOR RETAILERS

Would you please take the time to complete this short questionnaire. By doing so, you will assist us in our continuing efforts to provide you with a quality service that meets your precise requirements.

Q1 Do you advertise regularly (at least monthly)? ☐Y ☐N

Q2 Please list which newspapers or magazines you advertise in. ....

....

....

....

Q3 Do you use classified advertisements? ☐Y ☐N

Q4 Do you use display advertisements? ☐Y ☐N

Q5 What factors do you try to emphasize in your advertisements? ....

....

....

Q6 Do you use advertising to compete with the large department stores and discount stores? ☐Y ☐N

SAMPLE QUESTIONNAIRE: GOOD EXAMPLE

This questionnaire is an improved version of the example opposite. Here, the questions have been phrased clearly, and broken down into small segments. The answers should be simple to quantify.

Analyzing Competitors

A great deal of interesting and useful information can be derived from close observation of potential competitors. In one sense they are doing today what you are planning to do tomorrow. They should have already refined their product or service and learned from their mistakes – knowledge from which you can benefit. Furthermore, as they will be your competitors, it is wise to know their strengths and weaknesses. As you follow various avenues of research, compile a dossier on each of your competitors and add new information as you go along. This will make it easier to conduct your final assessment.

Data on Competitors
Prepare a checklist of information on each competitor. Fill in as many of the categories as you can, adding any other relevant details.

Competitor Assessment Checklist

Business name ....

Business address ....

Phone number .... Fax number ....

Email .... Website ....

Corporation, partnership, or sole proprietor? ....

Are they part of a larger group? ....

Year started in business ....

Names and locations of other branches/subsidiaries ....

Names of the proprietors/directors ....

Names of other key staff ....

Relevant details from their annual financial statements

....

What do they do? ....

Technical description of their products/services ....

Do the products/services have any special features? ....

What are their prices ? ....

What aspects do they stress in their sales literature? ....

What aspects do they stress on their website? ....

What advertising do they do? ....

What other promotions do they do? ....

What are their sales methods? ....

Assessment of their strengths and weaknesses ....

Proposals for most effective ways to enter into competition

....

Include the sales manager and marketing manager if applicable

For incorporated companies only, include annual financial statements

Describe their business in full

Include only products or services similar to yours

Include where they advertise and what they stress in their advertisements

Include incentives, discounts, credit terms, and guarantees

MARKET SHARE

When researching your competitors, consider the issue of market share. Try to work out how the market is currently divided up between competitors and how you can start to gain a share of that market. Your proposed business venture will either increase the likely size of the market (this is most commonly seen with new products or services) or succeed only at the expense of your competitors. Sometimes the success of a new venture can be due to a mixture of both, but the implications can be significant.

If you think you will be expanding the market it means new customers will be buying from you – where will they be coming from and what will attract them? Are you expecting them to stop buying something else to have the spare money to spend with you? If you are trying to break into an existing market, how will you win customers from other suppliers? One way of enticing customers away from competitors is to offer a better-quality product or service. Another is to undercut current prices. Think carefully about which you can deliver and which will be most profitable.

DIRECT OBSERVATION

If your intended business is retailing, then walk around the area in which you are thinking of opening a shop to look at the types of retail businesses nearby and to check out potential competitors. Talk to local appraisers, who will usually have a good idea as to the retail business in their area.

Once you have located a competitor, there are a number of techniques to use. If they are local you could sit outside their premises and observe the comings and goings; note down how many people go in and how many come out with purchases. In the case of industrial units, careful observation can reveal the names of suppliers and customers (conveniently written on the sides of vans) and the general level of activity of the business. Do this at several different times of the day or week, and for an hour or more at a time. If the competitor is a manufacturer, try to buy, rent, or borrow a sample of their product and check it out, noting any strengths and weaknesses. How does it compare with your own product in terms of appearance and features? What can

MARKET SHARE

This bar chart shows a fictitious market divided between garden centers in an area, and two possible results when a new garden center enters the market.

CURRENT MARKET SHARE
The market is divided unequally between three garden centers.

INCREASED MARKET SIZE
A new garden center increases the size of the overall market by attracting new customers.

CHANGE OF MARKET SHARE
The new firm captures a percentage of the existing market from the other garden centers.

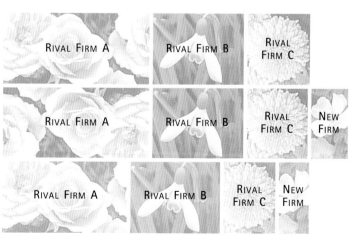

EXHIBITION
*Large exhibitions, such as
this auto show, are good
places to see a wide range
of exhibitors and to gain
an overview of an industry.
In addition to the large,
international companies,
there will be representatives
from firms of all sizes and
from numerous countries.*

you offer that the competitor does not? Note
any patent or registered design markings, since
these should be respected.

If the competitor is in the service sector, try
to use their service yourself, or ask friends to
phone as if they were customers. Enquire about
prices and how soon the service can be provided
(this may reveal how busy your competitors are
or provide a target for you to beat).

RESEARCHING INFORMATION

You can also use less direct means to find out
more about your competitors. If you have a
potential supplier, ask their sales
representatives who else they supply in your
area. Read trade magazines and attend the
relevant trade or consumer exhibitions, since
most of the businesses who are active are likely
to be there as exhibitors or visitors. Obtain
pamphlets, sales literature, and price lists from
shows or exhibitions. Here your competitors
are at their most vulnerable since their goods
are on display, and you can usually walk straight
onto their stands. Also, look at their
advertisements and check out their website. If
possible, speak to some past or present
customers. Try asking direct questions, such as
"How do you find...?" or "Do ... deliver on time?"
Sometimes the answers can be remarkably
candid. If a competitor is a corporation, they
have to file annual financial statements and
returns, which are available to the public.

Testing the Market

Test marketing can be thought of as putting a
toe in the water. This is not always
necessary or possible but can be very useful
where your other market research is rather
inconclusive. The function of test marketing is
simply to test the market reaction to a new
product or service with the minimum of
investment, and it is usually done at an early

TIME SAVER

When test marketing, focus your
energies on getting direct feedback
from potential customers, either by
showing a sample to potential
buyers, meeting buyers on your
exhibition stand, or getting
comments from a focus group.

stage before making a full commitment to the project. Test marketing acts as a bridge between having the big idea and launching a full-scale business. It can provide useful, possibly vital, feedback, but has the drawback that it may reveal your hand to a competitor.

In most test marketing an element of bluff is essential, particularly if you have not yet started your business. Since not everybody wants to deal with a business that has not yet opened or that is operating from a spare room, the use of a business name and a business address could be beneficial, although not essential. Operating under a business name is relatively easy but finding a temporary business address could present more of a problem. Try using a P.O. box number, or rent office space temporarily in a local business center.

METHODS OF TESTING THE MARKET

METHOD	WHAT TO DO	POINTS TO CONSIDER
ADVERTISING	Place an advertisement offering information about your product to customers who respond.	■ This is the simplest way for non-retail ventures to check for market response. ■ Avoid making misleading claims or statements in the advertisement. ■ Relies on people taking the trouble to contact you – response may be minimal.
SAMPLES	If you are making a product to sell to the industry, take samples to potential buyers and take orders before starting production.	■ Common practice in the fashion and gift industries where buyers are used to placing orders many months before receiving goods. ■ Allows you to quantify makeup costs and overcome technical problems.
MAILSHOTS	Send a letter to a potential customer asking whether they are interested in what you have to offer.	■ This is effective, especially if you have compiled a targeted mailing list, address the letters to named individuals, and sign and date each one. ■ May need a follow-up phone call.
LEAFLET DROPS	Put in mailboxes door-to-door, or insert into newspapers and magazines.	■ A less personal version of the mailshot. ■ Although leaflet drops can be cheap and targeted, the response rate is usually low.
EXHIBITIONS OR TRADE SHOWS	Rent a stand at an exhibition or trade show.	■ You can receive immediate feedback from potential customers to help you fine-tune your product or service or establish prices. ■ This can be costly, and reveals your venture to prospective competitors.
FOCUS GROUPS	Invite selected people to a showing of prototypes of new products or a description of new services.	■ Answers to carefully prepared questions and open discussion can provide very valuable data. ■ Focus groups can be quite inexpensive to set up.

Assessing Your Idea

Once you have completed your market research (which may take several weeks or much longer), you need to assess the situation. You will be faced with trying to make some sense out of a huge amount of information, some of which may be contradictory. If you do not carry out an assessment in an objective and rational manner, there is some danger that either your own feelings or someone else's chance remark might influence your final decisions. On the other hand, listening to your own feelings can be a good guide, particularly if secretly you are having misgivings.

No matter how successful your idea may look, bear in mind the danger of counterattack from existing businesses. This could include dropping their prices to engage you in a price war, poaching your key staff by offering higher wages, or interfering with your sources of supply. Most established businesses react with some hostility to a new business if they think they are going to lose customers. A few are surprisingly inactive – perhaps they simply underestimate the threat. In any event, if they try to attack your fledgling enterprise they will pose a serious threat unless you have enormous resources behind you. One survival strategy is to adopt a low profile and present as little threat as possible to a larger rival – at least until you become established yourself.

Carry out market research even when your business is up and running

APPLY THE FINANCIER'S TEST

A clearheaded way to assess your business idea is to take the same approach that an outside financier would take if he or she were looking at your proposed venture. A financier looks for three distinct features in a new venture:

1 DIFFICULT MARKET ENTRY This seems a contradiction in terms. Why should anyone want a project to have difficulty getting into the market? The answer lies in the fact that as soon as your business starts and appears to others to be successful it will encourage a rush of "me-too" imitators. This causes a dilution of the potential market and the possibility of price wars. It is therefore a considerable advantage to have a project that is not easy for others to copy. Note that a project requiring a high initial investment is not, in itself, a natural barrier to others.

2 HIGH MARGINS This is a fairly obvious requirement since high margins should translate into good profitability. But what this also means is that the business should enjoy good positive cash flow, have funds for future development, and should survive if margins are eroded by unforeseen events. Just what constitutes a high or low margin is difficult to say in general terms since it depends on many factors. Refer to the more detailed information on pricing (see pp. 84–8) to give you a guide, and take advice from your accountant and business development office.

3 LONGEVITY This factor is not often considered at the planning stage by small businesses, which tend to place too much emphasis on short-term results. Longevity in this context simply means a project which, once launched, is likely to continue to be competitive and profitable for a number of years without requiring substantial change or further investment. This justifies the initial investment required to launch the project. Thus "trendy" business ideas are discouraged, as are those that rely on too many volatile external factors, such as currency exchange rates or high-tech developments.

If your idea passes this test, a financier may be interested in looking more closely at the project. The market research you have done up to now will form a fundamental part of the business plan, which is essential for obtaining financing.

SUMMING UP
YOUR RESULTS
*Once you have collated
and processed all the
information gathered for
your market research,
draw up a summary so
that the end result of your
research is available in a
succinct form.*

Give a precise
description of your
target market

Provide calculations
and evidence of
customer acceptance
of prices

Give details and
suggestions of
your strategy

Outline and back up
your reasons why
some aspects of your
business would be
difficult to copy

MARKET RESEARCH SUMMARY

VIABILITY
Is there a genuine interest in your idea? ....
     Reasons: ....
Who is your target market? ....

What was your target market's response to your proposed venture?
....

Is your pricing correct? ....

What sales will you need to make to break even?
....

COMPETITORS
Who are your main competitors? ....
What key advantages do they have over you? ....
What are their weaknesses that you might exploit? ....

THE FINANCIER'S TEST
Market Entry:
     What aspects of your business would be easy to copy?
     ....

     What aspects would be difficult to copy? ....
Margins:
     What will be your likely operating profit margin? ....
     What are your trade sector's norms? ....
Longevity:
     Why do you think your business will still be trading in
     five years' time? ....

PREPARING A BUSINESS PLAN

One of the first steps in starting any new business should be the preparation of a business plan – a detailed planning document that sets out in both words and figures a proposed business venture. This can either be a new business start-up or a major expansion or diversification of an existing business. A business plan is as essential to the business that requires only $1,000 to set up as to one that needs $1 million. The principal role of a business plan is to persuade potential backers that your business is a sound proposition; it also helps you to plan and monitor the progress of your business.

A business plan should be drafted by the people behind the venture, with appropriate advice from an accountant. The purposes of a business plan are to:
■ transfer your thoughts to paper
■ raise financing
■ monitor the project.

KEY PURPOSES

When you start to plan how to set up a new business, there are many aspects to consider. By putting down the business idea in a structured plan, the situation will become clearer and you can start to assess the project more objectively. Furthermore, to complete the plan you will have to answer a lot of questions and this will make

Spend time on your business plan – it is as much for your benefit as for a financial backer's

you do the necessary research. The business plan is the key to opening financiers' coffers and so must contain all the information that is needed to answer their likely questions. It should also be neatly presented and clearly laid out. The document should be persuasive in tone, conveying your enthusiasm for the project, and it should emphasize the four key aspects that financial backers look for:
■ evidence of market research
■ proper planning
■ financial control
■ competence and commitment of the people behind the project.

CASE STUDY: Producing a Planning Tool

AFTER A CAREER in education, then industry, Margaret decided to set up her own training company. She had completed sufficient market research to conclude that there was a shortage of trainers in her area, and that there was enough work if she could market her company well. Although she was funding the venture entirely by herself, she decided to produce a business plan. This would help her to gather her thoughts and focus on exactly who she should be approaching to find training work, what her charges should be, and how much income she needed to cover her operating costs. She found that producing a break-even cashflow forecast for her business plan was a great comfort, as she knew that if she met those monthly targets she would survive.

Even if you do not need to borrow money in order to start up your business, the business plan could save you from losing your own funds, since the detailed financial forecasting required to complete the plan should help to highlight any potential problems in advance.

The plan lays down the path along which the business should be moving, for at least the first year – sometimes longer. When a business is starting up there are so many things to do that it is easy to delude yourself into thinking that the business is doing well just because you are busy. With the business plan at your side, you can take stock of the situation, at least monthly, and check to see if you are still progressing along the planned path (particularly in terms of the cash-flow forecast). If not, remedial action can be taken, and the sooner the better. Cash-flow management is discussed on pp. 140–42.

Choosing a Format for Your Business Plan

A number of different formats are suitable for a business plan, athough the information contained within each will be broadly similar. There is also software available for generating business plans in which you answer set questions, and the program creates the plan for you. These programs have obvious advantages (such as ease) and disadvantages (such as inflexibility),

PULLING TOGETHER RESEARCH
Writing your business plan involves gathering all the research you have done so far, looking critically at it, and making use of the information that is relevant. You will also need to do some additional research to provide a complete picture.

but the biggest danger of using such programs is that they may not sufficiently challenge the would-be entrepreneur.

On the following pages there is a fictitious business plan to illustrate one way in which a plan might be written and presented. The figures used are merely illustrative. Although this example has been written for a small shop, the layout and topics covered are applicable to virtually any business (including service- or manufacturing-based enterprises) employing either just the proprietor or several people. The usual format consists of a cover sheet, then several pages of typed text, followed by appendices. In some cases the business plan needs supporting documentation, which can be bound within the same covers or attached.

COVER SHEET

The cover sheet should give a professional look to the document. The information it needs to give comprises: the name(s) of the people behind the project; the proposed or existing business name; the business address, or the proprietor's home address if there is no business address as yet; and the accountant's name and address if he or she has been closely involved in preparing the business plan.

Ideally the plan needs to carry a recent date. Either keep the date current by printing out a fresh copy of the business plan when you present it to someone new, or do not date the document at all; if someone is given a plan with an old date, they may assume that someone else has turned it down already.

STEPS TO COMPLETING A BUSINESS PLAN

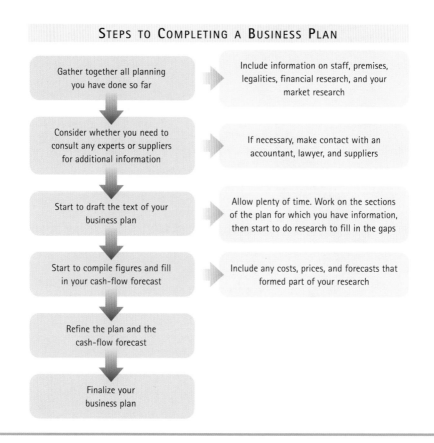

Gather together all planning you have done so far

Include information on staff, premises, legalities, financial research, and your market research

Consider whether you need to consult any experts or suppliers for additional information

If necessary, make contact with an accountant, lawyer, and suppliers

Start to draft the text of your business plan

Allow plenty of time. Work on the sections of the plan for which you have information, then start to do research to fill in the gaps

Start to compile figures and fill in your cash-flow forecast

Include any costs, prices, and forecasts that formed part of your research

Refine the plan and the cash-flow forecast

Finalize your business plan

SUMMARY AND CONTENTS

The summary is a one-page encapsulation of the key points contained within the business plan to allow the reader to see the gist of the plan at a glance. The larger the plan, the more useful this page is. A business plan with more than 10 pages benefits from a list of contents following the summary, with page numbers to enable the reader to locate a specific topic quickly. The example given here omits a contents page, since it is reasonably short.

FACT FILE

A business plan is usually written in the third person (for example, "the Directors," "the proprietor," or, as in this example, "Joan Smith"), although existing businesses may use the first person plural, "we." Write the text with a reader in mind who has never met you and who does not know anything about you or your business.

BUSINESS PLAN: SIMPLY PERFECT

SUMMARY

BUSINESS DESCRIPTION	New retail shop (ladies fashions for the over 50s).
LOCATION	Small provincial town.
PROPRIETOR	Joan Smith (trading as a sole proprietor).
STAFF	The proprietor only.
MARKET	The main market is ladies, over 50, living in the town (population 66,500). The nearest stores catering to this market are in the city, 28 miles away.
PREMISES	About 500 sq ft in a good location.
PROPOSED SHOP NAME	"Simply Perfect"
TURNOVER	First-year estimate: approximately $48,500. Second-year estimate: approximately $60,000.
FINANCING	Depending upon which shop is rented, capital of some $17,000 is required, of which the proprietor can raise $10,000, leaving a balance of $7,000 to be found. A three-year bank loan of $4,000 would be sufficient, together with an overdraft facility of $3,000 to allow for initial stock purchases.
TIMESCALES	The plan is to open by May 1, in time for the summer season, though stock will be ordered earlier.

2

SUMMARY
The essential details of the business plan are given on the summary page. Here, town and city names are not specified; in an actual plan they would need to be named.

Headings pick out key features of plan

Text summarizes the salient points only, leaving the detail for the main body of the plan

INTRODUCTION

This is a clear statement outlining the nature of the proposed business. For a manufacturer, the plan needs to mention the product's current stage of development and, if it is already in production, when it was first launched and how many have been sold. For a service venture, the plan needs to state if the business is a retailer, wholesaler, or whatever is relevant. If several phases of development are envisioned, this should also be mentioned.

BUSINESS HISTORY

Not included in this example, the business history section is needed only where an existing business is being bought or if the business plan is for a firm that is already in operation and is planning a major expansion or diversification. This section would mention the date the business started (usually the date of incorporation) and note any major recent events in the history of the business. In addition, the business history text would

INTRODUCTION

Here the purpose and scope of the business is stated briefly, along with a mention that the goal is to raise financing for the business.

Target market is clearly stated as the "over 50s age group"

Makes clear the need for the business among customers

Size of market is defined by stating population of town, and potential catchment area

Potential competition is listed with strengths and weaknesses

BUSINESS PLAN: SIMPLY PERFECT

INTRODUCTION

The objective is to set up a ladies' fashion shop in the town center. The shop will stock ladies' fashions targeted mainly at the over 50s age group. Garments will include dresses, skirts, blouses, coats, hosiery, hats, and accessories, and will be in styles and sizes appropriate to that target market. The purpose of this plan is to raise the financing for the venture.

MARKET RESEARCH

During her years in retail in the area, Joan Smith has observed that many of her older clientele complained that they were obliged to travel to the city, some 28 miles away, to find good clothing stores. This prompted her to investigate the market further. The population of the town is 66,500, but with several smaller towns nearby, the potential market is larger. The existing stores in the area that might present competition to her venture are as follows:

ICEBERGS — A large department store catering to a wide age group with only a limited range for the over 50s in its ladies wear department, although there is good availability of sizes and high stock levels.

CITY FASHIONS — A new upmarket shop but with relatively high prices, and fashions more appropriate to younger customers. Little stock is held in larger sizes.

3

comment on the business's current financial position and refer to the latest accounts (a copy of which would be enclosed at the back of the business plan). For larger projects the last three years' accounts may be required.

MARKET RESEARCH

Vitally important, this section, in most cases, should take at least a page of text and generally much more, especially with larger projects. This part of the plan summarizes the findings of the market research, including target customers, the size of the market and any assumptions you have made about it, how sensitive the market is to price, and an outline of the competition and their strengths and weaknesses. Pricing policy specifics can be covered in the financial section later.

For larger projects an independent market research report will give credibility to the plan; this would be attached to the business plan and referred to as necessary in the text.

BUSINESS PLAN: SIMPLY PERFECT

TOWN TRENDS   A small shop stocking fashions mainly aimed at younger customers, and priced at the middle to lower end of the range.

MISS JONES   A small boutique with only skirts and dresses for this age group. Joan Smith used to work in this shop.

There is at present little direct competition from stores in the town or nearby. The main competitors are the stores in the city. Joan Smith has questioned a sample of 50 women whom she knows and who would all be potential customers of her new store. Of this sample, 44 said they would be interested in a local fashion shop in preference to others 28 miles away in the city. The only reservations were expressed by six women whose work took them to the city anyway and who felt they would probably continue to visit the stores there.

In terms of price sensitivity, Joan Smith's retail experience indicates that her target market is relatively affluent and tends to be more concerned about the style, quality, and fit of clothing, rather than its price.

4

MARKET RESEARCH
This section covers all the key points connected with the market, showing that thorough research has been done to prove there is a potential customer base for the shop.

Text covers attitudes of members of target market to all relevant competition in catchment area

Indicates that other factors are more important than price for potential market

ADVERTISING AND PROMOTION

Details of planned advertising and promotional initiatives make up this section, along with a mention of costs. In some cases this section may take a page or more.

PREMISES

This section starts by stating the type of premises required (office, shop, industrial unit, and so on) and the floor area necessary. It also covers the desired location of the premises and other needs, such as large loading bays. If premises have already been found, this should be mentioned. It should also be stated whether the premises will be bought or rented, the length of lease, dates of the next rent and rate reviews (if known), and if building insurance is included.

PERSONNEL

This section gives the credentials of the proprietor(s) or director(s), providing details of their age, qualifications, personal means

ADVERTISING, PROMOTION, AND PREMISES

The advertising and promotion initiatives covered here are a mixture of larger events and smaller details. The premises section explains the requirements mainly in terms of location.

Includes a plan to monitor response to advertising

Indicates that proprietor has started to look for suitable sites

Text justifies why a noncentral and therefore cheaper site may still be suitable

BUSINESS PLAN: SIMPLY PERFECT

ADVERTISING AND PROMOTION

To promote the shop the proprietor plans to organize fashion shows at the local ladies lunch club when the shop opens in May and again before Christmas. These events will cost about $250 each. She will also advertise these special events in the local newspaper and monitor the response carefully, by asking a proportion of customers (such as one in every five) how they heard about the new shop. She would also change the shop window weekly, as she believes that is an important way to promote her stock. Finally, she would send regular press releases to the local newspaper's fashion writer.

PREMISES

A shop to rent of around 500 sq ft is required, sited preferably on West Street or Regent Crescent, or possibly Hill Lane. These are near the town center but do not attract the very high rents of Main Street. There are a number of nonconvenience-type shops on these streets, and they all have a high level of pedestrian traffic. There are two vacant shops that may be suitable, and the cash-flow forecast reflects the rent and rates of the shop at 12 Regent Crescent. This shop is available on a seven year lease (with rent and rates of $8,000 per year, including building insurance), and the next rent review is not for two years. Although this site is on the edge of the prime downtown shopping area, it is situated between the main parking lot and the downtown shops, so many people walk past.

(usually in terms of property ownership), other business connections, and, most importantly, any relevant experience. For a major project, complete resumés may need to be enclosed.

The plan should indicate how many part-time or full-time staff will be needed to start the business, and whether numbers will subsequently increase. In addition, their skill requirements, likely wages, and necessary training should be mentioned. In some projects this section might show a phased increase as the business grows.

MONEY SAVER

Although much of your plan is a result of careful research, some will be based on guesswork. Consult experts, such as accountants and appraisers, at this stage to make your guesses more accurate – this may cost money now but is likely to save unforeseen costs later.

BUSINESS PLAN: SIMPLY PERFECT

PERSONNEL

MANAGEMENT
The shop will be under the direct supervision of the proprietor, Joan Smith. After working as a primary-school teacher, Joan Smith, age 42, has spent seven years in the retail trade, initially as a sales assistant and more recently as assistant manager of the Miss Jones boutique in the town. She feels the timing is now right to start her own business. Joan Smith owns her own apartment. She plans to attend evening courses on elementary bookkeeping at the local college.

STAFF
The proprietor does not plan to employ any staff. However, her sister, who lives locally and has considerable experience working in stores, is able to assist her should the need arise.

PERSONNEL
In this plan, the personnel section is short because there are no plans to have any employees besides the proprietor.

Proprietor's personal means are indicated

Plan to remedy weakness in skills is mentioned

EQUIPMENT AND VEHICLES

This section discusses what equipment will be needed to run the business, and whether it will be purchased new or secondhand, bought outright or leased. The equipment suppliers may also be mentioned. Particularly where the equipment is expensive or extensive, it may be useful to list it in the Appendices. The transportation requirements also need to be mentioned, since purchase of a van or car often represents a significant part of a project's start-up and running costs. Include a description of the type of vehicle required, if any, its function in the business, how its purchase will be funded, and its likely annual mileage.

SUPPLIERS (AND SUBCONTRACTORS)

Many businesses rely on other businesses to supply them with their raw materials, stock, parts, or services. Any problems in obtaining these can spell disaster. Be careful of "single-sourcing" – relying heavily on one supplier. This section

EQUIPMENT, VEHICLES, AND SUPPLIERS
These sections provide a summary and justification of equipment needed and suppliers arranged. The financial details of both are left to the Appendices.

BUSINESS PLAN: SIMPLY PERFECT

EQUIPMENT AND VEHICLES

EQUIPMENT
Certain equipment, some purchased secondhand, will be required. In addition, the shop at 12 Regent Crescent requires its interior repainted. The exterior is satisfactory, though a new shop sign is needed. The start-up capital expenditure costs are listed as an appendix to this plan.

VEHICLES
The business does not require any vehicle. Stock ordered at trade shows or through suppliers' sales representatives will be despatched to the shop by normal parcel delivery services.

Plan states alternative transport method since no vehicle is needed

SUPPLIERS

Credit arrangements are covered

Joan Smith has attended two national fashion trade shows and has spoken to 15 potential suppliers who carry appropriate lines. They have almost all stated that they would normally offer 30 days' credit on receipt of satisfactory references. This credit is not reflected in the cash-flow forecast, as the suppliers stated that the credit facility would come into effect only after an initial order or two had been placed and paid for satisfactorily.

7

of the business plan details which suppliers and subcontractors the proprietor plans to use, and comments on discussions with them.

LEGAL ASPECTS

Any laws or regulations that might have a significant effect on the business should be commented on here. If a license is required, this should be noted along with who issues the license, the cost, the likely delay, and what criteria have to be met. If planning permission is needed, this would also be covered here, with comments on any likely delays and discussions to date with the relevant planning authority. For a patent, the stage the patent application process has reached should be mentioned.

TIMESCALES

Include proposed timescales, especially if there are any time-dependent or time-critical aspects. For example, a manufacturer may be planning to launch a product at a major exhibition.

BUSINESS PLAN: SIMPLY PERFECT

LEGAL ASPECTS

The situation regarding planning permission has been investigated with the local authorities. Since the intention is to operate out of premises which have recently been used for similar retailing purposes, Joan Smith has been informed that no application for planning permission is required.

TIMESCALES

It is hoped to take over the shop lease on May 1 and then to capture the summer market. As most summer stock levels at the suppliers will be low by this time, Joan Smith intends to order stock earlier, for delivery when the shop opens.

LEGAL ASPECTS AND TIMESCALES
Here, the legal aspects are quite straightforward. The timescale, however, is critical to the initial success of the business.

Planning situation has been thoroughly investigated

Details are included of special arrangements to ensure stock levels will be sufficient

8

FINANCES

This section can be divided into subsections:

■ **PRICING** This specifies how the product or service will be priced, what credit terms will be offered, and the likely "markup" or "margin" (see p. 86). It is usual to mention the norms of the industry and price sensitivity, if this has not been covered elsewhere.

■ **CASH-FLOW FORECAST** This comes near or at the end of the plan but could be commented on here, highlighting notable features and stating what assumptions have been made to arrive at the forecast.

■ **PROJECT RISK ASSESSMENT** This identifies and quantifies the risk associated with the venture. Potential risk factors include: a new competitor; changes in legislation; difficulties in obtaining stock or raw materials; changes in overseas conditions; foreign currency exchange fluctuations; sickness; or a flood or bad fire. A more mundane (and common) risk is that the expected level of turnover is

FINANCES

These pages are detailed and accurate, since they are the key to the business plan.

BUSINESS PLAN: SIMPLY PERFECT

FINANCES

PRICING

Garments and accessories in the store will reflect the markups that are typical of the fashion industry locally, which are generally 80–120 percent.

Range of figures is quoted

CASH–FLOW FORECAST

The attached cash-flow forecast shows a turnover in the first year of $48,500 at which the business is just above breakeven. It is thought that by the second full year of operation the turnover may rise to around $60,000. The sales estimates are based on two different calculations, which both arrive at a minimum turnover of around $50,000. In the first method, Joan Smith has estimated her proposed shop's first year's sales to be two-thirds of those done by the boutique Miss Jones, where she worked until recently. Second, she has calculated the likely turnover in terms of the rate of stock turn (which is defined as the turnover divided by the stock value, at retail prices). A rate of stock turn of 2.5 should be obtainable, and this would give a turnover of $50,000 with a stock level of $20,000.

Basis for calculations is given

not achieved. Try doing a second cash-flow forecast assuming 20 (or 30) percent fewer sales while the overheads remain the same. This could be commented on here with the new (low sales) cash-flow forecast attached as an appendix. This section should also give contingency plans for setbacks, such as who would take over if the proprietor(s) were ill.

■ **FINANCIAL REQUIREMENTS** These usually come as the last or penultimate paragraph and should state in clear, unequivocal terms the total money the project needs, how much the proprietor(s) are putting in, and if any loans are required. Loan requirements should be split into share capital (for a corporation), bank loans, and overdraft facilities. For each it should be stated when the money is required. In addition, the plan should outline in broad terms what the borrowed money is to be used for.

■ **PROFESSIONAL FEES** These should be estimated as closely as possible.

BUSINESS PLAN: SIMPLY PERFECT

PROJECT RISK ASSESSMENT

It is Joan Smith's opinion that the local market can sustain another specialist shop in addition to her proposed venture, so that should a second shop open at some future date her project would not be jeopardized. If sales were 20 percent less than forecast, the business would survive, albeit with difficulty. Finally, should Joan Smith become ill, her sister would run the shop.

Risks from competitors and low sales are covered

Contingency plan in the event of illness of the proprietor is included

FINANCIAL REQUIREMENTS

Depending upon which store is rented, approximately $17,000 capital is required, of which the proprietor can raise $10,000. A three-year bank loan of $4,000 would pay for setup costs (mainly equipment), while an overdraft of $3,000 would assist with the provision of stock.

Financial needs, including suggested term of loan, are clearly stated

PROFESSIONAL FEES

It is assumed that there will be lawyer's fees of $300 and $150 for an appraiser. Insurance has been quoted at $500 and accountant's fees of $400 have been allowed.

Fees from all sources have been included

APPENDICES

These are found at the back of the business plan. Appendices vary widely according to the type and scale of the business but, broadly speaking, can include:

■ **START-UP CAPITAL EXPENDITURE** This itemization of start-up costs is useful when they add up to a significant expense.

■ **PROJECTED PROFIT AND LOSS ACCOUNT** This is desirable for small projects, and essential for others. Also sometimes known

as a forecast profit and loss account, or abbreviated to a forecast P and L, this would normally be prepared by your accountant and is an important summary of the likely overheads the business will face and the profit it should make.

■ **CASH-FLOW FORECAST** This is essential for all projects (see pp. 54–7).

■ **PROJECTED BALANCE SHEET** This lists the projected assets and liabilities of the business and is essential for any larger project.

START-UP CAPITAL
EXPENDITURE
A detailed breakdown of the equipment section (earlier in the plan), this should include a thorough listing of costs.

Relatively small costs are included

Where relevant, secondhand equipment is indicated

APPENDICES

START-UP CAPITAL EXPENDITURE

FIXTURES AND FITTINGS

Shelving	$	300
Display units	$	580
Exterior shop sign	$	500
Repainting of interior	$	300
Extra lighting	$	200
Mirrors		
(for changing room)	$	60
Curtains		
(for changing room)	$	160
Sub-total	$	2,100

EQUIPMENT

Cash register	$	200
Pricing gun	$	50
Mannequins		
(secondhand)	$	200
Clothes hangers	$	50
Computer	$	750
Subtotal	$	1,250
TOTAL	$	3,350

▓ **TRADING ACCOUNTS** These are relevant only if you are taking over another business or expanding your own.

▓ **TECHNICAL DATA** This is needed only as appropriate, often by manufacturing firms.

▓ **MARKET RESEARCH** Include this in the appendix only where it has been done independently or if it is lengthy.

▓ **SALES LITERATURE, LEAFLETS, DIAGRAMS, PHOTOGRAPHS** Include anything available that will support your case.

MONEY SAVER

To make your start-up costs as accurate as possible, annotate confirmed costs, such as a piece of specific equipment, with a "c," and estimated costs with an "e." You can then assess how much of a contingency factor to allow.

BUSINESS PLAN: SIMPLY PERFECT

PROJECTED PROFIT AND LOSS ACCOUNT

SALES	$	48,500
LESS COST OF SALES	$	24,250
GROSS PROFIT	$	24,250
LESS EXPENSES		
Adverts and promotion	$	800
Banking charges/interest	$	622
Business insurances	$	500
Business rent and rates	$	8,000
Cleaning	$	0
Electricity/gas/water	$	600
Legal and professional	$	850
Loan interest	$	538
Car expenses	$	0
Postage/parcels	$	0
Repairs and maintenance	$	200
Staff wages	$	0
Stationery/printing	$	160
Miscellaneous	$	370
Telephone/fax	$	375
Travel	$	300
DEPRECIATION		
Fixtures and fittings	$	525
Equipment	$	312
SUBTOTAL	$	14,152
NET PROFIT	$	10,098

12

PROJECTED PROFIT AND LOSS ACCOUNT

This summarizes outgoings and receipts to estimate future profits (or losses). The net profit needs to equal or exceed the proprietor's drawings (allowing for Social Security and income taxes).

This figure is estimated from the value of stock sold (which produced the $48,500 of sales) using an average markup of 100 percent

Only the interest is tax-deductible. Here the $4,000 loan is repaid in 36 months at $160 per month (variable). The interest is: [($160 x 36) – $4,000] / 36 = $48.88 per month x 11 months (May–March)

For simplicity a 25 percent depreciation has been assumed, but there may be first-year allowances

CASH-FLOW FORECAST

Usually created using a computer spreadsheet, the cash-flow forecast is a key element of the business plan. A cash-flow forecast is just what it says – a prediction of the cash flowing in and out of the business, usually on a monthly basis. This forecast is normally done for 12 months, though a project with long lead times may need a 24- or 36-month forecast. In that case, years two and three tend to have the forecast done on a quarterly basis, as greater accuracy is unlikely.

The preparation of the cash-flow forecast requires estimates and assumptions, which should be explained in the business plan, together with hard facts derived from your research. The procedure for creating a cash-flow forecast is given on pages 56–7.

The golden rule with a cash-flow forecast is to be pessimistic and not underestimate your overheads

Rarely, if ever, is a cash-flow forecast right the first time. That does not diminish its importance, for the process of compiling the first cash-flow forecast forces you to face up to some harsh realities and make a number of important decisions. What makes a cash-flow forecast such an important tool for planning and controlling your finances is that you can update it regularly (at least monthly), and you can also experiment by inserting different figures to envision different scenarios.

FACT FILE

If it is very difficult to forecast your sales, do a break-even cash flow. Complete the whole cash flow, leaving the "sales" line until the very end. Then insert what sales you have to make to break even – that is, ensuring the bottom line of the cash flow is positive or within your overdraft limit. You then know what level of sales you must achieve to survive.

HINTS TO COMPLETE A CASH FLOW

The following hints are intended to help you to complete your cash-flow forecast:

■ **LINE 1 (SALES)** Here you estimate your likely sales (turnover) for the year ahead. If you are offering credit, you should show the payments in the month when you expect to receive the cash.

■ **LINE 20 (REPAIRS AND MAINTENANCE)** Note that vehicle repairs are covered on line 17.

■ **LINE 21 (EMPLOYEE BENEFITS)** Depending on the number of its employees, a small business may not have to provide benefits to its employees beyond wages. In this example, the business does not have to provide employee benefits or unemployment compensation. For businesses that are under such an obligation, this line is used for employee benefit expenses.

■ **LINE 23 (STOCK/RAW MATERIALS)** In many cases there will be an initial stocking-up phase, and subsequently this line should bear a relationship to the sales line since you cannot make sales without stock. If you are given credit by your suppliers, this can have a marked bearing on your cash flow.

■ **LINE 31 (NET CASH FLOW)** This is line 5 minus line 32. If the figure is positive it means that more cash was received than was spent during the month (good). If negative, more cash was spent than received (not so good).

■ **LINE 32 (OPENING BALANCE)** This always starts at 0 for a new business, and each subsequent month equals the closing balance of the previous month.

■ **LINE 33 (CLOSING BALANCE)** This is the forecast cash in the bank at the end of each month. If this line is negative, it means your bank account will be overdrawn. Either you need an overdraft, or you will need to cut down on expenses or boost sales income to get yourself "out of the red." The totals in this line represent neither a profit nor a loss. If you can keep the amount in this line positive (or at least within your overdraft limit), you will not run out of cash.

CASH-FLOW FORECAST: SIMPLY PERFECT

CASH IN	MAY	JUN	JUL	AUG	SEP	OCT	NOV	DEC	JAN	FEB	MAR	APR	TOTALS
1 SALES	1,500	2,000	4,000	6,000	4,000	3,000	5,500	10,000	1,500	2,500	4,000	4,500	48,500
2 BANK OR OTHER LOANS	0	4,000	0	0	0	0	0	0	0	0	0	0	4,000
3 OWNER'S CAPITAL	10,000	0	0	0	0	0	0	0	0	0	0	0	10,000
4 OTHER MONEY IN	0	0	0	0	0	0	0	0	0	0	0	0	0
5 TOTAL CASH IN	11,500	6,000	4,000	6,000	4,000	3,000	5,500	10,000	1,500	2,500	4,000	4,500	62,500
CASH OUT													
6 ADVERTISING AND PROMOTION	300	0	0	0	0	0	500	0	0	0	0	0	800
7 BANK CHARGES/INTEREST	0	50	50	100	50	50	50	72	50	50	50	50	622
8 BUSINESS INSURANCE	500	0	0	0	0	0	0	0	0	0	0	0	500
9 BUSINESS RENT	1,000	0	0	1,000	0	0	1,000	0	0	1,000	0	0	4,000
10 CLEANING	0	0	0	0	0	0	0	0	0	0	0	0	0
11 DRAWINGS/SALARIES	0	500	500	750	750	750	1,000	1,000	750	1,000	1,000	1,000	9,000
12 ELECTRICITY/GAS/HEAT/WATER	0	150	0	0	150	0	0	150	0	0	150	0	600
13 FINANCE CHARGES	0	160	160	160	160	160	160	160	160	160	160	160	1760
14 LEGAL AND PROFESSIONAL	450	0	0	0	0	0	0	0	0	0	0	400	850
15 CAR - FUEL	0	0	0	0	0	0	0	0	0	0	0	0	0
16 CAR - OTHER EXPENSES	0	0	0	0	0	0	0	0	0	0	0	0	0
17 OTHER EXPENSES	0	0	0	0	0	0	0	0	0	0	0	0	0
18 POSTAGE/PARCELS	0	0	0	0	0	0	0	0	0	0	0	0	0
19 REPAIRS AND MAINTENANCE	0	50	0	0	50	0	0	50	0	0	50	0	200
20 STAFF WAGES	0	0	0	0	0	0	0	0	0	0	0	0	0
21 EMPLOYEE BENEFITS	0	0	0	0	0	0	0	0	0	0	0	0	0
22 STATIONERY/PRINTING	50	10	10	10	10	10	10	10	10	10	10	10	160
23 STOCK/RAW MATERIALS	8,000	4,000	2,000	2,000	2,000	1,000	6,000	500	0	3,000	3,000	2,000	33,500
24 SUBSCRIPTIONS	0	0	0	0	0	0	0	0	0	0	0	0	0
25 MISCELLANEOUS	80	50	30	20	20	20	40	30	20	20	20	20	370
26 TAX PAYMENTS	0	0	0	0	0	0	0	0	0	0	0	0	0
27 TELEPHONE/FAX	100	50	0	0	75	0	0	75	0	0	75	0	375
28 TRAVEL AND SUBSISTENCE	0	0	0	0	150	0	0	0	0	0	0	150	300
29 CAPITAL EXPENDITURE	3,350	0	0	0	0	0	0	0	0	0	0	0	3,350
30 TOTAL CASH OUT	13,830	5,020	2,750	4,040	3,415	1,990	8,760	2,047	990	5,240	4,515	3,790	56,387
31 NET CASH FLOW	-2,330	980	1,250	1,960	585	1,010	-3,260	7,953	510	-2,740	-515	710	
32 OPENING BALANCE	0	-2,330	-1,350	-100	1,860	2,445	3,455	195	8,148	8,658	5,918	5,403	
33 CLOSING BALANCE	-2,330	-1,350	-100	1,860	2,445	3,455	195	8,148	8,658	5,918	5,403	6,113	

How to Do a Cash-flow Forecast

These pages show you how to create a cash-flow forecast on a computer spreadsheet as illustrated by the sample forecast on page 55. You start by filling in the estimated sales, which are likely to show seasonal variations and a gradual buildup. Next you estimate your outgoings. This should then reveal how much capital the business requires to get it started.

CASH IN	
1	Sales
2	Bank or Other Loans
3	Owner's Capital
4	Other Money In
5	TOTAL CASH IN
CASH OUT	
6	Advertising and Promotion
7	Bank Charges/Interest
8	Business Insurance
9	Business Rent
	Cleaning

1 Create the Rows First open a blank spreadsheet on your computer. Next, create line (row) headings similar to the sample but adapted, if necessary, to your own venture.

CASH IN	MAY	JUN	JUL	AUG	SEP	OCT	NOV	DEC	JAN	FEB	MAR	APR	TOTALS
1 Sales													
2 Bank or Other Loans													
3 Owner's Capital													
4 Other Money In													
5 TOTAL CASH IN													
CASH OUT													

2 Create the Columns Working across the top line, write in the months as column headings, starting from the first month of business. Add a final column for the annual totals.

MONEY SAVER

As you become established, you may find it useful to break down the initial categories of your forecast. This will help you to see exactly how much you spend on specific items (such as stationery costs) and to assess more easily where savings can be made.

CASH IN	MAY	JUN	JUL	AUG	SE
1 Sales	1,500				
2 Bank or Other Loans					
3 Owner's Capital	10,000				
4 Other Money In	0				
5 TOTAL CASH IN	11,500				

3 Enter the Cash In Now for the first month fill in the sales (line 1) – unless you are doing a "break-even" cash flow, in which case complete this line at the very end. Skip line 2 at this stage, but fill in lines 3, 4, and 5 for the first month only.

CASH OUT				
6 Advertising and Promotion	300			
7 Bank Charges/Interest				
8 Business Insurance	500			
9 Business Rent	1,000			
10 Cleaning	0			
11 Drawings/Salaries				
12 Electricity/Gas/Heat/Water	0			
13 Finance Charges				
14 Legal and Professional	450			
15 Car - Fuel	0			
16 Car - Other Expenses	0			
17 Other Expenses	0			
18 Postage/Parcels	0			
19 Repairs and Maintenance	0			
20 Staff Wages	0			
21 Employee Benefits	0			
22 Stationary/Printing	50			
23 Stock/Raw Materials	8,000			
24 Subscriptions	0			
25 Miscellaneous	80			
26 Tax Payments	0			
27 Telephone/Fax	100			
28 Travel and Subsistence	0			
29 CAPITAL EXPENDITURE	3,350			
30 TOTAL CASH OUT	13,830			

4 Enter the Cash Out Fill in lines 6 to 30, skipping lines 7, 11, and 13. Some of these expenses will occur in the first month only, although others, such as electricity, may be due monthly or quarterly.

5 TOTAL CASH IN	11,500			

30 TOTAL CASH OUT	13,830			
31 NET CASH FLOW	-2,330			
32 OPENING BALANCE	0			
33 CLOSING BALANCE	-2,330			

5 WORK OUT THE CLOSING BALANCE For the first column subtract line 30 from line 5 to get line 31, and then add line 32 to get line 33.

9 BUSINESS RENT	1,000	0	0	1,000	0
10 CLEANING	0	0	0	0	0
11 DRAWINGS/SALARIES	0	500	500	750	750
12 ELECTRICITY/GAS/HEAT/WATER	0	150	0	0	150
13 FINANCE CHARGES	0	160	160	160	160

6 WORK OUT YOUR WITHDRAWALS Insert in line 11 the minimum withdrawals on which you can survive for the month.

CASH IN	MAY	JUN	JUL	AUG	SEP	OCT	NOV	DEC	JAN	FEB	MAR	APR	TOTALS
1 SALES	1,500	2,000	4,000	6,000	4,000	3,000	5,500	10,000	1,500	2,500	4,000	4,500	48,500
2 BANK OR OTHER LOANS													
3 OWNER'S CAPITAL	10,000	0	0	0	0	0	0	0	0	0	0	0	10,000
4 OTHER MONEY IN	0	0	0	0	0	0	0	0	0	0	0	0	0
5 TOTAL CASH IN	11,500	2,000	4,000	6,000	4,000	3,000	5,500	10,000	1,500	2,500	4,000	4,500	58,500
CASH OUT													
6 ADVERTISING AND PROMOTION	300	0	0	0	0	0	500	0	0	0	0	0	800
11 DRAWINGS/SALARIES	0	500	500	750	750	1,000	1,000	750	1,000	1,000	1,000	1,000	8,000
12 ELECTRICITY/GAS/HEAT/WATER	0	150	0	150	0	0	150	0	0	150	0	0	600
13 FINANCE CHARGES													
14 LEGAL AND PROFESSIONAL	450	0	0	0	0	0	0	0	0	0	0	400	850
25 MISCELLANEOUS	80	50	30	20	20	20	40	30	20	20	20	20	370
26 TAX PAYMENTS	0	0	0	0	0	0	0	0	0	0	0	0	0
27 TELEPHONE/FAX	100	50	0	75	0	0	75	0	0	75	0	0	375
28 TRAVEL AND SUBSISTENCE	0	0	0	0	150	0	0	0	0	0	150	0	300
29 CAPITAL EXPENDITURE	3,350	0	0	0	0	0	0	0	0	0	0	0	3,350
30 TOTAL CASH OUT	13,830	4,810	2,540	3,780	3,205	1,780	8,550	1,815	780	5,030	4,305	3,580	58,005
31 NET CASH FLOW	-2,330	-2,810	1,460	2,220	795	1,220	-3,050	8,185	720	-2,530	-305	920	
32 OPENING BALANCE	0	-2,330	-5,140	-3,680	-1,460	-665	555	-2,495	5,690	6,410	3,880	3,575	
33 CLOSING BALANCE	-2,330	-5,140	-1,680	-1,460	-665	555	-2,495	5,690	6,410	3,880	3,575	4,495	

7 REPEAT STEPS 3–6 FOR EACH MONTH You will almost certainly have a lot of negative figures in your bottom line (line 33), which indicates that you need more start-up funding. If you have no negatives you do not need a loan, and lines 2 and 13 will remain zero.

8 ESTIMATE THE MONEY YOU NEED Assuming your line 33 figures are negative, try to estimate how much money you need for: capital expenditure (which would normally be funded by a loan, hire purchase, or lease), and the purchase of stock or raw materials (which would normally be funded by an overdraft). The cash flow should indicate a diminishing overdraft requirement as the months go by.

CASH IN	MAY	JUN	JUL	AUG
1 SALES	1,500	2,000	4,000	6,000
2 BANK OR OTHER LOANS	0	4,000	0	0
3 OWNER'S CAPITAL	10,000	0	0	0
4 OTHER MONEY IN	0	0	0	0
5 TOTAL CASH IN	11,500	6,000	4,000	6,000
CASH OUT				
6 ADVERTISING AND PROMOTION	300	0	0	0
7 BANK CHARGES/INTEREST	0	50	50	100
8 BUSINESS INSURANCE	500	0	0	0
9 BUSINESS RENT	1,000	0	0	1,000

9 ADD LOAN REQUIREMENTS Put any loan requirement figure into line 2 and add repayments on line 13. Check that the sum of line 2 together with any overdraft does not exceed your line 3 – banks usually prefer not to put more money into a project than that raised from other sources. Add figures in line 7 to cover normal bank charges, plus interest on any overdraft (the latter is usually charged on a daily basis).

Use your cash-flow forecast to monitor your cash flow monthly or even weekly

RAISING THE FINANCING

How much money do you need to fund your new venture? Putting together your business plan should have given you the answer to this question. To start raising the financing, you need to be clear about how much money you will need to get your business up and running, and how much you will then need to keep it going. This should be in addition to the money set aside for your living expenses, since the business is unlikely to generate any profits for some time.

The money you need to raise to cover the initial costs of starting a business is known as start-up capital, or sometimes seed money. This goes toward onetime costs, such as buying machinery or vehicles, developing or launching a product, decorating a shop, or equipping an office. You also need to raise working capital. This is the short-term borrowing needed by many businesses to cover the time delay between paying for stock and reselling it (in a shop), or between providing a service and being paid for it, or between buying raw materials and selling the finished product.

The amount of money that you can raise has certain limits. If you cannot raise the money that the business plan indicates is necessary, then you either have to scale down the project, change the concept, or even abandon it. Deciding how much you need to borrow is a fine balancing act; the key is to make the estimates in your business plan as accurate as possible. Most new businesses start undercapitalized, and this makes them vulnerable. It is easier to raise money before a project commences than after several difficult months in business, so it is important that your business plan allows for contingencies. If you start on a small scale and your business is profitable, then you should be able to attract increased financing for expansion at the appropriate time, usually after you have been in business for several years.

Raising the money to start your business will almost certainly require funds from a number of sources, each of which is covered in this chapter. Your accountant or business adviser can suggest which local banks and financiers you might approach. In virtually every case, however, one or more of the proprietors or directors will have to put up a reasonable proportion of the funds required.

DOS AND DON'TS OF RAISING FINANCE

✓ Do start to restrict your own personal expenditure – immediately.

✓ Do make plans to minimize long-term domestic spending.

✓ Do manage any existing personal debts very carefully.

✗ Don't borrow money unless you absolutely have to.

✗ Don't plan on taking any holidays for the foreseeable future.

✗ Don't give up your job until your business is ready to launch.

Using Your Personal Funds

Look first at your own resources for money to start your business. In addition to any savings you may have in the bank, savings and loan, or in the stock market, you can also raise money by selling possessions. Setting up a business can involve considerable sacrifice and a drop in your living standards until the venture is established. "Luxury" possessions, including antiques, stereos, photographic equipment, video cameras, and jewellery, could be sold to raise cash. If you own a relatively new car, another possibility is to sell it and buy a cheaper, older model (or a van, if that is better suited to the proposed venture), but obviously if your intended business involves a lot of driving then purchasing an old high-mileage vehicle may not be the best course of action.

Be cautious about getting into debt – check interest rates and repayment totals

If larger sums of money are required and you own your own home, you could consider selling your house and either buying or renting a more modest home – check first what the legal expenses of selling might add up to, as these may cancel out the gain. An alternative idea may be to take out a second mortgage on your existing home. This is only possible if the property is worth considerably more than the existing mortgage, allowing scope for a second mortgage on the unmortgaged part of the house value. Note that second mortgages tend to be expensive, and that your monthly repayments may become more than you can easily afford when you are starting a new business.

If you are considering options that affect your home, be sure to discuss all the implications with your family; it is essential to make them aware of all eventualities and to find out how much risk they are prepared to accept.

A final, cautionary point is that, if you need to borrow large sums of money, almost certainly you will be asked for personal guarantees (see p. 63). Should the venture fail, you will be called upon to honor the debt, which could ultimately bankrupt you or make you homeless.

HOW MUCH CAN YOU CONTRIBUTE?

If you have either no money or can contribute only a very small portion of the total required, then you may have difficulty raising the balance simply because potential financial backers, such as banks, do not like to feel that they are taking the lion's share of the risk. An alternative to bringing money to the business is to offer capital in the form of machinery, plant, vehicles, equipment, and even business premises, however modest.

In contrast to having no funds, if you have sufficient funds to finance the complete project yourself, you might not think of talking to your bank, accountant, or any other financial specialist. In some ways this can be a disadvantage because you miss out on the considerable expertise of these people. Also, because you do not have to convince would-be lenders of the viability of your project you may not prepare as conscientious a business plan.

CASE STUDY: Sources of Finance

AFTER RESEARCHING THE market for their proposed plant nursery and finding a possible location, Laura and Kate had produced a business plan to raise funds for their venture. It would need considerable capital to set up, and they also had to make provisions for domestic expenditure while the nursery became established and to allow for the seasonal nature of the business. They planned to finance the purchase of the land and buildings with a long-term mortgage, then get a bank loan for equipment, and an overdraft to fund the purchase of stock. They also asked some of their suppliers for extended credit to help their cashflow. Their own savings were needed to support themselves for the many months it would take before the business started making any profits.

You should always prepare such a plan and ask your accountant to read it through and make comments. Your bank will probably ask to see it when you approach them to open a business account. If anyone expresses doubts, then take another very hard look at the venture and make modifications if necessary.

Borrowing from Friends and Relatives

Many people shy away from this good source of money. Care is required to avoid family friction, so approach only those people who could afford to lose what you are asking. Show them your business plan, ask them for a specific amount, and mention that you do not expect an immediate reply as you would like them to think it over.

AGREEING TERMS

If your friends or relatives agree to help fund your business with a loan, it is essential that whatever is agreed is put down in writing. Unless it is a very small loan, the document should be drafted by a lawyer and it should specify the following:
- the amount of the loan
- when the loan is to be paid
- when the loan is to be repaid to the lender (be realistic here)
- how the loan is to be repaid if the business runs into trouble (usually the repayment period is extended)

MONEY SAVER

Try to think about the worst-case scenarios that might occur when your business is trading. Ensure that your cash-flow forecast permits you to repay loans at the rate and within the time agreed, even if bank interest rates rise and your turnover drops.

- what interest (if any) is to be paid and at what intervals
- to what extent the lender can interfere with the business
- who the money should be repaid to if the lender dies
- what should happen if the business closes.

In the case of a friend or relative wanting to invest in the business as a silent partner (see pp. 163–4), the conditions of the loan could be detailed in the partnership agreement; in the case of their buying shares in your company, the Terms and Conditions could cover these conditions.

CALCULATING INTEREST

What is the best way to calculate the interest on a loan? Choosing the bank base rate as a basis for calculating interest is useful as it is an externally determined rate that saves argument, is cheaper for the borrower (as banks charge more than the base rate), and it is also often a better rate of interest than the lender would receive from simply putting the money in a savings account.

The simplest approach is to use a fixed rate of interest based on the average bank base rate taken over the previous 12 months (this is to avoid artificial peaks and troughs in the rate). Alternatively, you could use the bank base rate current during the period of the loan; although this rate is more difficult to calculate, this is a much fairer method as it takes into account fluctuations in bank interest rates and is a more accurate reflection of the current economic

FACT FILE

Intrafamily financing is often the cheapest money you can borrow. It has other advantages over commercial sources: the lender is likely to be more sympathetic should your business struggle; and you may get sound business advice if the source of funds is already running their own business.

conditions. Note that you may be entitled to obtain tax relief on the interest you have to pay to the lender. In the case of an interest-free loan being offered by a close friend or family member, the loan would normally be repaid in months rather than years. Friends or relatives who provide a loan to help you to start up would not normally have any say in the running of your business.

OTHER OPTIONS

In the case of a friend or relative who becomes a silent partner in the business, the money they loan is invested as risk capital. A silent partner does not draw a wage, since they are not doing the day-to-day work of the business; however, they should have a say in how the business is run, and be aware of their liability for any debts the business may build up. At the end of the financial year, they should take a proportion of the net profits of the business (the profit after all expenses and your agreed wages have been deducted). One suggestion for working out how to divide up the profits is for them to be apportioned in the same ratio as the capital that was originally invested in the business. For example, if you put $3,000 into the business at the start and the sleeping partner puts in $6,000, then you could share the profits as one-third to yourself and two-thirds to your partner. This proportion of the profits would be in addition to your regular wage.

If you are starting a publicly traded company company, the friend or relative could opt to invest in the business by buying shares (see p. 65). Bear in mind that, in a publicly traded company, the person who is the majority shareholder can dictate how the company will be run. This is unlike the arrangement in a partnership, where (unless the partnership agreement states to the contrary) the partners are entitled to have an equal say in the way the business is run, even if their initial capital contributions vary.

Read over your plan critically, from the bank's point of view, before presenting it

Approaching Banks for Finance

Banks are in the business of lending money, so they are constantly on the lookout for good business propositions in which to invest. However, since new businesses present a considerable risk, banks are naturally cautious. They will want to know the full details of the proposed business and the people who are behind the project. Your business plan is precisely the document for that purpose.

In addition to reading the business plan, the bank manager may wish to meet not only the people behind the plan, but also their spouses and accountants. For, although a carefully prepared

GUIDELINES FOR REQUESTING A BANK LOAN

1 Ensure your business plan is up-to-date and accurate; avoid under- or overestimating the figures.

2 Make an appointment with the bank's manager or business adviser.

3 Present a crisp copy of your business plan several days before the meeting.

4 Think of questions you are likely to be asked by the bank, and plan out what your answers will be.

5 If you are nervous, try a rehearsal with a friend acting as the banker.

6 For the meeting itself, dress neatly and conservatively.

7 Don't be overawed by banks – they need your business as much as you need them.

8 If you are unsuccessful, think about what the bank says, review your plan, recheck the facts, then approach another bank. Don't give up easily.

Meeting Your Bank Manager
Banks are an important source of funding, advice, and information for small businesses. Presenting yourself and your business plan in a confident manner is vital to making a good impression on the bank manager.

business plan is important, the banker knows that if things should go wrong (and they often do) then it will be the caliber of the people behind the project and the support they get that will count towards redeeming the project and preventing a complete failure.

Banks prefer the risk of a new venture to be shared and rarely put up more than 50 percent of the capital. In the case of some well-known franchises, the banks are sometimes prepared to lend more, provided of course that the projected profits of the business can sustain the loan repayments. This generous attitude to selected franchises is simply because of their proven higher success rate, but taking on a franchise can be an expensive way to start a business (see pp. 24–6).

Types of Funding from Banks
Bank funding is normally in the form of loans and overdrafts:

■ **Loans** These are normally made to finance the purchase of the fixed assets of the business (plant, equipment, buildings, and so on). Loans can be at fixed or variable rates of interest and are repaid monthly or

Types of Security
Although you should not start by offering security, a bank will normally request this to cover any loan should the business fail. You should not agree to security in excess of the value of the loan you are requesting.

■ **Guarantor** Someone else, with suitable personal or business assets, guarantees to repay the bank should you default on your loan repayments.

■ **Your Home** If you own your home you may be asked to offer it as security for a business loan. Resist using your home as security if at all possible and offer an alternative: the bank is able to, and will, foreclose on the mortgage in the event of a business failing, no matter how small the

amount owed, and you may lose your home at the same time as your livelihood. Having a home potentially at risk is also an unwelcome additional strain on your family. If you do decide to offer your home, consult a lawyer.

■ **Your Work Premises** If you own your shop, office, or workshop, the premises could be acceptable security to offer to the bank. If the business fails you should still be able to retain your home (unless you have signed personal guarantees).

■ **Life Insurance Policies** Policies with a surrender value are most likely to be acceptable to the bank.

■ **Life Insurance** Depending on your age, the size of loan you require, and what other security is offered, a bank may require a life

quarterly over a preagreed term, usually two to five or more years (often considerably longer for buildings).

■ **OVERDRAFTS** These are for short-term working capital to cover inevitable cash-flow fluctuations. An overdraft, if granted, will cover up to an agreed amount. Never exceed this limit without prior permission from the bank, because the facility can be withdrawn at any time if the bank has the impression that you are mishandling your financial affairs. An overdraft is usually the cheapest money you can borrow commercially for your business, since you pay interest only on the daily balance in the red. This interest is deducted automatically from your business bank account, usually each quarter.

Many businesses require a combination of loan and overdraft facilities, as well as funding from other sources, when they start up. All banks publish and display their base lending rate, but as a small business you will normally be required to pay several percent more than the base rate for your loan or overdraft. Make sure you know what rate you are going to be charged, and remember that it is negotiable.

SHOPPING AROUND

Assuming your project is likely to be viable (in other people's opinions, not just your own), then if you do not get what you require from your own bank, or the conditions they want to attach to the financing (personal guarantees, for example) are unacceptable to you, then it is worth shopping around. Also, the way in which you present your business plan and your responses to questions may well improve with practice, so you have a good chance of succeeding on the second or third try.

Government and Other Organizations

I t makes good sense for anyone setting up in business to explore fully what government grants, "soft" loans, subsidies, and other forms of assistance are available. Soft loans are those with terms that are not strictly commercial, so the rate of interest may be lower than for a commercial loan, or the loan period longer, or the interest rate stepped from an initially low figure. A business plan will almost always be

USING YOUR WORKPLACE AS SECURITY
If you own your workplace, the bank may be prepared to accept it as security against a loan. This is a safer option for you than offering your home as security.

insurance policy payable to the bank to cover its loan should you die prematurely.

■ **PERSONAL GUARANTEE** This applies to incorporated companies only. The directors pledge to pay up from their personal funds should the business be unable to make the loan repayments. Doing so removes one of the advantages of incorporating and the limited liability protection it offers. If personal guarantees are sought, read the small print carefully and take legal advice.

■ **FLOATING CHARGES** This also applies only to incorporated companies. The bank has rights over specified assets of a company as these change (float up and down). So if a business goes under, the bank will take the assets (such as stock) and try to sell them.

required. It is advisable to approach the relevant agency before you set up your business, and your business plan should demonstrate a clear need for the assistance.

What government help there is comes from many sources (federal, state, and local government) and is channeled through many different bodies. It can also vary considerably from one area to another. For a significant majority of business start-ups there is little help available in terms of hard cash. Instead it may provide help with rent-free periods in industrial units, assistance with research and technology projects, and the training of staff, especially where these relate to the employment of long-term unemployed people, people with disabilities, or young people.

STOCK EXCHANGE
Equity financiers tend to invest in larger small businesses. Some equity financiers are large companies set up to invest in projects that they deem to be good risks – those likely to bring them a high return on their investment.

In addition to financial assistance available from the government, there are a number of other organizations which may be able to assist new business start-ups. Their help can range from business advice and mentoring to financial assistance. Your local business development organization or local authority will be able to point you in the right direction to obtain government assistance, or alternatively provide the names of other organizations to which you can apply for financial help.

Funding from Equity Financiers

This type of funding is available only if you plan to set up a corporation. It involves obtaining investment money by selling shares in your company privately. There are two very good reasons for having an outside investor in your business – first, they can contribute business knowledge and contacts and, second,

FACT FILE

Overgearing is when the ratio of loans to share capital is such that the profits cannot support the interest payments on loans and the business slowly sinks. The term is usually applied to a company with shares, but is sometimes used to refer to any business where the debts are too great.

by having the money invested as equity (shares) rather than loans you are not in danger of becoming overgeared (see box, above).

Many people want to retain total control and ownership of their new business because they are convinced that they will make their fortune from it, and they do not feel inclined to share the spoils. However, it takes a good deal of investment and business acumen to make your fortune, and those elusive millions are much more easily obtained if you are prepared to have a slice of a large cake rather than the whole of a small one.

An investor should contribute knowledge as well as capital to your business, so choose these partners carefully and ask what they can offer by way of expertise, and trade and customer contacts, in addition to money.

Equity finance can come from one or a combination of two main sources: private investors or venture capitalists.

Choose an investor you can get on with even if the going gets tough

PRIVATE INVESTORS

An individual invests directly in the business by purchasing shares, which are often a nominal $1 each. If the total capital being invested is $20,000, there will be $20,000 of "issued share capital." You may have decided to invest $12,000 of your own (you will therefore own 60 percent of the company), and to ask other shareholder(s) to invest the remaining $8,000. If you do not want to give up as much of the equity as this or if you want more funds, then

you could take out loans or set up more complicated financial structures. For example, different classes of shares can be issued, or a limited company can be split into several limited companies. Seek advice if you wish to find out more about these highly technical arrangements. Note that an investor is better protected if some of their money is in the form of a loan, because if the business fails they are more likely to get some of the loan money back, whereas the share capital is likely to be lost.

Private investors are sometimes known as "business angels." Generally you need to approach them and persuade them that your firm is a good one in which to invest. The drawbacks of accepting private investment are few, provided that you can work well with the individual in question, and accept that you are giving up (selling) part of your business.

VENTURE CAPITALISTS

Venture capitalists are individuals or companies (set up to invest in business) who may be interested in projects that are on the larger side of "small," with start-up capital in the $50,000-plus category, ideally more. You can find them through accountants, banks, or a local business development organization. Usually you have to pay fees for acquiring venture capital money. These may include "negotiation fees" (also called "commitment fees") for arranging the financing, which can vary from two to seven percent. Together with legal fees, these administration costs can reach ten percent of the sum raised. In addition, some organizations also charge annual "management fees." This makes it expensive money. However, an attractive aspect of equity financing is that companies, if empowered by their Articles of Association, can buy back their own shares out of capital, providing certain safeguards are met. This mechanism may attract investors, since they can make a capital gain and recover their

COMMON ERRORS WHEN RAISING FINANCING

1 Going ahead without raising sufficient funds for all your business needs.

2 Predicting a higher or faster rate of sales than is likely.

3 Not providing for an escape route, financially.

4 Borrowing so much that the interest and the repayments become onerous.

5 Putting your assets at risk unnecessarily by not considering other security options.

6 Not providing financially in your plans for expansion of the business.

7 Underestimating funds needed for domestic bills.

8 Not considering a possible downturn in the economy.

9 Not allowing for the cash-flow effects of any quarterly payments.

10 Thinking that raising the financing is the hardest part of starting a business.

investment (assuming the business is successful) by selling back their shares to the company at a profit. Venture capitalists are therefore really only interested in projects with huge growth potential.

Hire Purchase and Leasing Firms

Generally this is a more expensive way of raising financing than using a bank. However, it can be useful for acquiring high-value items such as cars, vans, or machinery if you have difficulty raising the required capital. Because the finance company usually retains ownership of the vehicle or equipment, they may be prepared to offer the financing to you even when your bank borrowing is at its limit. Obviously there is no point in trying to negotiate a finance deal if you think you may have difficulty in meeting the repayments.

There are tax differences between hire purchase (HP) and leasing, which will require an accountant's advice. In every case, get quotes from several HP or leasing firms and read the small print carefully, as their interest rates and conditions can vary markedly.

Making Use of Trade Credit

Another excellent source of financing is trade credit: a supplier allows you time before you have to pay for the goods or services they have provided. If you do your cash flow assuming no credit, and then do the same cash flow assuming your suppliers will give you 30 days' credit, you will be amazed at how this can improve your figures dramatically. One snag is that a new business is often asked to pay up front as it is an unknown credit risk, so if you can negotiate any credit period it will be a great help. Once you are in business you may, by negotiation, stretch the normal 30-day period to 60 days or even longer. You should, of course, pay your bills by the agreed date. Failure to do so is not only poor business ethics, but your supplier will note this and may either eventually remove your credit facility or simply be less accommodating on other matters.

Unfortunately, trade credit can also work the other way if your customers expect credit from you (even if you are a new business). This will be a problem for your cash flow, and it can be aggravated by one or more customers either being very slow to pay or simply defaulting. In these circumstances, credit control is vital to your cash flow (and survival). Issue your invoices promptly and send out statements at the end of the month, as many companies pay only on statements rather than invoices received.

COMBINING SOURCES OF FINANCE FOR STARTING A BUSINESS

In practice, most businesses raise the funding they need by a variety of means. Except in unusual cases, such as franchises, banks are not prepared to loan more than half of the total funding needed; *the remainder needs to come from one or more other sources. This chart shows some of the possibilities; percentages relate to the total funding required by the project, and are merely illustrative.*

EXAMPLE	YOUR CAPITAL (%)	INVESTOR OR GRANTS (%)	BANK LOAN (%)	OVERDRAFT (%)
For a very small project where the proprietor has no capital, a bank may be prepared to provide a small overdraft, particularly if there is adequate security.				100%
Where the proprietor raises the start-up capital, perhaps from friends and relatives or their own funds, the bank may provide an overdraft to meet the working capital requirements.	50–100%			50–0%
Where there is a grant available, the maximum likely bank funding may be increased in amount, but still within 50 percent of the total.		50–100%		50–0%
Where the proprietor puts up at least half the necessary money, the bank may be likely to provide the rest, partly as a loan and partly as an overdraft.	50–100%			50–0%
In the case of a franchise, the bank may be prepared to lend up to 60 or even 70 percent of the capital requirements.	30–100%			70–0%
A company in the $50,000+ league may attract an outside investor, possibly a venture capitalist.		50–100%		50–0%

FINDING AND EQUIPPING PREMISES

Small businesses need small premises, and these can be hard to find. Premises are usually the second highest overhead cost after staff wages, so it is vital to find the right place to work. The key points to consider are location, cost, size, and layout, as well as, in some cases, whether to rent or buy. Once you have found the right workplace, there are some equally important decisions to make, including what equipment to buy – from computers and phone systems to storage and manufacturing machinery.

Your business will need premises, even if it is just the front room of your home. In fact, working from home is probably the cheapest, simplest, and quickest way for many businesses to start, and is a very popular choice. Your home may not be appropriate for the type of business you are proposing, however. The alternatives to working from home depend on the nature of your proposed business, but range from offices and shops to industrial units.

Working from Home

This is an easy and cost-effective way for many businesses to start. Working from home can be ideal for a number of service businesses, particularly those that are computer-based. If you go to others' premises to supply your work – if you are a consultant or decorator, for example – it is also easy to work from home since you will mainly need your office for administration.

On the other hand, most people's homes have little spare room, and even the humblest business venture takes up some space. There are also domestic aspects to consider, since family members may resent the intrusion of a business – after all, homes are designed to be lived in rather than used as places of work. If the business is likely to be noisy, smelly, or to upset your neighbors, then it is probably not a good idea to work from home. Despite these hurdles, many businesses operate quite happily from home. They usually maintain a very low profile, with few visiting customers or suppliers.

CASE STUDY: Putting Location First

MICHELLE WAS A TRAINED printer and wanted to set up her own business, but had problems finding suitable premises. She needed to attract passing trade, which meant a retail site. She could not afford prime-site rental costs, so looked for a site near the periphery of the town's shopping area. Most of the properties that were available were quite run-down and unattractive, while other shops that could have been improved had no parking nearby. She located two streets with suitable premises and decided to postpone her start-up until the right property there became available. During the time she was waiting for premises, she was able to shop around for good deals on the equipment she would need, buying some in advance and pinpointing good sources for the rest.

If you are considering working from home, your first requirement is space. Unless your home already has a study or office, you need to think about where you are going to work. The spare bedroom or basement are popular options; otherwise, can you use an alcove or corner of a room where your desk or other equipment will not be too obtrusive?

Next, you can consider the utilities, such as heating (or cooling), lighting, electricity, and phone connections. People work more efficiently, and make fewer mistakes, if the temperature is about 20°C, with adequate fresh air. Ideally the room would not get full sun, which produces glare on computer screens and paper. Domestic room lighting is usually inadequate for prolonged close work or reading. You need good background lighting, which can be provided by fluorescent strip lighting, and then halogen desk lights for reading or other close work. Strip lights have the advantage of being relatively cheap to run, although some people dislike the quality of light that they produce.

If you are thinking of working from home, you should always let your insurance agent know exactly what you are doing. There are special policies for home-based businesses. Also there are legal constraints and possible tax considerations (see p. 171).

Finding Premises Outside the Home

There is seldom one organization that lists all the commercial properties available to buy or rent in an area, so you need to consult a number of sources, including:
- your local business advice center
- the local government business development office (especially for industrial units)
- commercial property advertisements in the local newspaper
- real estate agents specializing in commercial properties.

POINTS TO REMEMBER WHEN LOOKING FOR PREMISES

1 Do not be in too much of a rush. This is one of the most important start-up decisions you have to make.

2 Do not even consider a property in a poor location.

3 Do the math and keep within the budget you have set yourself.

4 Think about the layout of the workplace and do not choose somewhere with unusable or wasted space.

5 Be realistic about the size and timescale of possible expansion.

6 Read the small print in the lease, and seek professional advice.

7 All terms of the lease may be open to negotiation, including the length of the lease, and sometimes common charges.

8 Get advice from insurers and quotes for security, and work them into the equation – these can often be surprisingly expensive.

You might also consider taking out an ad in the local newspaper in the "Properties Wanted" section. A meeting with a local real estate agent can be informative. Such agents can advise you on areas, rents, and so on. When you locate premises (to rent or buy) you would be advised to have them surveyed. Check also about planning permission and fire safety regulations (see p. 171).

THE LEASE
If you are going to rent a property, read the lease very carefully. It will cover the period of lease, the rent, all responsibilities – including those for insuring and repairing the premises (normally up to the tenant) – statutory liabilities, when rent reviews are due, and the use and transferability of the lease (you want to

be free to pass on the lease). Many leases permit the landlord to raise the rent by a fixed amount whenever a lease is reassigned. If the lease states that you are responsible for the dilapidations (deterioration of the building) during your tenancy, you should get a survey done and its conclusions agreed with the landlord (it is also a good idea to take some photos). Leases are not set in stone, so challenge hostile or unreasonable clauses and question any you do not fully understand. Find out if there is a real estate agent who is managing the property, what their charges are, and if there are further common charges.

Never sign a lease until you have secured your financing and taken legal advice

Far too many businesses find it very difficult to get out of a lease if their business is not doing well, and the tenancy can then become a financial nightmare. Check the get-out clauses (there may be none) and think very carefully about the length of lease you are taking on; unless you can reassign the lease, you may be obliged to pay the rent for the whole period of the lease. If you are in business as a corporation, you may be able to get out of the lease if your business goes into liquidation, but landlords often make company directors sign personal guarantees.

FINDING OFFICE SPACE

Suitable small office premises can be difficult to locate. Two initial considerations are whether or not you need a downtown location, and the

COMMERCIAL PREMISES

Before starting to look for premises, you need to think about a number of issues. There are also tax and legal implications that will affect your choice (see p. 171). The most important aspects to consider are the following:

■ **COST** Perhaps the biggest disadvantage of commercial premises is that they are expensive to rent or buy and therefore add considerably to your overhead. In addition to the rent there are maintenance fees and sometimes common charges (for cleaning, utilities, security, and so on), which can add up. These charges continue even if your business is making no sales (prior to start-up) or few sales (as you have only just started up), and can erode your funds quickly. Shops in good sites have particularly onerous costs.

■ **TO RENT OR BUY?** When you start a business you probably do not want all your money to be tied up in bricks and mortar, so you will have little choice but to rent. In time, if you can afford it, and if you are planning to remain at one location for several

years, it may be better to buy the property, because it will provide more security in the longer term and may be an investment rather than simply an ongoing expense. If you are taking over a hotel or guest house, it is more usual to buy the property at the beginning.

■ **LOCATION** This is crucial. Ask "Where is the best place for my business?" Think about what your business needs to succeed – how customers will find you, which services you need to be near, whether you need easy access to a highway or train station to receive deliveries, and so on. Do not limit yourself to premises near where you live – that may lead to setting up in a poor, or at best marginal, location. The best place may be in an adjacent town or county.

■ **SIZE** What you pay generally relates to the floor area of the shop, office, or industrial site. It makes sense, therefore, to take on the smallest property you can manage with the proviso that, if you think your business's growth may require larger premises, you take that into account.

CHECKING OUT OFFICE PREMISES

If you are interested in a particular office space, look at it critically, bearing in mind all your needs as a business. It may be useful to sketch out a rough scale floor plan to help you visualize the office furnished and check that there is sufficient room for the equipment you need. You can also note down important features.

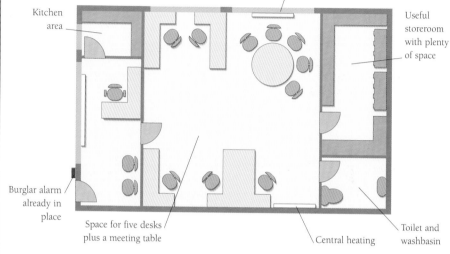

Windows provide good natural light and some ventilation

Kitchen area

Useful storeroom with plenty of space

Burglar alarm already in place

Space for five desks plus a meeting table

Central heating

Toilet and washbasin

POINTS TO CHECK

■ **FLOOR AREA** Note the total area as well as the area of each room.

■ **DECOR** Study the condition of the decor, and decide if you will need to redecorate before moving in.

■ **LIGHTING** List how many lights, their location, and the type of lighting. Note if there is good natural lighting, and if windows have locks or security bars.

■ **CONDITION OF FLOORING** Make a note of the type of flooring, and whether it needs any repairs, or replacing altogether.

■ **HEATING** Check the type of heating installed, if there is any.

■ **ELECTRIC SOCKETS** Note the quantity of sockets and their locations.

■ **TELEPHONE OUTLETS** Note the quantity of sockets and their locations.

■ **BUILDING CONDITION** Note the age and state of repair of the building.

■ **FLOOR ON WHICH OFFICE IS LOCATED** What is the access from street level, and does the office door lead into a shared area?

■ **SIGN** Check if this is easily changed.

■ **RENT PER YEAR** Find out the review date, whether there are any rent-free concessions, and, if so, for how long.

■ **BUILDING INSURANCE** Who is responsible for paying this insurance?

■ **LEASE** Check the length, expiry date, and notice period.

■ **COMMUNAL SERVICES** If there are any, check how much you would be required to contribute.

■ **LOCATION** Where will customers come from, how will suppliers reach you, and are potential staff likely to live nearby?

■ **PUBLIC TRANSPORTATION** Check out routes and frequency.

■ **PARKING** How many spaces are there?

Shop Premises

When looking at shops, the most vital consideration is location, then the shop's interior space. Finally, you need to check that office and storage space behind the scenes is adequate. Producing a scale drawing and noting the essential features can help to make a decision.

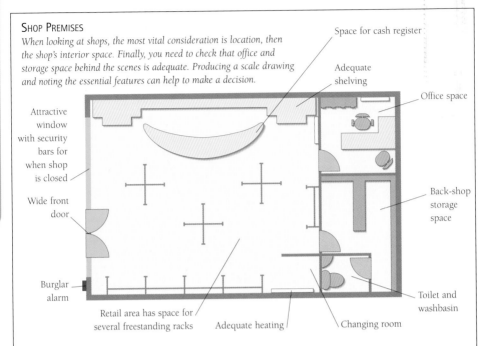

Space for cash register

Adequate shelving

Office space

Attractive window with security bars for when shop is closed

Wide front door

Burglar alarm

Back-shop storage space

Toilet and washbasin

Retail area has space for several freestanding racks

Adequate heating

Changing room

Points to Check

■ **Retail Area** Note its size and shape.

■ **Office Space** Check if this is sufficient.

■ **Storage Space** Check that it is sufficient.

■ **Interior Decor** Note the type and condition of the decor.

■ **Lighting** Check types and levels of lighting in the shop and the shop window.

■ **Condition of Flooring** Note the type of flooring, and its condition.

■ **Heating** Check the type of heating installed, if there is any.

■ **Electric Sockets** Note the quantity of sockets and their locations.

■ **Telephone Outlets** Note the quantity of sockets and their locations.

■ **Building Condition** Note the age and state of repair of the building.

■ **Sign** Can this be easily changed?

■ **Security** Check if there is a burglar alarm and whether there are adequate bars on the window.

■ **Rent Per Year** Find out the review date, whether there are any rent-free concessions, and, if so, for how long.

■ **Buildings Insurance** Who is responsible for paying this insurance?

■ **Lease** Check the length, expiry date, and notice period. Is a premium payable?

■ **Communal Services** If there are any, check how much you would be required to contribute.

■ **Site** Is it a prime downtown location, near the downtown, in a shopping center, suburban, or remote? Is it near a school, office, factory, or hospital?

■ **Customer Parking** If there is any, is it on a street or in a parking lot?

■ **Public Transportation** Note the nearest bus stop and pedestrian crosswalk.

■ **Access for Deliveries** Check if this is restricted to certain times of day.

■ **Shops Nearby** Look at the types of shops and other businesses in the area.

floorspace you require. A lesser matter relates to the image your new business needs to project, which will affect your requirements for location and appearance of the building. If you expect visitors, then you need to check there is adequate parking and public transportation nearby. Be wary of top-floor offices with no elevators. In any office building be aware of your responsibilities for common repairs and any joint management charges for security, cleaning, heating, and so on, all of which can be expensive. Think carefully about your requirements and the priority you would place on each, and keep these clearly in mind as you look around potential premises. If you plan to employ anyone you must meet all regulations (see the guidelines on pp. 172–3).

FINDING RETAIL SPACE

The retail industry is subject to continuous change: many of the chain stores and retail giants have great financial and marketing strength; new shopping malls are shifting the retail centers of towns, sometimes out of the town centers altogether; offices are encroaching on previously exclusive retail sites; shopping has become more of a family leisure activity; and there is the growth of online shopping over the internet. A street that was good for shopping a few years ago may now be in decline. The choice of location for a shop should be closely related to the findings of your market research.

Walk around the shopping areas to develop a feel for which streets are suitable, which end of the street is better, and even which side of the street has more people walking along it. Look for "For Rent" signs. To assess a site, talk to people in the trade and other shopkeepers nearby, and take the advice of a local chartered surveyor. If you are considering a particular site, go there on different days and at different times and count the passers-by. Are they

Inform the local authority, post office, and utilities when you take over new premises

carrying shopping bags? Are they to be seen in the stores or just walking past? Do they look like your potential customers? Check that there is suitable parking and access so stock can be delivered easily. Discuss the proposed site with an insurance broker, as certain areas and certain types of stock may be regarded as high risk from a security point of view, and this could make your contents insurance expensive. Insurance companies might also insist on a burglar alarm or other security, such as roller grilles, when you are closed, which can add up to an additional expense.

The demand for good sites can be such that you may have to pay a "premium" for the benefit of taking over a lease. This is a onetime payment for the privilege of taking over a desirable lease, and it can be expensive. If the rent was set several years before and the next rent review is not due for a couple of years, then the incoming tenant may get the lease at the existing rent, which could be lower than the current market rate. In this case, a premium is more likely. A premium is highly negotiable, especially if no other party is interested in the site. Finally, in retailing, the correct location is so critical that if a site is not available it is wise not to consider one that is second best, as you could be wasting your time and money.

WORKSHOP OR INDUSTRIAL UNIT

Usable space for production is the main need in this case; you might also consider requirements for heavy machinery or access by large trucks. Drawing a plan will help you to map out the best way to use the available space.

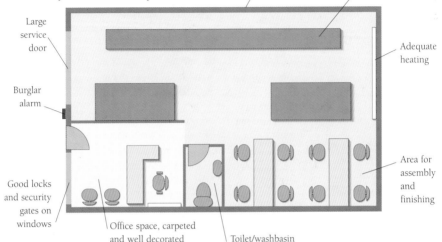

No windows in unit, but several large skylights

Machinery will fit well on workshop floor, with sufficient space around

Large service door

Adequate heating

Burglar alarm

Good locks and security gates on windows

Office space, carpeted and well decorated

Toilet/washbasin

Area for assembly and finishing

POINTS TO CHECK

▨ **WORKSHOP FLOOR AREA** Note the size and shape of the floor area, including the amount of clear space and any awkward corners.

▨ **FLOORING** Check the material of the underlying flooring, and whether it can carry sufficient weight.

▨ **ROOF HEIGHT** Check that this is adequate.

▨ **OTHER FACILITIES** Is there a large enough office space, and what is the condition of its decor?

▨ **LIGHTING** Check types and levels of lighting, from windows or skylights.

▨ **HEATING** Check the type of heating installed, if there is any.

▨ **ELECTRIC SOCKETS** Note the quantity of sockets and their locations.

▨ **TELEPHONE OUTLETS** Note the quantity of sockets and their locations.

▨ **VENTILATION** Is the building adequately ventilated, especially around machinery?

▨ **BUILDING CONDITION** Note the age and state of repair of the building.

▨ **SIGN** Is this easy to change?

▨ **SECURITY** Is there a burglar alarm or other types of security?

▨ **DOORS** Note the main entrance and other service entrances.

▨ **RENT PER YEAR** Find out the review date, whether there are any rent concessions, and, if so, for how long.

▨ **BUILDINGS INSURANCE** Who is responsible for payment?

▨ **LEASE** Check the length, expiry date, and notice period.

▨ **COMMUNAL SERVICES** If there are any, check how much you would be required to contribute.

▨ **LOCATION** Check proximity to customers, suppliers, and staff, and ease of access for deliveries. If you need staff, is there a likely source nearby?

▨ **PARKING** How much is available?

CAFÉS, RESTAURANTS, AND BARS

As with shops, location is crucial. Whereas a fast-food outlet requires a prime location, a good restaurant or bar can afford to be elsewhere, but not just anywhere. A key factor is grouping: if there are already other restaurants and bars on the same street and they appear to be doing well, then that is a very good indicator. Setting up in a solitary location is much more risky unless you have excellent local knowledge and prior experience of the same type of business. Parking is likely to be vital.

WORKSHOPS AND SMALL INDUSTRIAL UNITS

There are new, old, and refurbished units widely available, but in a few areas there may be a shortage of the most popular units (under 1,000 sq ft). Unless there are particular reasons for being on your own, there are often advantages to being located with other businesses in an industrial or office park. Neighboring businesses can be helpful and useful (there may be equipment, such as a van or forklift, that you can borrow occasionally), and inter-trading can take place.

The golden rule is to choose the smallest premises you can get by with, but ensure that your lease allows you to move to a larger unit, if required, without attracting financial penalties. Rents (in terms of cost for floorspace) tend to be lower for older premises or larger units.

SMALL HOTELS OR GUEST HOUSES

Choosing the location for a hotel will depend on the type of clientèle you are hoping to attract – mainly tourists or people on business, for example. To attract mainly overnight bed-and-breakfast visitors, you need to be in a highly visible location on a busy road. For mainly longer-staying tourists, you need to be located in a popular tourist area. If the likely clientèle is mainly business people, the proximity to businesses or major roads is probably the key factor. In every case, contact the local tourist information to find out who comes, from where, at what times of the year, what accommodation they look for, and whether the total numbers are rising or falling. An indication of typical room rates, occupancy levels, and recent trends would be useful, too.

Before you either take over an existing hotel or convert a building into a hotel, a great deal of market research must be done, because once you buy you are heavily committed. If you own your own home, you may consider selling it and putting the money toward the purchase of the hotel. Ads and real estate agents are the best sources for finding places to buy. Always have a full appraisal carried out, consult an architect if necessary, and check on zoning regulations before signing anything.

Equipping Your Workplace

For many people, the selection of equipment for their new business is both challenging and exciting. There is a real sense of progress being made and dreams becoming a reality. However, it is important not to become so focused on this aspect of starting your business that you neglect other, more important, aspects, such as starting to make sales. There is unfortunately a natural tendency to become engrossed in the selection, installation, and commissioning of new equipment – it is fun, under your control, and, as you are the

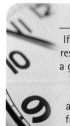

TIME SAVER

If you are planning to set up a café, restaurant, bar, guest house, or hotel, a good approach is to buy an existing business and alter it over time to your own style. This has many advantages: a proven track record; fully equipped premises; no zoning issues; and less risk.

customer, the sellers treat you well. It is easy to put off starting the business because you tell yourself that you are not quite ready yet.

Another factor to remember is that it is very important to keep your setup costs to a minimum. A characteristic of successful entrepreneurs is that they usually manage to equip their new businesses on a shoestring and actually take pride in how little they have spent to achieve their overall objectives. This whole aspect of being careful with your funds cannot be overemphasized. It is not smart to spend your hard-earned, tax-paid money (or expensive borrowed money) unnecessarily, even more so before your venture has actually started to make a profit.

Seek effectiveness, not just low cost, when choosing equipment

There are a number of key factors to bear in mind when selecting equipment:
▍ alternatives
▍ features
▍ financial considerations
▍ warranty and backup
▍ used equipment.

ALTERNATIVES TO CONSIDER

The first thing to think about is whether you are able to get by without the equipment. Are there alternative ways of working that make the purchase of the equipment unnecessary? Would it be cost-effective to pay someone else to do a portion of the work requiring specialist machinery? Maybe you can decide to put off purchasing the equipment for a while. This will help your cash flow and also establish whether or not you really need the item. If you conclude that you really must have a particular item, then see what rival products there are. Business publications often carry out tests on equipment where several rival models are put through their paces. These articles are usually illuminating. They not only compare the models themselves, but also highlight aspects of

the models that may not be evident from the manufacturers' brochures.

FEATURES

When choosing equipment, such as a computer, cash register, or piece of machinery, there is usually a wide variety of models available, ranging from the basic to the fully featured top-of-the-range model. You need to be clear about which features you think are essential, and which are merely desirable for your own purposes. The only unknowns will be if you think the business may grow or alter, and these requirements might therefore change. As with any big decision, it is best to think about it for at least a few days before committing yourself. Some items can be upgraded – ask the supplier if this is possible, and at what cost.

FINANCIAL CONSIDERATIONS

The real price of any piece of equipment is not simply the purchase price, but must also take into account the equipment's depreciation and running costs. For simplicity, even if you disregard the depreciation, you ought to consider the running costs, as these can vary enormously between rival products.

A big question is always whether to buy equipment outright or to rent or lease it. Since renting or leasing involves borrowing money and paying interest on that borrowed money (whatever the deal is called), it is usually best avoided. The exceptions are: if you are offered a genuinely interest-free deal; if you must have a piece of equipment but do not have the cash up-front; or if you are fairly sure you will have to change the equipment within a couple of years. For this last option, be sure that you are offered a rental or lease arrangement that allows you to change the equipment without penalty.

WARRANTY AND SUPPORT

All equipment breaks down at some time, and it usually seems to occur at the most critical moment. So you need to know what is covered by the warranty, for how long a period of time, how prompt the service will be, and the cost. Although greater bargains may be had purchasing some equipment by mail order or over the internet, it is when something breaks down that you may be relieved you bought it locally and can get it repaired or replaced relatively easily and without delay.

USED EQUIPMENT

Generally, secondhand business equipment has very little resale value, which is precisely why the smart entrepreneur should be able to pick up some bargains. In particular, office furniture – such as desks, chairs, and filing cabinets – can be bought from suitable auctions for a fraction of their value when new. Slightly scratched filing cabinets can be resprayed if necessary. If you are buying secondhand furniture, you need to weigh the savings you make against the image you want to project in your office – if a stylish or coordinated appearance is important, or you expect to receive a lot of visitors, it might be wiser to buy new furniture.

Computers and business machinery can be purchased, with a limited warranty, from companies that specialize in selling these goods secondhand. They advertise in appropriate business publications. Unless you really need the latest state-of-the-art machine, you can obtain good value here – although do check that the model you are buying is still supported in terms of service and parts, and that it comes with full instructions. One phone call or email to the manufacturer should give you the answer.

HOME OFFICE

This home office has space for two, and has been simply and effectively equipped. Storage comprises built-in shelving as well as desk drawers. Natural lighting is a key feature, but there are lamps to supplement light levels.

Equipping an Office

Whether your office is at home, in a commercial premises, or at the back of a shop, one of your first requirements will be furniture. You probably need a large table or desk (tables are generally considerably cheaper), a comfortable, adjustable chair, some shelving or cupboards, and possibly a filing cabinet. Note that filing cabinets when full are very heavy, so ensure your floor is strong enough to support the extra weight.

If you are planning to have a computer in your office, and particularly if you are employing others to use computers, ensure that the setup of each workstation is adjustable, and allows for good posture and distance from the computer keyboard and screen. This will affect the size and height of the desk, in particular. You need to comply with relevant safety regulations (see p. 171).

COMPUTERS
When buying a computer, do plenty of research first. Ask for advice from computer users you know, and shop around to compare the advice given about the specification you need for your business. For general use, the choice of software is usually more important than the choice of hardware. Think carefully about the functions you need the software to perform (word processing or accounting, for example), then compare the applications available in terms of features, ease of use, and price. There are some "office" sets of software available that combine all the basic office functions in a bundle. If there are programs that are standard in the field in which you work, this will probably dictate your choice.

For internet access, you will need a modem; some computers come with an internal modem, or you can buy an external one. Computers fitted with internal modems also allow you to send faxes directly.

Printers vary hugely in cost and quality. If you need to print highly visual material, a good-quality laser printer may be a worthwhile investment. Otherwise an inkjet printer should be more than adequate for your needs.

You may need to consider networking either between machines within your office, or between suppliers and customers. Get advice about the most flexible and reliable systems. Finally, if you are very reliant on your computer system, look into the question of computer support. Much software and some systems come with free technical support for a set period of time. It is often worth paying an additional fee to be able to phone up or call out a specialist at short notice.

TELECOMMUNICATIONS EQUIPMENT
Telephone systems range from basic phones with an answering facility to complex switchboards, and prices vary accordingly. Many systems can be adapted to your precise requirements. Make inquiries with several firms to compare the deals offered, and compare installation costs, standing charges, and call charges; this is a very competitive market. You should also consider how many lines you will need – if you use a fax or modem a lot, it may be worth getting a separate line for one or both – and whether you need a high-speed data link, such as an ISDN line.

SECURITY
Do not forget about the physical security of your office, since computers and other expensive office equipment attract thieves. You need to make arrangements to keep backup copies of critical computer files at a separate location, and if you have to keep critical documents, you might consider storing them in a fireproof security box. If you are looking after valuable items in transit, you may need to obtain specialist, flexible insurance that covers them while they are in your care. Talk to your insurance agent about the requirements, and obtain quotations for any new security systems.

A WELL-EQUIPPED SHOP
This wine shop uses highly functional, specialty units and simple boxes to make an appealing permanent display. Its long, straight aisles and low central display are likely to discourage shoplifters.

Equipping a Shop

Equipping a shop requires specialist retail and shopfitting knowledge. If you are new to retailing, this is the stage at which to seek and employ professional help. Retailing is a highly competitive business, and customers expect high standards of design and layout. You may be setting up a modest enterprise, but your customers will not wish to experience an amateur effort. Key factors to consider are:
■ shop layout
■ interior display
■ point of sale
■ window display
■ exterior sign
■ security.

LAYOUT AND DISPLAY
The shop layout is the starting point. The design needs to allow for a natural flow of people around the shop so that they can enter, move around easily to see everything on display, make a purchase, and leave, all without any difficulty. Access should be good to all parts of the store. Note that customers can be reluctant to go to upper or lower floors, even if there are elevators or escalators (unless it is a large department store). The layout also needs to take into account the security of particularly valuable stock, which should not be exposed near the door or in areas of the shop hidden from staff. Not only will there be pilferage of stock from the main retail area, but the storage area may also be vulnerable.

The interior display needs to show off the goods to their best advantage and yet be quickly changeable to meet alterations in stock. The need for security must once again be considered. Often quite a simple procedure can thwart thieves; for instance, in clothing stores garments can be hung up with alternate coat hangers facing in opposite directions, thus preventing a thief from grabbing a whole rail at once. High-value stock needs electronic tagging, an alarmed wire, or – even better still – a wire and small padlock.

One question to resolve is where to put spare stock. It may be that you resupply daily, or have a storeroom at the back of the shop, or perhaps use high-level shelving above the normal retail displays.

A key part of the interior layout is the point of sale, where the cash register is located. This needs to integrate into the rest of the layout. There are many schools of thought about the best location: having the register by the door allows staff to monitor customers; on the other hand, by the rear of the shop is more secure, and ensures that customers walk through the shop. The exact positioning needs careful thought and will depend on the shop space available, the planned layout, and the sort of business you are in. The choice of cash register needs to reflect your method of keeping your financial statements, the sales information you want, and the requirements of the tax authorities.

EXTERIOR ASPECTS

The overall image that the shop projects sends an important signal to a potential customer, and as a result of that image, they may or may not choose to enter. Seeking professional advice is not simply about getting the shop "to look good," but about making it actually work and be a viable business. Get the design wrong, and the business will suffer badly or fail. Have a

closer look at shops similar to the one you propose so that you can get an idea of what may be involved. In particular, look at branches of successful retail chains to see what their professional designers and decorators have done, and weigh up the task that confronts you.

Together with the storefront and sign, window displays are critical in attracting customers. Professionally arranged window displays require props, which can be made or purchased from specialist suppliers. Sometimes sales representatives will provide sales material to promote their goods that you can use in your window displays. A good rule of thumb is to change the window display every week. This is not only a simple discipline to keep the shop's appearance interesting, but is based on the assumption that many people shop on a weekly basis. Note that any external sign may be subject to restrictions by landlords, mall operators, or local bylaws.

Equipping a Workshop or Small Industrial Unit

When you are buying equipment for an industrial unit, the key factors you must first consider are:

◼ storage of raw materials
◼ workflow
◼ storage of completed goods
◼ regulations
◼ security.

Storage can be a bigger problem than many anticipate, and the need here is to have ease of delivery coupled with ease of access for production. Most goods travel around the country loaded on pallets, though small quantities are usually packed in cartons. Your goods inward area may require some form of pallet handling, though the alternative is to break a pallet down. There are plenty of solutions to handling goods, the snag being that the equipment, such as pallet trucks, fork-lifts, racking, and possibly conveyor systems,

MONEY SAVER

If your tools are central to the work you produce – for example, if you are a carpenter or craftworker – buy the best versions you can of your basic tools. Keep them in optimum condition. Long-term, this will save money, as you will need to replace them less frequently than cheap tools.

The key to equipping a workspace is to ensure that the layout is geared toward ease of production. Here, a simple workbench has been situated by a window that provides good natural light.

can be quite expensive. However, if you need them, they should more than repay their cost in terms of efficiency. Another potential problem is protecting the goods from the weather and from damage due to poor handling, either while in storage or in transit.

In terms of workflow, the choice of equipment and its precise placement in the unit should be to facilitate efficient production and to establish a safe working environment. Compliance with the many safety regulations is essential, and unless you have experience in this field, it is vital to get professional advice. Experiment on paper with different layouts drawn to scale before finalizing your purchases. Industrial units are often the targets of thieves or vandals; this needs careful consideration and professional advice from security experts.

STARTING out

Launching your venture means making potential customers aware of what your business has to offer and beginning to make sales. Be prepared for a steep learning curve as you start to put your plans into action. A flexible attitude and a willingness to keep rethinking and improving on your business are essential. As your business grows, you may need to consider different ways of expanding at home or abroad.

MARKETING

You have a business only if you can make sales, and the whole process of getting those sales involves proper marketing. Good marketing is vital to every business. It covers the whole process of selling goods or services, including correct pricing, appropriate advertising, useful promotion, and, finally, effective selling. These four aspects need to be in harmony to work successfully, which is why a marketing strategy is essential for the best results. The first two aspects are covered in this chapter, while sales and promotion are covered on pages 98–113.

Doing the market research for your business should have enabled you to assess whether there is a market for your proposed business and if it is big enough to support you. Even if this is so, your business will not succeed unless you market it properly. Market research is a key element of marketing and should be an ongoing process once your business is up and running.

There are innumerable different ways to market your product or service. For instance, if you were publishing a trade magazine you could distribute it free and rely on the advertising revenue to make a profit, allowing you to guarantee a wide circulation to your advertisers. An alternative marketing strategy would be to charge readers a subscription; your circulation will be less, which might put off some advertisers, but you would have a more reliable income from the subscriptions. Even a fairly straightforward business can market itself in different ways. An instant print shop located in a downtown area, for example, could simply rely on passing trade, or the proprietor could go out and visit businesses to bring in more printing work. When you start your business you need to come up with a marketing strategy that relates to your market research and business plan. Once you start in business you can adjust and improve the strategy as necessary.

Spend time developing a marketing strategy

Pricing a Product or Service

The first basic aspect to consider is pricing. This is difficult to get right. A key element of working out pricing is understanding your costs. Once you know your costs, you can use this as an element in the pricing calculation. Two types of costs are relevant here:

■ **FIXED COSTS** Also known as overhead, these refer to business expenditure, which is basically constant or fixed irrespective of the level of trading. Rent, most salaries, and insurance, are examples of fixed costs.

■ **VARIABLE COSTS** Also known as direct costs, these comprise expenditure which varies directly in relation to the level of business; for instance, the costs of raw materials.

The price you choose needs to meet your fixed and variable costs, and then make a surplus (your profit) on top. This is the minimum you need to make from your sales to stay in business. With fixed costs it therefore makes a good deal of difference whether you sell one item or a hundred items per year, or provide a service for one day or a hundred days, since the entire fixed costs have to be recovered on those sales. Dividing the fixed costs by one, a hundred, or whatever, obviously has a huge impact on the end price. Be very cautious in predicting your likely sales in terms of units sold or chargeable time.

Fixed costs must always be kept to a minimum as they can float upward and soon overwhelm the profitability of a business (see pp. 142–4). Businesses are usually better at controlling their "variable costs." For example, when a supplier raises their prices, most businesses take notice and, where the rise is unjustified, they will challenge it or find a new supplier.

SENDING THE RIGHT SIGNALS

While costs are an important element in calculating a price – one you should never lose sight of – there are numerous other factors you need to take into account. For instance, your selling price can send an important signal to your customers. In the absence of other indicators, the price tells them if you are offering a cut-price deal or if you are at the top end of the market. To decide where your own price should lie demands knowledge of your target market and what the likely buyers are prepared to pay. This requires prior experience of the industry or accurate interpretation of your market research results.

In general terms, if you price slightly on the low side you will make more sales, but with a lower margin, and if you price slightly on the high side, you will make fewer sales but with a

DOS AND DON'TS OF PRICING

✓ Do put a realistic price on a product or service.

✓ Do make sure you include all the costs in your pricing calculations.

✓ Do take into account the true value of your own time.

✓ Do compare actual costs incurred on a job with the invoiced price.

✓ Do react quickly but thoughtfully to a competitor changing their prices.

✗ Don't forget to increase prices in line with inflation.

✗ Don't make the price hard to find in your sales literature.

✗ Don't price low just to get the work.

✗ Don't discount too much, too often.

✗ Don't think the customer is concerned only with the price.

greater margin, so the net profit will remain the same. The problem is, of course, knowing what constitutes a "high" or a "low" price; if you have existing competitors they will have already created price norms in the market. Finally, if you have one major customer, they may simply dictate what price they will pay, in which case your calculations will tell you if that is sufficient for your business to be viable.

CASE STUDY: Developing a Marketing Strategy

ONCE HE HAD left his job in the civil service, Michael began to set up his wine business, selling directly to consumers. His first task was to get his prices right. He had to be sure that he was including all his overhead, not overestimating likely sales, but at the same time establishing prices that would be attractive to buyers. His market was sensitive to price in that many of his potential customers would be very well aware of what their wine should cost. To coincide with the opening of his business, Michael also produced a press release, which he sent to his local newspapers; he backed this up with some targeted advertising in the same papers. He then considered incentives for customers to encourage them to introduce him to their friends; he would be relying on the personal touch and word of mouth to give him an edge in this highly competitive market.

UNDERSTANDING MARKUPS AND MARGINS

A markup is the amount added to the cost price to reach the selling price; a margin is the amount of profit you are making on an item. The calculation for a markup is:

$$\text{Markup (\%)} = \frac{(\text{selling price} - \text{cost price})}{\text{cost price}} \times 100$$

The calculation for a margin is:

$$\text{Margin (\%)} = \frac{(\text{selling price} - \text{cost price})}{\text{selling price}} \times 100$$

Markups and margins vary from industry to industry, and in different parts of any supply chain. Learn the norms for your business; the only way to do this is to ask others in the business, either through a trade association, or contacts. Beware of a common error: sometimes people say their markup is 200 percent, meaning that they buy something for one price, and sell it for double that price. In fact, this is a markup of only 100 percent.

DISTRIBUTION AND PRICING

How you distribute your product can make a great difference to your pricing. The main

options for selling a product are selling directly to the customer, using an agent on commission, or distributing through a wholesaler or retailer. Each method is appropriate to a particular industry, and you should know the markups of the different distribution stages relevant to you so that you can work out your "end-user" price to see if it is competitive. Some people, when starting a business, begrudge using wholesalers or retailers, because they feel they will take too much of the overall profit to be made on an item. However, selling direct to the customer takes both time and effort on promotion, neither of which is cheap. It might actually be better to sell indirectly through wholesalers or retailers, who already have the outlets and the customers.

PRICING FOR WHOLESALERS AND RETAILERS

A straightforward way to price a product for wholesale or retail purposes is as follows:

$$\text{Selling price per unit} = \text{net cost price} + \text{markup}$$

For example, if you buy an article for $4.65, and if the typical trade markup is 85 percent, then the selling price would be calculated as follows:

$$(\$4.65 + 85\%) = \$8.60$$

There are several other points to consider:
■ You may consider rounding the price up or down to a figure (such as $8.50, or perhaps $8.99) that sounds more appealing to a customer.
■ Keep your prices in line with those of your competitors.
■ Check that your cash-flow forecast reflects your markups, in terms of the relationship between the top "sales" line and the "stock/raw materials" line lower down. For example, if you are using a 100 percent markup, then your "stock/raw materials" line should be about half the value of the "sales" line, or you will be destocking or overstocking gradually.

PRICING FOR MANUFACTURERS

If you are a manufacturer, a straightforward calculation to price a product is:

Selling price per unit =

(cost of raw materials + direct labour + overhead contribution) + markup

You can calculate the elements in this sum in the following way:

■ **COST OF RAW MATERIALS** This should be relatively easy to calculate per item, but do remember to allow for wastage.

■ **DIRECT LABOR** This is the realistic cost of employing staff to make the units. Staff costs should include about one-third as much again on top of the wage to allow for Social Security, paid vacation, and so on. If you are self-employed, do not be tempted to price your own labor costs cheaply – if you do, and you take on staff at a future date, you will either have to raise prices or take a drop in profits to cover the extra cost.

Price to achieve the maximum profit possible

■ **MARKUP** To work this out, insert a known markup appropriate for your trade into the pricing equation (see opposite) to obtain your selling price; you can then make slight adjustments to the final price as necessary. The markup needs to provide a small surplus (say five to 10 percent) to provide funds for future expansion, new product development, or simply to save for any future contingencies.

■ **OVERHEADS CONTRIBUTION** This considers the overhead (fixed costs) of the business, which obviously has to be supported by the production. To work out the overhead contribution per item, use the following calculation:

$$\text{Overhead contribution} = \frac{\text{total overhead}}{\text{total production}}$$

An important point to note is that this calculation assumes that everything that is produced is subsequently sold.

CASE STUDY: Working Out the Unit Price

ELLEN IS self-employed, making children's garments. The raw materials cost $10 per unit (allowing for wastage), and each item takes one hour to make, so in a 40-hour week she might make 35 such items (allowing for downtime, time spent on administration, and so on). The labor cost is $500 – equivalent to what it would cost to pay an employee to do the job, plus one-third extra for paid vacation, sick leave, and so on. So the direct labour cost would be:

$$\frac{\$500 + \$165}{35} = \$19 \text{ per unit}$$

Assume total overhead comse to $8,000 a year, and total annual production is 1,680 items (for 48 weeks' production, allowing for some vacation). The overheads contribution is:

$$\frac{\$8,000}{1,680} = \$4.76 \text{ per unit}$$

Finally a markup is added of ten percent. The selling price, therefore, is:

($10 + $19 + $4.76) + 10% = $37.14

Ellen might choose to sell at more or less, depending on the competition and the market.

PRICING SERVICES

The pricing of services is usually based on hourly labor rates plus material costs. For consultancy or freelance work, this is usually called "fees plus expenses."

■ CALCULATING HOURLY LABOR RATES

$$\text{Hourly rate} = \frac{\text{(total overhead including all wages)} + \text{markup}}{\text{total likely productive hours}}$$

First of all, find out the typical "going rate" for what you are planning to do. If you plan to employ anyone, allow an adequate hourly wage for them out of the amount you are planning to charge, making allowances for downtime and profit. Work out overhead and an appropriate markup. To calculate your productive hours, assume you (and any employees) will be productive (doing work for which you can actually charge) for approximately 75 percent of the working week. The actual figure may be lower. Being productive for 75 percent of the time means that in a typical 40-hour week you will only be charging for 30 hours, but having to pay your staff for 40. The remaining 10 hours are absorbed in getting sales, doing paperwork, traveling, buying materials, and so on. Do the calculation, and insert that figure into your cash-flow forecast. If the cash-flow forecast figure looks good, and your labor rate is

CASE STUDY: Working Out an Hourly Rate

PAOLO AND GEORGE run a small car servicing and repair business as a partnership with no employees. Their overhead is $25,000 per year, and their basic workweek is about 50 hours. They estimate that they can do productive work for 40 hours (administration and cleaning taking up the balance of time). They take four weeks' vacation per year and, when possible, draw $50,000 a year each. The equation, assuming a 10 percent markup, would then be:

$$\frac{(\$25,000 + \$50,000 + \$50,000) + 10\%}{2 \times (40 \text{ hours} \times 48 \text{ weeks})}$$
$$= \$35.80$$

The hourly rate is very dependent on them achieving a full 40-hour productive week with no time lost. In practice, they also make a useful profit on the spare parts sold.

about that for the industry, that is a good start. If not, see what you can adjust.

■ **MATERIALS** These are usually charged "at cost," but charging your customer the price you paid ignores the time you take to locate the materials, the cost of travel to collect them, materials held in stock, and so on. So most businesses define "at cost" as the retail price; they purchase the goods at wholesale prices, giving themselves some margin.

CASE STUDY: Looking at Different Options for Charging

CAROLINE IS A graphic designer who wants to freelance. She plans to work on her own from home and to visit clients as necessary to get work and to discuss projects. She calculates the minimum hourly rate she must charge to provide an adequate "wage," and to cover any overhead she has. She needs to allow for time lost due to traveling, getting work, and administration. Any materials used she will charge at cost. She may be able to quote her hourly rate for some jobs, while in others she may be given a budget to work within or be asked to quote an overall price. Her difficulty in the latter situations would be estimating how long the job might take. She plans to keep a time log, and at the end of a fixed-price job, she will use it to calculate the actual hourly rate she achieved – this will help her with future estimates.

ESTIMATES AND QUOTATIONS

Service businesses usually operate by providing customers with an estimate (or quotation) which, if accepted by the customer, forms the basis of the contract between the two parties. An "estimate" is the approximate price for doing a job, but usually a buyer will ask for a "quotation" in writing. A quotation is a fixed price, and, if agreed, is binding for both parties. You may be able to quote on a separate basis for each client, but always look at previous quotes to a client before submitting a new one so that you can keep the basics consistent.

MONEY SAVER

Avoid unnecessary friction with customers by advising them in advance if a price is likely to change (often prompted by the customer changing their specification). Since all quotations involve some guesswork, carefully record the actual time and materials you spend on fulfilling each contract. In this way your guesses should get more accurate with experience.

QUOTATION
If you have to do a large number of quotations, it can be useful to have a standard template so that you can fill in the relevant details. Always put the date on the quotation, and make clear for how long it is valid. Be clear about exactly what is covered in the quotation, and include your payment terms.

Quantity and specification are described in detail

Length of time for which quote is valid is included

Payment terms are made clear

Secure
Gates

10 Sellers Lane
Any City, Any State, ST 54321
Tel: 555-4321

Mrs. S. Nixon, Manager
Excellent Products
Unit 3, Industrial Place
Any Town
Any State, ST 54321

June 21, 2001

Dear Mrs. Nixon,

WINDOW GATES - QUOTATION

Thank you for taking the time to meet me yesterday. I now have the pleasure of providing you with a quote to supply and fit window security gates for your factory unit.

QUANTITY	Four windows, all to the rear of the premises.
SPECIFICATION	Mild steel expanded mesh as per sample left with you. Gates to be attached to window surrounds by one-way security screws.
PRICE	$623.00 + tax. This quotation is valid for 30 days.
TERMS	Payment is due 30 days from date of invoice.
GUARANTEE	We guarantee our workmanship and materials for 12 months.

If you have any questions please do not hesitate to call me. I look forward to hearing from you in the near future.

Yours sincerely,
Paul Wilson
Sales Manager

Different Methods of Advertising

You can have a desirable product or service at an attractive price, but if nobody knows about it, it is unlikely to sell. There are many ways of advertising to find customers, and even a small business should try to use a combination of these. Some advertising methods are more costly than others, while some are more effective. Cost and effect are not always clearly related.

The function of advertising is to arouse interest in specific readers and to encourage them to take the next step (to visit you, phone you, or buy your product). With most advertising you are trying to target the message at the person who can make the buying decision. It is therefore essential to choose the best medium for your message. To target your advertising, look back at your market research to help you ascertain who your customers are, where they live or work, what they like, what makes them different. This might help you to form a picture of the places and publications in which they are likely to notice advertising.

Your advertising needs to be part of a campaign. People tend to forget most single advertisements almost as soon as they have seen them, unless they happen to have a need for the product or service at the time they see the ad. A successful advertising campaign requires regular advertising. You do not need to take out large ads, in fact a little and often is likely to give a better result.

As with any endeavor that will take time, money, and effort, you need to formulate a plan. This should set simple goals (such as an increase in sales of 10 percent within six months), a budget, likely timetables, and a means of monitoring the success of the plan. The clearer you are about your goals at the outset, the more likely you are to be able to measure your success and improve upon your campaign in the future.

COMMON ERRORS WITH ADVERTISING

1. Assuming one big advertisement is all that is necessary.

2. Placing an advertisement in response to pressure from advertising salespeople.

3. Advertising in the wrong place (or at the wrong time).

4. Advertising without a clear idea as to the objective.

5. Using your business name for the advertisement's headline.

6. Designing an advertisement that promotes image, then expecting a response.

7. Placing an advertisement too hastily, and not as part of an overall plan.

8. Omitting a clear call for action at the end of an advertisement.

9. Allowing too small a budget for advertising.

10. Continuing to place advertisements without monitoring the results.

ADVERTISING IN A NEWSPAPER, MAGAZINE, OR DIRECTORY

Before placing an ad in a publication, check to see if similar firms are advertising. If not, check again whether the publication will reach your target market. Directories can be a good place for small businesses to advertise, as long as the directory is one your target customers are likely to use. Many industries have their own directory. Ask businesses (not direct rivals) already advertising in a directory if they get much response from their entry. Some directory entries are simply a listing of the business name and address; if there is space for a comment, give it as much thought as you would for any other advertisement. Most directories are annual, so try to be sure your details will not change during the life of the directory.

CHOOSING AN ADVERTISING METHOD

METHOD	COST	ADVANTAGES	DISADVANTAGES
DIRECT MAILSHOT LETTER	Low	■ Targeted audience ■ High response rate (2–5 percent)	■ Time-consuming to locate or produce a good mailing list
SMALL POSTER	Low	■ Large readership ■ Long life	■ Limited locations ■ Message must be short to make an immediate impact
MAILBOX LEAFLET	Low	■ Can be part-targeted	■ Low response rate ■ Post office distribution is most effective but increases the cost
INTERNET WEB SITE	Low/ Medium	■ Potentially huge audience ■ Full color, sound, and some animation possible	■ Difficult to stand out in the crowd
DIRECTORIES	Low/ Medium	■ Ad life is one year ■ Allows comparison with competitors ■ May have wide circulation	■ Can only make changes annually
DIRECT MAILSHOT LEAFLET	Low/ Medium	■ Targeted audience	■ Response rate is variable ■ Time-consuming (but less so than direct mailshot letter)
AD IN LOCAL PAPER	Medium	■ Local audience ■ Can repeat often ■ Supporting editorial is possible	■ Readership much larger than your target market
AD IN TRADE PUBLICATION	Medium/ High	■ Targeted ■ Editorial often possible ■ Publication can have long life	■ If publication is relevant, none, except price
AD ON LOCAL RADIO	High	■ Wide audience	■ Ad time very brief, so needs repeating frequently
AD IN NATIONAL MAGAZINE	High	■ National audience ■ Color may be available	■ Editorial unlikely ■ Expensive

To place an advert, check the advertising rates. For classified advertisements, rates will usually be quoted as cost per word or line, while display advertisements are usually quoted as cost per single column centimetre (scc) – a space one column wide and one centimetre deep. Larger display adverts are also quoted in terms of one-eighth, one-quarter, a half- or a full page. Check the deadline for submitting your advertisement. Ask for a rate card, which will give all this information plus details of the circulation of the publication. If you are booking an advert, send in a press release at the same time, to try to obtain extra coverage in the editorial (see pp. 96–7). It is often more effective to take out two or more different adverts in the same issue than one long one.

PUTTING TOGETHER AN ADVERT

First, think about the content of your advert. It is tempting to try to address all readers – this is a scattershot approach and is rarely effective.

SAMPLE DISPLAY ADVERTISEMENT

This eye-catching ad focuses on particular items for sale. An incentive is offered to encourage a prompt response, and a 24-hour phone number is given.

Good-quality photograph is used both to attract attention and to show items for sale

Call for action by offering an incentive

Design is simple, with no clutter to detract from the basic message

Principal objective is to stimulate customers to request a brochure or visit the website

Headline promises a benefit and may therefore catch the attention of more prospective customers than a specific heading such as "Patio Furniture"

Contact details are provided

10% OFF ORDERS PLACED BY MAY 31

ENJOY THE OUTDOORS
Top brands of patio furniture in teak, cast iron, aluminum, etc
■ WIDE RANGE, ALL IN STOCK ■

For your free color brochure call our
24-HOUR ORDERLINE
1-800 555 6789
or visit our website at **WWW. .... .com**

John Smith Garden Center
Rose Street, Any Town

Instead, address the ad to a specific section of the readership who will at least consider your product or service. Your ad must be honest, and never misleading; you must avoid applying false descriptions to goods or services, and you must be able to prove any performance claims you make.

Do not clutter the ad in an attempt to squeeze in all sorts of information about different products. To encourage potential buyers to take the next step, you could try putting a closing date or using words demanding action. If you are giving a phone number in the ad, ensure someone will be there to answer it.

Keep your advertisements simple and to the point

Designing ads demands time, thought, creativity, and experience. It is all too easy to get it wrong and to produce an ad that costs money but produces little result. Look for eye-catching ads in previous issues of the publication in which you plan to advertise, and try to analyze what makes them successful. If you are using a classified ad, it needs a catchy heading. If you are placing a display ad, a good photograph or image is often more informative and enticing than text.

Many new businesses give prominence in an ad to their company name. However, unless the name is very descriptive, that is largely wasted space; an unknown name has little impact or meaning. Building brand or company name awareness takes a very big advertising budget – usually out of the question for a new small business. However, if your business represents or sells a well-known brand name, it may be useful to give that prominence (check first with the company concerned – they may even pay a portion of the cost of the ad).

An effective style of display ad is the advertorial, which looks and reads like a news item or feature article. In most cases it will be necessary to have the words "Paid Advertisement" at the top. If written skillfully, it can be worthwhile, but it must not be misleading. This type of ad tends to cost more than others, because it is generally larger.

LEAFLETS AND BROCHURES

The purpose of a leaflet (also a pamphlet or brochure) is to convey a message in a lasting form. Leaflets can also carry a much longer, more detailed, message than an ad, and can be distributed to a targeted group of people or sent out in response to an enquiry. Distribution of leaflets is very dependent upon your product or service and your likely customers. The most obvious way is to insert them in mailboxes yourself or you could use the post office, who will distribute them along with the post for a fee. An alternative is to pay to have them inserted loose in a newspaper or magazine. This is particularly popular in trade publications. If your target market is local consumers, your local newspaper may, for a small charge, include them with the paper round. Finally, you could hand them out at special events that attract your type of customer (for which you should have the organizer's permission), or distribute them in the street (for which you may need a permit). To design a leaflet or brochure, consider the following:

■ **SIZE** This will be determined by the amount of information you need to convey, the

TIME SAVER

Producing an effective, quality advertisement takes time and expertise. It may save you time (and ultimately produce a more effective advertisement) if you use a designer to help you. Look at adverts the designer has produced in the past, to form an idea of their work. Provide a detailed written brief as to your requirements, and ask about his or her likely charges.

intended method of distribution (for example, does your leaflet need to fit into an envelope?), and the amount you can afford to spend. Your leaflet is best kept to a standard size, and can be flat or folded, printed on one or both sides.

▪ **Cᴏʟᴏʀ** A full-color leaflet is expensive. It is, however, justified if the product or service you are offering is itself expensive, or needs color to show its features fully (for example, a wallpaper leaflet would be pointless in

black and white), or if it needs to be in color to compete with a rival's full-color leaflet. Note that you need full-color printing only if you are incorporating color photographs. If full color is not essential, great effect can be achieved by using two colors for a much lower price. Be careful of printing black on brightly colored paper, since this is often used to advertise cheap products or services. If you have a computer and a good-quality color printer you can create your own

Sᴀᴍᴘʟᴇ Lᴇᴀꜰʟᴇᴛ

This sample leaflet to promote patio furniture in the spring attracts attention by offering a benefit. Information follows about the range of furniture available, prices, and contact details.

Introductory comment clearly explains what is being offered

Main part elaborates on the offer. Enough information is given to arouse interest, and prices are given

Call for action by offering an incentive

Business name and contact details are clearly stated, but not unnecessarily prominent

MAKE THE MOST OF SUMMER
WITH YOUR FAMILY AND FRIENDS

PATIO FURNITURE – HUGE STOCK

We can now offer a complete choice of attractive, comfortable, and yet affordable patio furniture in pine, aluminum, or plastic. Elegantly designed and carefully made to be enjoyed and admired. Chairs from $19.95, tables from $49.95.

SPECIAL OFFER 20% DISCOUNT
If you bring this leaflet and buy at least one table and four chairs before May 31.

We also stock a full range of pots, plants, potting soils, tools, seed, hoses, fertilizers, gravel, seedling trays, sprays, garden sheds ....

John Smith Garden Center
Rose Street, Any Town Tel: 555-6789
www. ... .com

Fᴏʀ ᴛʜᴇ Gʀᴇᴇɴᴇsᴛ ᴏꜰ Gᴀʀᴅᴇɴs

Headline promises a benefit and may therefore catch the attention of more prospective customers than a specific heading such as "Patio Furniture"

Professional photograph is included

Text is arranged in well-spaced blocks so that it is easy to read

Additional items in range are mentioned, but should only be included if there is space

Business slogan is an optional extra

leaflets. This is best done only when the numbers of leaflets needed are small – probably 50 or fewer.

■ **MATERIAL** Look at several weights of paper before making your decision. A glossy or semi-matt coated finish and thicker paper are more expensive, but give a high-quality impression.

■ **CONTENT** This will obviously vary hugely, but there are a number of guidelines you can follow in most cases. Think of a catchy heading to focus the reader's mind. It can either be descriptive ("Patio Furniture"), questioning ("Need Stylish New Patio Furniture?"), assertive ("Patio Furniture Now in Stock"), or indicating a benefit ("Make the Most of Summer with Your Family and Friends"). Add some text explaining the heading; make it as short as possible, and keep it interesting. You are producing the leaflet because you want it to trigger some reaction. The end of the leaflet should therefore urge the reader to do something, such as contact you, so your address, email address, and phone number should be given clearly. A simple reply coupon can be useful in some cases. Include a map if you are not near to downtown or are hard to find.

■ **DESIGN** For a leaflet to achieve maximum effect, the design must be professional. It is a good idea to employ a designer to help.

■ **FOLDER** This is a specialized style of leaflet, suitable where you are dealing with a small customer base (under 100 or so), and the product or service you are supplying is either complex or changing. The idea is to print a stylish folder of lightweight card stock, usually slightly larger than $8^{1}/2$" x 11" in size. Into this folder you can slip sheets of information, possibly an introductory letter, and, where applicable, photographs. The folder gives impact to your presentation while maintaining maximum flexibility by allowing you to add to or change the information sheets within it.

DIRECT MAIL

Consisting of a letter, a leaflet, or (most often) both, direct mail is targeted at consumers or business customers. Its strength, or weakness, lies in the quality of the mailing list on which the mailshot is based. Direct mail is particularly useful for selling to existing customers whose details you already have on record, and can be used to notify them of new products and services, price changes, special offers, or anything else that might encourage them to place an order. You might also use it as a reminder for customers who order regularly.

POSTERS

A small business is more likely to use small posters aimed at the local market rather than large posters on billboards. The best use of posters is to advertise a specific event, such as a sale, or an opening. Usually permission should be sought from the local authority before putting up posters. Decide the sites you would like to use, then design the poster accordingly. If the people who will read the poster are on foot, the design can be slightly more detailed. For passing cars, the text needs to be brief and readable from a distance.

INTERNET

Having a presence on the internet with a website is an important marketing tool for many businesses. It is vital to recognize that your website is an advertisement like any other and should therefore be designed with that in mind. In addition to having your own website, you might consider paying to have an ad on someone else's web pages, especially their home page; the effectiveness of such advertising is uncertain, but it may be worth experimenting with if you have the budget. See pp. 101–5 for more details on websites.

LOCAL RADIO

Commercial radio can be an effective advertising medium for a wide range of local consumer and business-orientated products or services, and is a suitable place for small businesses to advertise. Start by speaking to the radio station's advertising manager and ask which times of day are best for your particular business to advertise.

Costs are based on airtime, and you need to add about 10 percent to cover the production costs of making the commercial. Research shows that the length of the commercial makes little difference to its impact, so choose as short a slot as your message requires.

Most local radio stations can help you to produce the commercial in their studios. A common mistake is to try to squeeze in too many words: in a 30-second slot with a brief jingle, there is only time for about 100 words, spoken quickly. Research has shown that commercials with dialogue between two or more people achieve higher impact than a single voice. The radio station will also have free library music that you can use. Ask for a demo ad, so you can hear in advance how your ad will sound.

MONITORING RESULTS

Few businesses, large or small, make enough of an attempt to monitor the results of their advertising. In fact this is crucial to testing and refining your advertising strategy. There are basically three direct ways and one indirect way in which you can monitor responses.

The simplest way is to ask the customer who phones or calls in person how they heard about your business. Alternatively, if a customer is replying by post, you can add an extra line (such as a name or a room number) to the address you give; as you receive replies you can detect the source of the enquiry. You can also see which ads have produced a response if the reader is invited to bring or send a coupon or form from the ad; this is particularly useful in a retail context. Finally, the indirect method is to see if your overall sales change, all other factors remaining the same; in practice this is rarely the case over a long time span, but you may be able to detect a trend.

TIPS FOR YOUR PRESS RELEASE
1   Try to tie in your news with some bigger event or story that the publication is already running.
2   Submit the press release well before the publishing deadline.
3   Keep the press release short (ideally under a page).
4   Write to catch the eye and hold the reader's interest.
5   Put the most important aspect in the first paragraph, since any editing is usually done from the bottom up.
6   If possible, include a good photograph or two with the press release.
7   Follow up the press release by phoning the appropriate editorial department – this is not always a popular strategy with journalists, but it can work and may give you some feedback, too.

Public Relations

This is a term for all the activities aimed at communicating an image and message about your business and products into the marketplace. If you can afford it, you can employ a PR consultant. For most small businesses, however, the main method of PR is to compose a press release and send it to relevant publications whenever you have a story that is newsworthy. The publication may then use the text from your press release to form a story or feature. Since the story is in the main body of the publication, this is not perceived as advertising, and often appears authoritative and therefore effective. Remember that the publication may or may not use your news item, they may choose to use it days or weeks later, and they may write the article in their own words and with their own bias. Trade publications are more likely to use your press release than the consumer press, and tend to be less ruthless in their treatment of stories.

Write your press release carefully, adjusting it as necessary to the tone or emphasis of the publication. Avoid superlatives or making suspect claims. Journalists prefer to have advance warning of events, but if you do not want premature publicity you can request the publication not to print anything on the subject until the date shown. Whenever possible, include clear, sharp photographs or transparencies, preferably taken by a professional photographer. Some local papers prefer to send their own photographer, so ask before you incur unnecessary expense. If you are sending a photograph, attach a clear description of what it shows (especially the names of people).

PRESS RELEASE

Keep your press release short, factual, and to the point, but ensure that it includes all the information a journalist is likely to need to write an article.

Headed notepaper is used, with contact details

Since press release ties in with a specific event, it indicates the earliest date for publication

Subject of press release is clearly indicated in heading

Start with the newsworthy event, then put it into context

Quotations and comments are included from relevant people

Indicates that photographs are included

Direct contact details

SPEEDY *RALLY CONVERSIONS*

8 Main Street, Old Town

PRESS RELEASE

NOT FOR PUBLICATION OR BROADCAST BEFORE MAY 2ND

LAUNCH OF NEW RALLY CAR BUSINESS

At a short ceremony in the downtown today, Bobby Millar, the rally driver, launched a new rally car preparation business called Speedy Rally Conversions.

SRC, located at 8 Main Street, will take high-performance road cars and prepare them to full rally standards. This will entail completely stripping down the original vehicle, strengthening the body shell, and adding a protective roll cage, then carefully installing the new, highly tuned engine, transmission, and running gear.

Jim Smith, the proprietor of the new business and a former amateur rally driver, said: "At present many rally drivers have difficulty in finding the right expertise in this part of the country. I hope SRC will meet their needs."

Bobby Millar, who now lives in the town, said: "I need my rally cars to be prepared to the highest standards and I am confident that SRC has the very people to do this for me in the future."

PHOTOGRAPH attached

FOR MORE INFORMATION:

Contact: Jim Smith

Tel: 765-4321

SALES AND PROMOTION

Selling your products or services is one of the most crucial aspects of running a small business. Advertising and PR let potential customers know that you exist and encourage sales, but there is no substitute for excellent promotional and selling skills when it comes to making a sale. This chapter covers a variety of promotional techniques, different selling forums, ways of negotiating, and tips for building a good working relationship with your customers over the long term.

There are almost as many ways of promoting sales as there are business ideas. Promotion differs from advertising in that it is much more proactive; it aims to stimulate the buyer into making a purchase at once. Although often cheaper than conventional advertising, promotion still costs money. In recent decades, consumers have been subjected to a flood of promotional gimmicks, so really effective promotion has become increasingly difficult, especially on a small budget. Wholesalers are not quite so saturated, but are perhaps more cynical. Promotions are also time-consuming. When you do a promotion, monitor its progress to decide if the resulting sales justify the time spent.

It is important to note that how you promote sales can depend on the circumstances and the timing; for the best results you need to focus

Keep trying out innovative forms of promotion to appeal to new and existing customers

on achieving a particular objective. If you wish to counter a competitor who has dramatically reduced their prices, for example, then you can either engage in a price war (not usually a good idea) or start a promotion that stresses why your product or service merits the apparently higher price. A different approach would be required to increase market share; in this case you would need to concentrate on the best ways of enticing customers away from your rivals. If you are promoting a new and innovative product, you may need to concentrate on drawing attention to the nature and purpose of the innovations.

Many of the most successful methods of promotion are covered in the chart opposite. Exhibitions and seminars are among the most useful and productive promotional means for small businesses and are covered in more detail on p. 100.

CASE STUDY: Choosing Promotional Methods

ANDY HAD RETIRED from the military. He was a talented painter, specializing in military subjects, and now wanted to make a living using this skill. His initial market research indicated there was a niche market, which would be best met by a mix of prints and commissioned originals. His target market would be not only serving and retired members of the

armed forces, but also members of the public with an interest in military matters. There was additional interest from overseas. He therefore decided to create a website offering online ordering, and to try to make sales in person at military events that were open to the public. He also planned to create a mailing list of customers who might be interested in purchasing prints on an occasional basis.

PROMOTIONAL TECHNIQUES

TECHNIQUE	DEFINITION	POINTS TO CONSIDER
MAILSHOT	A personalized letter or a leaflet is sent to a customer introducing a special offer	■ Useful for both consumer and wholesale customers ■ Cost is average compared to other methods, but depends on complexity of design ■ Response rate variable and unpredictable
SAMPLE	A sample of a product is sent to an individual	■ Effective when sent to someone with major buying power in an organization, or to someone who influences buyers, such as the editor of a magazine ■ Follow up with a phone call a week or so after sending
FREE TRIAL	The customer tries out a product before buying or as an incentive to buy	■ Most suitable for high-value onetime-purchase items, which the customer tries for a set period of time, or for low-value repeat-purchase items, such as consumables ■ Can be very effective with target market
COMPETITIONS/ RAFFLES	A raffle is organized with prizes of the products to be promoted	■ Requires legal advice to comply with regulations governing raffles, and permits to sell the tickets ■ Prize must be suitably attractive (or expensive) for people to enter the raffle
IN-STORE DEMOS	A manufacturer or importer organizes a demonstration of a product in a store	■ Store is usually carrying the product, so the demo often results in immediate sales ■ Demo needs to be carried out with enthusiasm
OPEN DAYS	An office, workshop, or studio is opened to the public	■ A lot of organization is needed to make the day successful ■ Need to put on special displays to interest visitors ■ Event must be publicized well in advance ■ Check you are covered by insurance for visitors
VIDEO/CD	Information about a product is made available on a video or as video clips on a CD-ROM	■ Ideal for conveying a complex message or to demonstrate how a product works ■ A CD-ROM could have an interactive element and a Frequently Asked Questions (FAQ) section ■ Expensive to produce and to alter
FASHION SHOW	Used in the fashion and accessory industry, a show is put on to display new products	■ Requires considerable time, skill, and money to stage an impressive show with the right venue, experienced models, and good-quality sound and lighting ■ A good way of influencing wholsalers and public buyers

Exhibitions and Seminars

For nonretail businesses, sales generally have to be made on a one-to-one basis, which is very time-consuming. However, there are two special opportunities where such a business can meet potential customers *en masse* – at an exhibition and at a seminar. In the case of an exhibition, your business has to show its wares alongside competitors, while in the case of a seminar you are the organizer and usually the only business giving a presentation.

EXHIBITIONS

These include consumer shows and trade fairs, and have increased hugely in importance. For nonretail businesses they can provide regional, national, and even international exposure. Do not pitch your expectations too high – many new exhibitors are disappointed with the

results of their initial showings. This is usually due to inexperience, although if you are getting consistent feedback about the viability of your product or service, ensure that you listen to it. Approach all exhibitions with an open mind and be ready to learn from other exhibitors and from your own mistakes.

Making the most of exhibiting requires a great deal of preparation, an adequate budget, and hard work before, during, and after the event. Because exhibiting can be time-consuming and expensive, the decision to participate should not be taken lightly.

During the show you and your staff need to pace yourselves, especially if the show lasts for several days. Take time out to rest, eat, and sit down whenever you can. Depending on the industry, the selling opportunities vary. At some exhibitions you make sales on the spot; at others you may just take orders; at others the main purpose is to make buyers aware of what you have to offer. Be sure in advance what you need to offer, and be ready as appropriate with supplies of stock, the facility to handle cash, checks, or credit card transactions safely, or order forms for taking names and addresses so you can follow up after the show. Each evening you should have a review of how the day went and make whatever adjustments are necessary ready for the following day.

After the show you need to allow time to follow up the sales leads you have made, and to catch up with all the other routine paperwork that will have been mounting up in your office while you were away.

PREPARING FOR AN EXHIBITION

1 Visit a number of similar exhibitions and talk to the organizers.

2 Decide which show or shows are the most appropriate for you.

3 Read the small print of the exhibition terms and conditions.

4 Design your stand or stands to be eye-catching and sufficiently interesting to keep someone from just walking past.

5 Organize what you will display on your stand and have leaflets to give away.

6 Decide on any pre-exhibition supporting publicity to encourage people to come and visit your stand.

7 Work out staffing rosters and book local accommodation.

8 If necessary, train staff on how to sell effectively from the stand.

SEMINARS, TALKS, AND DEMONSTRATIONS

These are events organized by you where you invite carefully chosen people who are likely buyers of your product or service. The key is to get the right audience. Once you have your captive audience, you can give them your sales pitch. Such events can be very useful for many different businesses, including both service-based and manufacturing concerns.

If you are selling to wholesalers, you may be able to tag your seminar onto some other event (such as a trade association or chamber of commerce meeting). If not, to get the buyers to come, you need to make the occasion sound interesting and appealing – offering lunch or drinks at a venue such as a local hotel may help to encourage their appearance.

It is vital to ensure that the presentation itself is entertaining and of a high standard. Whether you are doing the presentation yourself, or hiring a professional speaker, take the time to prepare high-quality visual aids (such as slides,

HOLDING A SEMINAR
In this small seminar, visuals are used in order to show the key features of a product. The restricted number of participants means that the salesperson can take the time to answer individual questions in detail.

a video, or a multimedia presentation), samples on display, and leaflets for people to take away. Rehearse at least once at the venue to get used to the conditions, time the presentation, and to iron out any technical hitches.

Internet and e-commerce

There is little doubt that an increasing amount of business is being done over the internet. The word "e-commerce" simply means carrying out business transactions over the internet. The relationship between customers and suppliers is being radically affected by the internet; customers can place orders electronically and then track the progress of the goods right into their warehouses or homes. The rapidly expanding internet market presents opportunities and threats to small business. On the one hand, it can give a small business a window to the world for its products (and services to a lesser degree) and a presence equivalent to its larger rivals; on the other hand, it poses the challenge of competition from far and wide.

BUSINESS USES OF THE INTERNET

The internet is an exciting and potentially highly beneficial tool for businesses. Nevertheless, it is important to consider what you want to achieve through this new medium, just as it is for any other new venture. Typical tasks carried out by small businesses through their websites include:

■ Sending and receiving emails (both internally and externally).

DOS AND DON'TS OF WEBSITES

✓ Do make it clear what you do and what you are offering on the home page.

✓ Do include some background information on your business on your site.

✓ Do have a "return to home" button on each page.

✓ Do provide an opportunity for feedback by email or telephone.

✓ Do give your full postal address, to establish credibility.

✓ Do ensure your site is registered with all major search engines.

✓ Do offer added value on the site, with useful information and free downloads.

✗ Don't include too many photos on your opening page, as they slow it down.

✗ Don't have too many layers requiring a great deal of mouse-clicking.

✗ Don't insist on registration simply to get on to your site.

✗ Don't be anonymous – provide contact names and email addresses.

■ Sourcing services, stock, raw materials, and consumables (the internet throws your buying net wider).

■ Publishing online sales catalogs (which have the big advantage that they can be updated easily and quickly and can also be used for publicizing special offers).

■ Selling goods online.

■ Providing technical support and backup (this reduces time-consuming phone calls from customers with problems, and provides customers with a more efficient service).

■ Carrying out market research (there is a huge amount of information available online, much of it free).

■ Checking out competitors (the amount of information available can be stunning and revealing).

■ Exchanging order information with customers and suppliers (this reduces the amount of paperwork and provides trading partners with increased information about the other party, such as stock levels and despatch details).

■ Managing a bank account (including paying business bills by internet banking).

WHICH BUSINESSES CAN BENEFIT FROM USING THE INTERNET?

All businesses will benefit from at least some of the business uses of the internet that are listed above. While many business websites simply provide information, there is a huge growth in the number of businesses who are selling their products and services online. The internet is changing fast and maturing in the ways in which it is used, but at present the main growth area is in business-to-business trading and the slowest rate of growth is in businesses providing services in person to consumers. A service-based company might nevertheless use a website primarily to promote their business.

To some extent, selling via the internet is like selling through a catalog that can be constantly updated, and permits the customer to place orders electronically (and, in some specialized

RESEARCHING WEBSITE DESIGN

Look at a variety of websites set up by large and small businesses. Note features that you like and that make the site easier to use. Explore other pages apart from the home page to understand the site layout.

A "Help" guide is useful where a site contains numerous pages, or to assist with an interactive process such as selling

Name of business is a prominent feature of the web page

Navigation buttons make it easy for the user to find information and connect to other pages on the site

A "Search" feature is useful on large sites or on those containing complex information

Users can choose whether to access more information

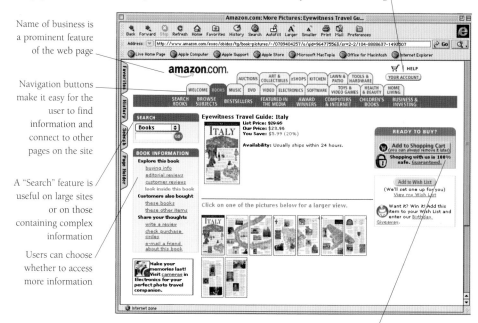

Shopping process is clearly indicated, and security aspects are emphasized

cases, such as software and music, to take delivery electronically as well). As always, the big question is: Will a professionally designed website generate enough online business to justify its cost and the time taken to set it up? The setting-up costs are dropping dramatically, thereby reducing the risk. At the same time, with secure credit card transactions now possible, customers are more prepared to buy online. A key factor is how committed your business is to moving in this direction.

CREATING A GOOD WEBSITE

If you have seen other business websites, you will certainly know that the quality and ease of use of different sites varies considerably. Some

are straightforward to use, while others are far less so. Visit a variety of websites and note features that appeal to you and that you find easy to use. Analyze how the site is structured and the usefulness of the various links. As with the design of any advertisement, keep in mind your target market and their needs, as well as your own e-commerce objectives.

Your opening home page should load quickly, have your business name clearly visible, and make a firm and direct statement as to who you are and what you do, so that the visitor knows if the site is relevant to them. You want not only to attract the right visitors, but also to keep them interested enough to browse your other pages. A home page benefits from buttons that give clear options for moving around the site and locating further information, and ideally does not require scrolling down.

Promotion of your website is as important an activity as the creation of the website itself. Merely creating a website is unlikely to generate sufficient visitors. Right from the start you should consider the keywords for the search engines to find. Look at rival sites to see what keywords they use. Include also common misspellings of your keywords. Ensure that your new website is registered with all major search engines. Once it is up and running, be sure to promote the site through any other advertising you do, giving your website address on all your correspondence and literature, business cards, products, and even your van sides, where appropriate. There is also proactive marketing of your site, in which you look for other sites that relate to yours and suggest a hypertext link directly to your site. This is a time-consuming but potentially very worthwhile process.

SETTING UP A WEBSITE

Register your domain name

Are you clear what your e-commerce objectives are? → If not, establish key objectives and a related budget

Is your business set up to sell over the internet? → If not, get a reputable outside adviser to help you, particularly with security and receiving payment

Create your website with the help of a web designer → Test out your website thoroughly

Set up the system for receiving, processing, and despatching orders

Register your website with all major search engines and relevant directories → Promote your www address by adding it to your promotional material, letterheads, invoices, and so on

Go online

Keep your website up to date, both in terms of your product prices and with latest website technology

Finally, for many businesses, the internet offers a new sales channel, but you should use it as an additional means rather than neglecting traditional channels in its favor.

SELLING ONLINE

If one of your objectives is to sell online, there are several issues you need to consider. The first of these is how to have secure credit card or debit card transactions. This is relatively easy, but requires specialist knowledge to set up properly. Another issue is that your business should be structured to process these new orders and to take care of the extra workload associated with the many emails (some of them junk ones) that are inevitable. It is difficult to anticipate likely demand in terms of orders, and in fact initial demand is likely to be slow, but you should be fully prepared to react as the situation develops. If you are selling a product, it is vital not to run out of stock.

UPDATING YOUR WEBSITE

After putting a great deal of thought, effort, and money into creating your new website, you need to keep it up to date to maintain its effectiveness. Having out-of-date information on a website reflects badly on the business concerned. For certain businesses, such as real estate agents, having out-of-date information makes the site useless. People will not visit a poor site twice. If you do not have the time or resources to dedicate to updating detailed information on your website, then keep it simple; the site could act as an initial point of contact, telling visitors how to contact your business through other means.

In addition to keeping the content of your site current, you need to monitor the major search engines to ensure they not only locate your site, but give it a high ranking when the right keywords are typed in. From time to time arrange to have your site checked over from a technological point of view, to ensure that it remains compatible and easy to use with the latest browser software.

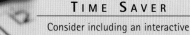

TIME SAVER

Consider including an interactive element if an aspect of your website is to sell a complex product or a service with different options. Offer a form for the customer to fill in their requirements; in return they will quickly receive a personalized proposal or estimate.

Face-to-face Selling

With the exception of former sales staff, most people who start their own business have not had to sell to others before, and may feel somewhat daunted by the idea. There are many basic selling techniques that can easily be learned and, when put into practice, will result in good sales. Even the most reluctant salesperson can get a real buzz out of making a sale, particularly where clinching the sale depended on their sales technique.

There is a saying that "customers buy benefits, not goods or services." Once you have understood that basic concept, the whole art of selling begins to make more sense. What the saying actually means is best illustrated by an example. Two football fans may buy a video recorder because they want the benefit of being able to replay their favorite games. If there were some better way they could do that, they might not buy a video recorder. In other words, it is not really the video recorder they need and are buying, but the benefit it gives them.

Your starting point is to know your product inside out, and to be fully aware of all its potential benefits to buyers.

FINDING NEW CUSTOMERS

When you start up in business you may have a few key customers in mind, but will need to find more to expand. As the business grows, it is important to keep building on your list of customers. In some cases, potential customers will find you as a result of a recommendation from a satisfied customer, and they are very likely to become buyers. Usually, however, you will have to find customers yourself. This can be by direct means; for example, if you are a service business, you can find potential customers from listings in business directories then contact them directly. You can also find customers, both other businesses and the general public, by indirect means, such as through your advertisements or other promotions.

Getting an Appointment

To get an appointment with a prospective customer (or "prospect"), the best strategy is first to find out the name of the person who has the buying authority. You can usually do this by phoning the business concerned, explaining that you wish to write to the buyer, and asking for the buyer's name. Occasionally, you will be put directly through to the buyer even though this is not what you asked for, so be prepared for this eventuality. Once you have the buyer's name, write a letter enclosing relevant sales information. In the letter, state that you will phone to discuss the contents in about a week's time (if you ask the buyer to call you, you will rarely get a response).

About a week or so after sending the letter, telephone the buyer to make an appointment. Be positive and friendly, but not pushy. Some buyers will be willing to see you, others will refuse directly, others may simply avoid you. Try a few times, and if you are not successful then try another business, and make a note to approach the original buyer again in a few months to see if their needs have changed.

Preparation

It is vital to prepare carefully for any face-to-face selling appointment. Make sure that you are familiar with background information concerning the person and the business you are going to see, and that you have thought through their possible needs and requirements.

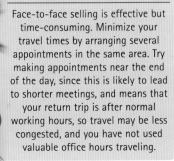

TIME SAVER

Face-to-face selling is effective but time-consuming. Minimize your travel times by arranging several appointments in the same area. Try making appointments near the end of the day, since this is likely to lead to shorter meetings, and means that your return trip is after normal working hours, so travel may be less congested, and you have not used valuable office hours traveling.

Gather together your sales material and ensure that you know it thoroughly. Sales material is a key element of face-to-face selling. It consists of samples, brochures, your business cards, order forms, and possibly a calculator or laptop computer if you need to come up with estimates or quotations on the spot. If you do not have a good brochure and it is not possible to carry samples due to their size, an effective substitute is good-quality photographs neatly presented in a folder or album. Letters of commendation, relevant newspaper cuttings, certificates of technical competence, and so on, can also be useful when presenting your case. Have your price lists ready and ensure that you know your bottom price – the price below which you are not prepared to go.

If dealing with a buyer from another culture, research the norms and etiquette in their culture for selling and negotiation. Their way of doing business may be very different from yours, so you need to build this into your plan. There are numerous books dealing with this subject. An alternative is to use an agent or other representative who is familiar with that culture and who can advise you on your best approach.

Opening the Sale

Arrive at your appointment in plenty of time. To open any sale (see also pp. 108–9), use the same friendly gestures as you would on meeting anyone new for the first time. Smile, make direct eye contact, and start with a genuine "hello" and a warm handshake. Hand over your business card if you have not met before and, if appropriate, ask for theirs.

Maintain open, nonthreatening body language and a positive attitude throughout the meeting. Try to sit close enough to be friendly, but not so close as to be overfamiliar – respect personal space (and note that perceptions of personal space vary from culture to culture). It is conventional to discuss briefly topics that are not controversial, such as your journey, before getting down to business. Find out the prospect's needs at an early stage so that you can tailor your explanation of the benefits of your product or service to those needs. Take a positive "Can do" approach and attempt to resolve any queries and clarify any points that need further explanation. If the prospect raises objections, that may be a sign of interest. Listen carefully, perhaps jotting down what they say so that you can overcome the objections one at a time without missing any.

Do not reveal all your tactics at once when negotiating

NEGOTIATING SKILLS

Your ability to negotiate comes into play once the customer is interested. The skill is not to lose the order but equally not to give too much away. At this stage you have one important factor in your favor – the buyer obviously wants what you have to offer. Your position is weakened if you have a competitor offering a similar product or service at a better price, but do not be panicked into giving away unnecessary concessions.

Negotiating successfully can be fun. Once you have a fixed bottom price in your mind, all you need to remember is, first, to keep calm and do not show your excitement about getting the order, and, second, every time the would-be buyer asks for a concession, ask for something in return. When the prospect starts to show a definite interest and is at the stage of

wanting more information, including exactly what the cost will be, introduce your starting price. It should flow naturally in the conversation but, if not, then create the right moment by saying something like: "I know you will want to know the cost, so..." and perhaps taking out your price list at the same time.

The buyer is likely to say that your price is too high. You might defend the price by explaining the high quality of the product or service, or making clear its benefits once more. The buyer may then harden their position by stating what they are prepared to pay. Your starting price should have allowed for a little discounting anyway, and an experienced buyer will presume this. Take your time before replying as your reactions will be carefully assessed. Again defend your price, but offer a reduced price as an introductory offer (or some other scheme which does not create a precedent) and ask for the customer to pay sooner or buy a greater quantity. In other words, you are granting a discount but asking for something in return. Another alternative is to negotiate on non-money issues, so you could reduce your price, but equally offer a shorter guarantee, or omit one of the lesser features.

The best deals are where both buyer and seller feel they have done well – a "win-win" situation. This is not only fair on both parties but is good business, for the buyer is more likely to come back to you, will also act as your ambassador, and neither party will have driven such a hard bargain as to jeopardize the other's business. In all your negotiations, avoid confrontation. As a new small business, it is unlikely to achieve anything.

SALES TO AVOID

Be wary of a buyer if the top price they are prepared to pay is much lower than your stated price. If their price is below the minimum you have in mind, then this is not a good sign. Ask again about what exactly the buyer requires to help you form a better idea of their situation and needs, and maybe gain a clue as to why their offer bid is so low. Also, watch out for the "why don't we just split the difference" offer which, at first glance, may sound fair. Work out if the final figure is in fact still above your bottom price.

Finally, sometimes it is better to lose the sale altogether than to enter into a working relationship with a difficult customer or to get into a deal that makes you no money. Experience has also shown that customers who are difficult to deal with are frequently poor payers too – so be warned and, if you are unhappy or have a bad feeling about the deal, trust your instincts and just walk away.

TECHNIQUES FOR CLOSING A SALE

Learn to sense when a customer is ready to buy. He or she may start to ask detailed questions or talk about methods of payment. Listen carefully to the questions and answer them fully. Then you can attempt to close the sale by, for instance, taking out your order book and asking something like "How many do you want in your first order?" or "On what date would you like your first order delivered?" (then discuss quantities). Another technique is to bypass the Yes/No decision completely by discussing details of the order, getting the customer involved, and then taking out your order book. Once the order has been agreed, ask the buyer to sign a duplicate copy of the order form, which should include the agreed price, terms, and timetables.

MAKING A SALE

Salesman smiles and makes eye contact

Buyer touches chin, revealing thoughtfulness and interest

Salesman explains benefit of products

Tense posture indicates some hostility to the product

Salesman listens carefully to objections

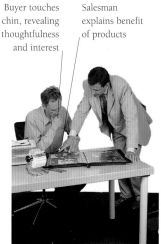

1 OPENING THE SALE
The salesman approaches the buyer confidently, gaining his complete attention. He introduces himself clearly and shakes his hand firmly.

2 SHOWING THE PRODUCTS
After asking about the buyer's needs, the salesman shows the buyer photographs of the relevant products, pointing out key features and potential benefits.

3 MEETING OBJECTIONS
The salesman has captured the buyer's interest in one particular product but the buyer has doubts, which he expresses. The salesman listens, considering his possible responses.

If the customer says he or she needs to think it over or otherwise delay making a decision, then try to leave something like your personal catalog (marked as such) or samples, which you arrange to collect the next day or the day after. This tactic allows you to see the customer face to face again, which gives you a second opportunity to close the sale. It is much more difficult for the customer to turn you down in person than over the phone.

If the customer is unsure because he or she needs a boss's or colleague's opinion, ask for that person to join your discussions or arrange to come back and see them all – try not to let them decide in your absence. If you need to check on any details or cannot come up with a quotation for something a customer has asked for on the spot, then you have not yet closed the deal. In many businesses a number of meetings are needed before a deal is finally agreed. Be aware of consumer regulations that provide for a cooling-off period, in which agreements covered by the regulations can be cancelled by the consumer.

Selling in a Retail Context

Small retail outlets fall into two categories: "convenience shops" (such as a newsstand, corner shop, or pharmacy), and "specialty shops" (such as a boutique or gift shop). In a convenience shop the customer tends to make most of their purchasing decisions before entering, while in a specialty shop the customer tends to make decisions after entering. That is a simplification, but it emphasizes the differences required in selling technique. In the former case there is less opportunity for selling, as you are primarily responding to the customer's requests; selling can still play a part as you can encourage the customer to buy additional (often complementary) purchases.

In specialty shops, active selling plays a greater role. Here are some suggestions:

■ **GREETING** Acknowledge the presence of a customer soon after they enter the shop, by a nod, smile, and a "Hello" or "Good morning," even if you are dealing with another customer. This makes them feel more at home on unfamiliar territory (especially if they have not visited the

Buyer leans forward, expressing cautious interest

Salesman offers alternative features

Buyer makes sure salesman understands his exact requirements

Salesman listens as he takes down order

4 NEGOTIATING
The salesman overcomes the buyer's doubts, explaining how he can have some features adjusted to meet the buyer's specific needs. He then raises the subject of prices.

5 CLOSING THE SALE
The salesman has gotten the buyer involved in detailed negotiations. He takes out his order book and starts writing out the order, while discussing the quantities needed.

shop before), and it also tends to hold them until you are free to help them. It is a simple, effective strategy.

▪ **FINDING OUT MORE** Let the customer browse for a short time and then approach them. Avoid saying "Can I help you?", as you will probably get the universal reply "No, I'm just looking," which stops your sales pitch dead in its tracks. Instead, try using a question more related to the situation. For instance, in a clothing store you might ask what color the customer is looking for. In a gift shop, you might ask if the customer is after something for himself or herself or for a present. The point of these questions is that they tend to open up a dialogue, which has several advantages: first, it is likely to prevent the customer from rushing around the shop

MONEY SAVER

Pay attention to details to achieve the best results when buying stock. Listen to your customers and try to balance meeting their needs with financial considerations. Buy direct from manufacturers to get the maximum margin and order based on past sales figures projected forward.

and disappearing out of the door; second, it allows you to find out what the customer needs, enabling you to offer your goods to match those needs; finally, the customer perceives you as being helpful. Being too pushy can, of course, lose sales.

LAYOUT AND DISPLAYS

The shop layout is important in assisting your selling and should be discussed with contractors who know about retailing your type of goods (see p. 79). Sales material you should have includes placards and posters or stickers

HELPING THE CUSTOMER
The salesperson has found out that ease of aftercare is important to the shopper, so is giving her a leaflet detailing washing instructions. Meeting the customer's needs ensures that the shopper feels her concerns have been answered, and she can buy the item with confidence.

that are produced by the suppliers of the stock you are carrying. Suppliers may also provide leaflets to be given away free. Particular thought should be given to point-of-sale displays, since these can contribute significantly to your turnover. Point-of-sale displays usually consist of relatively low-priced and often small products that are either an impulse buy or closely related to what the customer is already buying. The main reason why they work is that the customer already has their purse or wallet in their hand, ready to buy, and may be open to buying something else.

The display window is a crucial factor in selling from a specialty shop; it is the magnet that draws people in as they pass by, very often on an impulse. It should be bright and well-lit, attractive, and all the articles on display should be clearly priced. Displays with a theme, such as a seasonal event, or a common color, are often eye-catching. Your suppliers may offer free display material that you can use to promote a new product (see also p. 80).

TIPS FOR TELEPHONE SALES

1. Try to keep a smile on your face – it makes your voice sound friendlier.

2. Keep your product or sales information in front of you.

3. Remember the customer will be thinking "What's in this for me?" Stress the benefits of what you are selling.

4. Understanding the customer's needs is half the battle.

5. Since there is nothing in writing, always summarize what has been agreed and later confirm it in writing if necessary.

6. Be polite if rebuffed – never be rude or allow yourself to get angry.

7. At the end of the call, pause, then put the phone down after the other person.

8. Keep a brief record of what is said in all your calls.

Selling by Telephone

The telephone can be a most useful tool in your sales drive, but to use it effectively requires skill and practice. Telesales are often used to sell expensive onetime-purchase items such as sunrooms, financial products, and customized kitchens to the general public. They are also used extensively for selling trade advertising and other general business products and services to businesses. When selling by telephone to the public, there is a very low level of uptake. The success rate for businesses is slightly better, but still relatively low.

The main advantages of selling by phone are that you can contact a large number of people in a relatively short period of time, and you can often get through directly to the decision-maker. The main disadvantages of telesales are that you cannot show your product or other sales material to the customer, and you cannot accurately gauge their reactions from seeing their face or body language.

As with any sales work, preparation is essential. Know the name of who you are calling and what you are trying to achieve with the call. Handle the phone conversation in very much the same way as you would any sales meeting. In your opening statement, identify yourself and your business and state clearly the purpose of your call. Rehearse this opening statement so that it sounds clear and confident, but do not recite it parrot-fashion. Then concentrate on fact-finding and getting across your sales message. Be prepared to answer numerous questions and to enter into negotiations if the caller is interested.

If you are planning to make unsolicited calls to private numbers, there are various legal restrictions, and you must not call a phone number that is unlisted.

Selling by Mail Order

This method of selling allows a small business to have customers located almost anywhere. The first problem is finding those customers. Useful techniques are either to acquire a good-quality mailing list, or to advertise (including on your website) and hope for a response. You need to carry sufficient stock to meet orders promptly, because customers expect a rapid turnaround. Handling phone orders takes a lot of time, but should be made a pleasant experience for the caller, so do not rush them. Payment should be by credit card or by check with order, since giving open credit can create problems even if the sums of money are small. Packaging and distribution costs are high, but customers are resistant to paying much for "postage and handling", so the product prices need to carry some of the distribution costs. Mail order succeeds mainly when the products are such that the customer is unable to buy them easily from local stores.

Customer Care

Customer care is about developing a long-term relationship with a customer. It is seeing beyond a single purchase so that the customer becomes a regular purchaser. Your customers provide your income and your staff's wages, so they are your lifeblood. This fact should determine your after-sales service, and be central to your attitude and that of your staff. In addition, in a competitive market, the way you treat your customers can be crucial to keeping them. Customer care is more than being friendly to customers and giving them good deals. It involves being concerned about them and their business problems, and taking steps to make their lives easier and offer solutions. An enthusiastic "Can do" approach is more appreciated by customers than a sceptical approach – the customer knows best what they want and, if you cannot supply it, another business probably will.

Good communication is important to good customer care. A typical situation to avoid is when a long-standing customer phones in to talk to their usual contact in your company, only to be told that the person has left. This can come as a shock to the customer and could have been avoided by a simple letter or email notifying them of the change. Take time to phone customers at regular intervals to check that they are pleased with your product and enquire about their current needs. Listen to their ideas – they can often help you in spotting new trends and gaps in the market.

As with all relationships, there may be ups and downs. If you make a mistake, ensure you rectify it promptly, and, just as importantly, apologize to the appropriate person. If a customer is angry, remain calm and put all your efforts into resolving the cause of their anger.

CREATING A CUSTOMER DATABASE

Preferably from day one, you should create and maintain a database of customer particulars. This should record the obvious details such as contact names, addresses, phone, fax, email, and mobile phone numbers, plus, more interestingly, details of their orders, credit record, and any other relevant information, such as dates of visits and outcomes of any problems. Ideally you will be able to pull up this information on your computer screen when the customer calls, so you can respond to whatever they are requesting with the benefit of background knowledge. There are regulations governing confidentiality that you must observe (see p. 170).

REWARDING CUSTOMERS

The reward that is most beneficial to customers is consistent good care and keeping promises. You might like, in addition, to invite selected buyers, one at a time, to your business premises, assuming they work nearby and your premises are relatively impressive. Alternatively you could invite them to lunch or dinner at a local restaurant. The latter approach has the advantage of you meeting them on neutral territory in a low-key, relaxed situation, which allows them to gain insight into you and your business, and vice versa – do not spoil the occasion by trying to sell them anything.

Many businesses like to offer seasonal presents to their customers. Before doing this, ask yourself if handing over a present makes any real difference to your business relationship with the recipient. Once started, it is difficult to stop, as customers might wonder why they received something one year but not the next. If you decide to give seasonal presents, each

should be effective and appreciated. Ideally presents should carry your business name, be useful and reasonably long-lasting, and should be accompanied by a personalized message. There are tax considerations with gift-giving, so check the implications with your accountant.

DOS AND DON'TS OF CUSTOMER CARE

✓ Do follow up on inquiries.

✓ Do provide quotes or estimates quickly.

✓ Do ensure you can access details of your customer when they call.

✓ Do let a customer know if the work is running late or if there is a problem.

✓ Do keep them informed of relevant changes in the personnel of your business.

✗ Don't always leave it to customers to make contact with you.

✗ Don't take regular customers for granted.

✗ Don't leave customers in the dark.

✗ Don't be sharp with customers.

✗ Don't be rude or impatient with customers.

EXPORTING

Businesses start to export for different reasons, but the main one is usually the desire to make the most of a good product or service that is applicable to a wider market than just the home country. Another good reason to try exporting is to spread your risk by widening your customer base. Some companies actively pursue an export policy and produce a business plan with that venture in mind, while other companies slip into exporting on being approached by overseas buyers. Like any other major change to your business, exporting needs market research and careful advance planning.

Exporting can be exciting, providing huge opportunities for even the smallest business. The most likely small businesses to undertake exporting are manufacturers – as long as they have the right products to sell. Exporting is not usually a good move for firms that are having problems selling their products at home, unless there is firm evidence that a new market has a larger demand for that product.

There is much official encouragement to go into exporting, but the proprietor of a small business, especially a new business, cannot afford to be dazzled by government promotions. It is important to ensure before you start that exporting will be profitable for your business, and that the structure of your business can support it. As a small business it may be wise to focus initially on one small export area or country and build from there. You may choose to start by exporting to neighboring or nearby

countries, and it is often a good idea to avoid areas with severe transportation difficulties, at least until the export side of your business becomes more established.

WHO MIGHT CONSIDER EXPORTING?

A small business with a suitable product or service should probably not consider exporting unless it is well established in its home market (making it financially strong enough to set out on this new adventure), or at least one of the proprietors has been in exporting before and already has some of the contacts and necessary experience. Beginning to export is almost the equivalent of starting a new business in terms of the time and cost it can take to set up properly. You will need substantial funds, either from profits or from an injection of new capital, and management needs to have the time available that moving into export demands.

CASE STUDY: Making Initial Exporting Arrangements

FIONA OWNED A successful screen-printing business. After a number of years in business, she was approached at a national gift trade show by a foreign buyer who placed a significant order. This made Fiona think about exporting, as she felt her firm was now well established at home. She had spoken at some length to this overseas buyer and thought that there was scope to sell more in that particular country. Unfortunately, the buyer wanted to secure an exclusive arrangement so Fiona had to consider other territories. She wrote to the overseas buyer confirming her terms and decided to add that the exclusive arrangement would be for an initial period of two years and would depend on the buyer's company placing regular orders and paying on time.

Getting into Exporting

As with any new business venture, the first thing to do is to find out more about the market by doing some market research. There are specialists who can help – speak to your local small business authority or trade association. Also try reading economic reports produced on various regions of the world and tourist guides for the country concerned, to get a better idea of the local culture.

GOALS OF MARKET RESEARCH

One key issue to establish is whether there are any differences between the requirements of the export market and your home market. The differences may be due to cultural, climatic, regulatory, or other reasons, and some can be quite surprising. Other aspects to research are the likely size of the market, the strength of any local competition, the way in which the particular trade operates (there may be a strong trade association that has preferred suppliers), and the established means of distribution in the country or region concerned. Find out, too, the prices of competitors' products so that you can work out if your own prices are likely to be acceptable within that context. Check whether or not you will require an import license for the destination country, if there are any import duties, and if you will require an export license from your own country. As when undertaking any market research, keep an open mind and assume nothing.

ADVANTAGES AND DISADVANTAGES OF EXPORTING

ADVANTAGES		DISADVANTAGES	
MARKET SIZE	One of the biggest advantages of exporting is that the potential market is much larger than that of your own country.	HIGH COSTS	Traveling abroad to get orders is expensive in time and money. Shipping goods and agents' fees may also raise your prices.
MARKET MATCH	The product or service you are selling might suit certain overseas markets better than your own country's market.	MARKET MISMATCH	Cultural differences can be such that a successful product or service in your own country might have little appeal elsewhere.
DIVERSIFICATION	Selling in markets beyond your own country provides a possible safeguard against a downturn in your own country's economy.	REGULATIONS	You need to find out about local regulations. There may also be import restrictions or onerous duties.
CURRENCY	Exchange rates can give you an advantage if your currency is weak against that of your customers (or a disadvantage if your currency is strong).	SHIPPING	Speak to a shipping agent at an early stage. Note that the expression "shipping" includes both trucking and air freight.

One of the best and most direct ways in which to obtain information on the potential market is to visit an appropriate trade show in the country concerned. At the show, speak to as many people as you can, make contacts, take notes, observe potential competitors closely (including other exporters from your own country), and obtain copies of any relevant foreign trade publications from which you can have selected articles translated later. Although many people will be more than happy to offer advice and assistance, bear in mind that exhibitors are there to do business and are likely to have time to speak to you only if their stand is quiet.

As part of your research, assess whether your product needs modifying to suit other markets

DOING AN EXPORT BUSINESS PLAN

An export business plan is exactly like any other business plan, except that it is primarily concerned with the exporting intentions of the business. For clarity, the plan should show the export funding and cash flow separately from the main business. In practice, there would be no such separation, unless you were to open a foreign currency account to stabilize your prices. The currency used in your plan and cash flow would be your normal one, as you may be dealing in a number of export currencies. When you start exporting, your accounts should show export sales separately for the tax authorities and for the purposes of your own information.

GETTING STARTED IN EXPORTING

Do initial research to establish which country to export to first

→ Seek professional advice

Find out more about the trade in the target country

→ Consider visiting a trade show in that country

Find out about competitors and typical local prices

→ Consider another export market if research results are worrying

Decide on your preferred method of distribution

→ Consider the likely impact on your existing business

If applicable, arrange visits to selected major potential customers or distributors

Produce an export business plan

MAKING CHANGES AT HOME

If you are going to start exporting seriously, it will have an impact on your existing business. A major factor will be that the proprietor will have to spend a great deal of time setting up the whole export operation. Overseas sales trips take much longer, cost more, and are much more exhausting than taking a sales trip around your own country. Can your business afford to lose a key person for so long, or will it slowly atrophy through neglect? Only you can decide. One option is to take on new staff, either to keep things running at home or to visit the export market. This is a big step, and probably worth considering only once the exporting side of the business is up and running.

DISTRIBUTION

Assuming your market research results are encouraging, you need to consider how best to approach the market.

For a service business, the options depend very much on the type of business concerned; you may have to open a branch office or store in the country concerned to provide your service. Recruiting and supervising local staff can be a challenge, so franchising might be one solution. Certain types of service businesses may generate good sales leads via their websites. Manufacturers have several options:

■ **AGENT** An agent will visit potential customers, take orders on commission (which is typically ten percent), and then you ship the goods directly to the customers and invoice them individually. You will therefore be responsible for getting payments. Finding a hardworking, reliable agent and controlling customer debt are the main problems. If the agent represents another (noncompetitive) business from your country, ask him or her for a reference. Agents often start with enthusiasm, but this can wane if they find that selling your product is going to take some perseverance or if they realize that they are unlikely to earn much from your sales (being a new, small business).

■ **DISTRIBUTOR** A distributor not only goes out taking orders, but also stocks your goods, so you only need to ship to and invoice them, rather than to numerous individual customers. This usually works better than simply having an agent, but the distributor will require a significant discount, and you need to ensure your distributor is reliable and likely to pay you on time. One way to find a distributor is by recommendation through your trade association or other businesses they represent. Do get a credit rating for them, too. As with agents, they should not only sell your goods, but also provide important customer feedback.

■ **DIRECT SALES** To sell directly you can take a stand at a trade show abroad or visit selected customers in person. You may also generate export sales from your website. In all cases, you would have to ship and invoice each customer individually. Follow-up sales might be difficult or just too expensive for you to undertake, but if you attend the trade shows regularly, your customers will expect to see you there.

■ **COLLABORATIVE PROJECTS** A completely different and often useful approach is a collaboration with an overseas business. This might take the form of providing certain facilities or contacts for them in your country in exchange for the overseas business providing the same services for you.

■ **MANUFACTURE UNDER LICENSE** In this case, an overseas manufacturer agrees to make and sell your product locally. You could supply them with parts, specialized tooling, or even the whole product in kit form. Alternatively, you may just get paid a royalty. This is complex legally, and you will need good professional advice to explore the implications and set up an agreement. It is essential to check out fully the other party's track record, financial status, and integrity.

Sales and Marketing for Export

Many aspects of selling your goods and services at home apply when selling them abroad, but often with slight modifications. Some of these can be learned as you become more experienced, but it pays to be aware of possible pitfalls before you start.

TRAVEL AND ACCOMMODATION

Costs of traveling abroad and the necessary meals and overnight accommodation can be high for a small business, so it is worth taking the time to find cheaper flights and places to stay. In fact, the ability to travel to some countries more cheaply than others might influence your decision as to which countries to target first.

Look for cut-price tourist package deals on flights and accommodation

TRADE SHOWS

Even the smallest of businesses might consider participating in international trade shows. At these shows you will have direct contact with potential buyers and can receive valuable feedback. If you go on an initial trip to do your market research, you can assess the show and any likely competition at the same time. There will also be international trade shows in your home country that attract foreign buyers; you can make a tentative move into exporting by exhibiting at one of these.

> ## FACT FILE
> It is vital to know each country's precise import documentation requirements and to ensure your paperwork is complete and accurate; otherwise the goods will not be released by customs. The customer may then get excess storage charges, which they will pass on to you.

Security can be a problem at trade shows, where competitors may attempt to steal your commercial secrets. Some experienced exhibitors keep sensitive items locked away and remove them at the end of each day.

If looking for an agent or distributor when exhibiting abroad, you might display a small "Agent Wanted" sign at your stand. If you plan to make your contacts through an annual overseas trade show, a good rule of thumb is that the first year you will not make enough sales to cover your costs; the second year you may, with luck, break even; and in the third year you may achieve profit.

INTERNET

A website is increasingly essential for exporters. One way to show different markets that you are serious about exporting is to have your site available in appropriate languages. On your web pages you can offer simply a description and pictures of your products, and a means of contacting you.

Alternatively, you can use the internet to provide easily accessible information about your business and sales for agents, distributors, and customers. The internet is likely to be particularly beneficial as a selling tool for those businesses with a specialized product or service; potential buyers looking for such a product should be able to find your site relatively easily when searching on-line by using relevant keywords.

ADVERTISING AND WRITTEN INFORMATION

In addition to using your website and taking a stand at a trade show, what other ways are there of promoting your business to overseas buyers? The normal rules of advertising and promotion apply, but all the material you use, such as leaflets, brochures, and press releases, must be accurately translated into the appropriate language, preferably by a professional translator. Poorly translated material tends to look amateurish and is likely to convey a bad impression of your business.

Sending a press release in the appropriate language to trade publications in the export country concerned is a cheap and effective way of advertising your presence in the market and what you have to offer. If you include a contact address, try to have one in the relevant country, such as that of your distributor. If instructions are enclosed with a product, ensure that they are clearly translated into the relevant language, also with a local contact address.

PRICING

The extra costs associated with the process of exporting inevitably make your products more expensive abroad than they are at home. These additional costs may include:

■ freight charges
■ the often onerous handling and shipping agent fees
■ shipping insurance (always more expensive than when simply moving the goods within one country)
■ import duties, where applicable
■ bank charges
■ an overseas agent's commission, where applicable.

As an exporter you can price your goods as ex-factory, FOB, or CIF (see the definitions box below). Large customers usually prefer the first option if they are filling a container from a

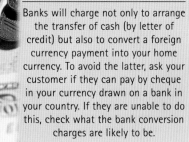

M O N E Y   S A V E R

Banks will charge not only to arrange the transfer of cash (by letter of credit) but also to convert a foreign currency payment into your home currency. To avoid the latter, ask your customer if they can pay by cheque in your currency drawn on a bank in your country. If they are unable to do this, check what the bank conversion charges are likely to be.

number of suppliers, while CIF is popular when the customer is just buying from you, as they know in advance exactly what your goods are going to cost them. As a new exporter, it is vital to get advice from a shipping agent. Shipping costs, together with the associated paperwork, can be very expensive in relation to the cost of the goods being shipped.

The "off-the-shelf" price will clearly be much more than the cost of the product at home, due to all the extra costs of exporting. This can obviously diminish the appeal of your product unless your chosen overseas market can withstand the higher price.

An important decision to make is in what currency to quote your prices. Most overseas customers prefer to be quoted in their local currency, as they are used to it, and it will not fluctuate. A common alternative is to quote in US dollars.

EXPORT TERMINOLOGY

BILLS OF LADING This is the name given to the very detailed shipping documents that need to be prepared, prior to transporting the goods, by a shipping agent (for plane, ship, or truck transport).

CONSOLIDATION This is where your goods are consolidated (grouped) with others (often in a container) to get the benefit of cheaper shipping rates.

LETTER OF CREDIT This is a common form of payment for exports, controlled by the bank.

PRICE CIF CIF means "cost, insurance, freight," so your price includes the cost, insurance, and freight costs.

This can be very difficult to calculate accurately in advance when providing quotes.

PRICE EX-FACTORY This is your price with the goods sitting at your factory, packed up, and ready for dispatch. The buyer is responsible for arranging and paying for collection and shipment.

PRICE FOB FOB means "free on board," so your price includes carriage to and loading on board the specified transportation (plane, ship, or truck) at an agreed port in your own country. For example, a purchase order might state "FOB New York".

Sending Goods Abroad

For most products there are likely to be two main options:

- **MAIL** If the goods are lightweight, you may be able to send them by mail. This can be by airmail (which is relatively expensive but quick) or surface mail (which is cheaper but takes many weeks to reach most places). The advantages of mailing goods are that you have no handling agent's fees and there is less onerous paperwork. For small orders, this can be quite useful.

- **AIR AND SEA FREIGHT** These are effectively the same method as far as efficiency is concerned. A good shipping agent is essential for handling the often complicated documentation associated with air and sea freight, and to advise on the best route and carrier – the most direct way is not always the best. Shipping costs are usually quoted in terms of US $/kg; air is, unsurprisingly, the more expensive. The paperwork must meet the destination country's requirements, or there can be delays and penalties for the importer.

SEA FREIGHT
Goods travel between countries by a variety of methods to keep down costs and maximize efficiency, often being moved from one means of transport to another en route.

PACKAGING

Appropriate packaging is essential as goods that arrive damaged create ill will with customers, take a lot of your time to resolve, and the insurance may not fully cover your financial loss. What constitutes the correct packaging depends on the goods you plan to send and on what you have agreed with your customers. If the goods are flexible (such as garments) the packaging should flex to absorb ill-treatment, and should be waterproof. If the contents are vulnerable to physical knocks, they need to be isolated by using an inner and outer carton with a gap between the two, and if they are fragile they need an absorption medium in the gap. Generally it is wise to assume that your packages will get rough handling unless you are paying for a premium courier service. Furthermore, warning signs on your packets or cartons such as "Fragile" are universally ignored. Usually, goods on pallets survive better, provided they are kept well within the

TIME SAVER

Packaging can take a large amount of time and money. Try out several standard packaging options to compare the unit cost, ease and speed of use, and weight. When you have found the best method, order the materials in bulk to keep down unit costs.

IMPORTING

This is an entirely different activity from exporting, with its own particular risks and rewards. The main areas a small business is likely to explore are importing stock or raw materials, and arranging for an overseas manufacturer to make your products.

■ **IMPORTING STOCK OR RAW MATERIALS** The main risks are unscrupulous or inefficient suppliers (a common problem is that they substitute when they are out of stock of the item you had asked for), misunderstandings due to language, and unexpected shipping charges.

■ **MANUFACTURING OVERSEAS** Having goods created to your design raises its own particular issues of compliance with your instructions, quality control, and meeting the deadlines you have set.

Ideally, visit the supplier or deal with an agent in your own country. Always discuss with your insurers who should insure the goods while in transit.

pallet edges, but you should ensure that the shipper is equipped to handle the pallet size you plan to use (there are standard sizes). If you are using air freight, the weight of the packaging becomes relevant, and in many cases the sheer cost of the packaging itself can be significant. Experiment with different methods, and take advice from specialist packaging companies.

Getting Paid on Time

It is one thing to succeed in getting an export order, but it is quite another matter actually to get paid for it. Some countries are known for being particularly good or poor payers in business, although individual companies can differ. For small orders, request payment by credit card or in advance by proforma invoice.

For larger orders, as credit card and proforma offer no protection for the buyer, request payment by letter of credit or other documentary collection; these are handled by the bank and are relatively safe for both parties, but costly.

If you plan to offer credit, take up references just as you would with any local customer, but do so with even greater attention to detail, and get a credit rating too. Be wary of the customer who places increasingly large orders, always paying on time, but ultimately fails to pay for the last (by now huge) order.

In the event of nonpayment, use normal debt collection procedures – issue statements then follow up with a letter, then phone calls, and finally consider visiting the customer abroad if the size of debt warrants it. Some customers assume that because you are far away they can simply ignore you. Arriving in person usually has the desired effect.

EMPLOYING STAFF

Almost all businesses need to employ staff as they grow. Taking on a member of staff is a major step in the life of any business, so it warrants careful planning. Recruiting, training, and supervision will all take up a significant amount of your time as an employer. Staff also add substantially to your costs – in addition to wages, you also need to pay for vacation and sick leave, and overhead usually rises too. Finally, related paperwork will increase. On the plus side, good staff will enable a business to expand, will free up the time of the proprietor, and can bring new expertise to your enterprise.

When a small business takes on its first employee, it marks an important stage in the development of that business and has far-reaching consequences. Many new businesses think only of the amount of new work the recruit can do, and seriously underestimate the amount of time it takes to enable the new staff member to learn the ropes and perform at full capacity. Whereas the proprietors who set up the original business may initially work long hours for little or no wages, an employee will – not unreasonably – expect to receive a regular wage for set hours, and this can impose strains on a fledgling enterprise.

Another consequence is that, since the new recruit will require training and supervision to carry out their work properly, for some months the proprietors may have less time available for

DO YOU NEED TO EMPLOY ANY STAFF?

Although your business may be overloaded, there may be an alternative to taking on a full-time member of staff, especially if the need for extra help is intermittent. Here are some suggestions of cheaper and more flexible options:

■ **TELEPHONE ANSWERING** An answering machine and a mobile phone are essentials if you are out of the office very much. You can also use a telephone answering service to take messages and pass them on to you – sometimes by email or by sending a text message to your mobile phone.

■ **TYPING** With computers at the center of most workplaces, it is often best to learn to type yourself. If you need occasional typing you may be able to ask a friend or relative to

Choose new employees who will bring fresh ideas and enthusiasm to your business

do it for a small fee; or you can try an office services company to find someone to type what you need.

■ **DOING OFFICE WORK** If you have a rush of office work, try using a temp from an agency. Temps can work when you want, so are flexible and bring instant expertise, though they will require some initial supervision. If this is going to be a regular requirement, you could ask the agency to send you the same person each time. Although the hourly rate will be much higher than if you were to employ someone yourself, you will not have to find work for this person to do during quiet periods, nor will you have any of the additional overhead to contend with.

■ **BOOKKEEPING** It is a good discipline to do the bookkeeping yourself to keep in touch with their own work. Whereas the proprietors can make executive decisions as the need arises, the new employee will require guidelines and procedures to be drawn up, usually in writing, to avoid errors and misunderstandings.

Recruiting Staff

Before you start recruiting, you should draw up a detailed job description, including the skills required, the experience needed, the tasks to be performed, the responsibilities, and the way that the job might develop in the future. This will help you to be completely clear as to what you want the new person to do and how this will relate to your own work. The job description will dictate the qualities you need to look for in a prospective applicant.

Quantify how much extra work you need the new recruit to take on, and consider whether a part-timer might be sufficient to begin with.

CASE STUDY:
Planning Recruitment

MIKE AND GRAHAM had been laid off from a car assembly plant and were now well on the way to setting up their own precision engineering company. They knew they would need to take on skilled staff to assist them, so they decided to advertise in the local newspaper, and to make personal contact with good machinists they already knew. To find the best, they were offering a higher rate of pay than was the norm locally, and put in place a rigorous selection procedure. This included a practical machining test for each applicant. They also planned to use a number of part-time staff since this would give them flexibility, particularly while the business developed. Planning ahead, they thought about setting aside time to train their newly employed staff and using a system of production-related bonuses so their output would be maximized.

---

the finances of your business. Freelance bookkeepers are available, however; ask your accountant for contacts.

■ **MAKING DELIVERIES** The first option is to use one of the many parcel services to collect or deliver goods; most give national and even international service. For occasional bulk deliveries you could rent a van with a driver.

■ **SELLING** This is sometimes a difficult job to farm out, as selling is such a key activity, and, if you do it yourself, you will form good relations with customers and learn from their feedback. If you want an experienced professional, some organizations specialize in marketing other people's products and services, or you could use an agent (on commission) – try to find these by recommendation.

■ **MANUFACTURING/ASSEMBLY** If you need help with your manufacturing or assembly, you could consider subcontracting the work.

Different firms specialize in everything from heavy engineering to electronics. Another way of subcontracting is to use piece workers, who work at home – they are used particularly for knitwear and garments. Take professional advice: many piece workers are now deemed to be employees under employment law. Find such workers via ads in the trade press.

■ **SUBCONTRACTING/OUTSOURCING** In general, subcontracting or outsourcing any aspect of your business can be very worthwhile, particularly in the early stages of your enterprise, as it gives you flexibility and expertise while requiring little initial outlay. With today's internet connections, this process can be relatively straightforward – email allows the quick transfer of documents, and it is possible to link up with a firm's database or server remotely.

The advantages of using a part-timer rather than a full-timer include: a lower wages bill; some flexibility; and, more importantly, you may be able to recruit a higher-caliber person than might otherwise be attracted to a new small business, because the employee prefers a part-time commitment.

METHODS OF APPLICATION

Many businesses request a resumé as a means of finding out about each applicant, and this is an effective and easy method. An alternative that takes up more time at the outset, but provides information more tailored to your needs, is to compile an application form. When compiling the form, aim to obtain all the information you need in one place, so include a space for full personal details, educational qualifications, and work experience, as well as your own more specific questions. When you have a large number of applicants, it is easier to process standard forms than individual resumés.

LOOKING FOR STAFF

There are several ways to find staff:
■ **BY RECOMMENDATION** Friends, relatives, and colleagues are often eager to recommend potential recruits. This has advantages and disadvantages, but the key point is that you must scrutinize such an applicant in just the same way as any other. If you take on someone on a recommendation from a friend or relative and ultimately need to dismiss them, it is likely to prove embarrassing.

FACT FILE

It is illegal for your job advertisement to state or imply any preferences on the grounds of gender, race, color, ethnic or national origin, or on the grounds of disability. Neither should you treat any job applicant less favorably on any of these grounds at any stage of the application process.

GUIDELINES FOR EMPLOYING STAFF

1 Take on new members of staff only if you absolutely have to.

2 Consider timing: beware of recruiting in anticipation of demand.

3 Use part-time staff where this is more appropriate to your needs.

4 Interview carefully and advertise again if you do not find the right person.

5 Take time to encourage, train, reward, and keep good employees.

6 Get rid of bad employees as fast as is legally possible.

■ **NEWSPAPER/MAGAZINE ADS** For most recruitment this will probably be the main method. It may be more expensive than other methods, but it casts your net wider. Choose a newspaper that your potential applicant is likely to read. For specialized jobs an ad in a trade or professional magazine may be more appropriate. Before you advertise, check several copies of the publication to see if there are similar advertisements from other businesses, and compare the wages they are offering. Looking at those ads may help you with the wording of your own. Your ad should state briefly what the business does, describe the job, stating the experience and qualifications required, give the wage or salary offered, and have a closing date for applications. State whether applicants need to send a resumé or request an application form. Give the name and job title of the person who will process the replies, and the address. Using a box number can be off-putting as applicants like to know where they may need to travel for an interview or a job. Give your phone number only if you are willing to deal with telephone inquiries. Your ad may be contractually binding, so needs to be accurate; for legal reasons it is wise to avoid the phrase "permanent employment."

▓ **RECRUITMENT AGENCIES** For vacancies requiring specialized skills, or for more senior appointments, you could use a recruitment agency. Many specialize in certain industries or areas of expertise. This can be a quick and efficient way of finding suitable staff, as agencies often have a number of people on their books, and they will do the initial interviewing and screening of applicants. On the other hand, they can be expensive, since they charge for the ads they place plus a fee related to the annual salary of the recruit.

▓ **INTERNET** A growing number of businesses, and a huge number of recruitment agencies, use the internet as a means to recruit staff. This is a worthwhile method to explore, particularly if the type of employee you are seeking is likely to try this method of looking for work.

▓ **JOB CENTERS** These can be a very useful source of potential staff and may, if required, do initial interviewing and screening for you.

Assessing an Application

This is the first stage leading up to a job interview. The actual process depends on whether you have requested a resumé or a completed job application form.

RESUMÉS

Resumés are produced by applicants to present themselves in the best light, so there may be some exaggeration of skills and experience, while there may also be some omissions to hide less desirable aspects of their employment record. You should be able to assess a resumé in under a minute (personnel professionals do it even quicker), sorting the resumés into piles of unsuitable and possible applicants. Go through the possible pile again much more thoroughly, with a critical, questioning eye, grading applicants in terms of suitability. Select the top few to call for interview.

CHECKING AN APPLICATION

When assessing an application, draw up a list of questions for yourself so that you can check how each applicant matches your list. This will help you to make a more objective assessment. The following questions form a good starting point:

▓ Is the resumé or application form neatly and cleanly presented?

▓ Are the applicant's qualifications adequate?

▓ Is any of the applicant's previous work experience relevant?

▓ Does the applicant stay in one job or appear to change jobs frequently?

▓ Can you tell why the applicant left each of the previous jobs?

▓ Are there any unexplained chronological gaps in their employment record?

▓ Is the applicant's health satisfactory?

▓ Will a driver's license be necessary to do the job?

▓ Will the applicant have to travel far to work for you?

▓ How does the applicant's pay in their last job compare with the rates that you are offering?

▓ Is the applicant available to start work now, or is a period of notice required by their current employer?

Use the information contained in the resumé or form, and the questions it raises, as the basis for a list of interview questions. If an applicant does not have exactly the skills you are looking for but seems suitable in other ways, think about whether training can fill the gap, and if his or her other skills might be equally valuable in different ways.

APPLICATION FORMS

In many ways application forms are easier to assess than resumés as the applicants are responding to questions designed specifically to check their suitability for the job. As with a resumé, look at the overall presentation of the form to see if it is neatly and carefully filled in, and try to spot gaps of information as well as desirable aspects.

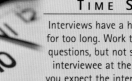

TIME SAVER

Interviews have a habit of going on for too long. Work to your set list of questions, but not slavishly. Tell the interviewee at the start how long you expect the interview to last, and have a clock that you can both see – looking at your watch can be very off-putting.

Conducting an Interview

Once you have drawn up a shortlist for interviewing, you need to make contact with the applicants to arrange an interview. An interview has two objectives – it allows you to assess the applicant, and it allows the applicant to assess your business. To save time, and to reduce a long shortlist, you might do an initial telephone interview; this can be especially helpful in borderline cases where you are not quite sure about whether to interview someone. Prepare a number of key questions before you phone and write down their answers as you talk, leaving space on your sheet for other comments, which you can add afterward. Telephone interviewing is very time-efficient and screens out unsuitable applicants quickly.

PREPARATION

To conduct a face-to-face interview you need somewhere comfortable and quiet where you will not be interrupted. You could try your business premises at the end of the working day, or hire a function room at a nearby hotel, or, if you are in a business center, there may be a meeting room you can book in advance.

Make certain each applicant knows where and when their interview is to take place. If

SUGGESTED INTERVIEW QUESTIONS

Before an interview, make up a list of questions to ask each applicant – this can be a standard list, or one prepared as a result of reading their application or talking to them on the phone. The following are suggested questions, some aimed at simple fact finding, others at drawing out the candidate to find out more about their personality and attitudes:

■ Please tell me about your current job (or last job if not currently employed).
■ What are your responsibilities in your current (or last) job?
■ What do you like best and least about your current (last) job?
■ How do you get along with your current (last) boss?

■ Why do you want to change jobs?
■ Why have you left your previous jobs?
■ What do you know about our business?
■ What attracted you to our job vacancy?
■ What do you think will be the positive points of the job?
■ What do you think will be the negative points of the job?
■ What do you think are your own strengths and weaknesses?
■ What do you consider to be your greatest success at work so far?
■ What would you say motivates you at work?
■ Are you ambitious?
■ Where do you see your career going over the next five or 10 years?

you are interviewing several people one after another, you need a separate waiting area for them, and a second person (such as the receptionist, if you are using a hotel) to handle the new arrivals. Allow at least an hour for each interview, longer for key managerial jobs, plus time for a break between interviews for you to make notes before you see the next person.

An applicant will want to know specific details of the business and the job offer. If your business has produced a leaflet or brochure, have a copy to give each applicant to illustrate what your business does. Also equip yourself with the following information:

- job title, and precise job description
- how soon you need someone to start
- the usual hours for work and if it includes weekends or evenings
- the wage or salary (per hour/day/week/month) and method of payment
- the possibility of any overtime (at what rate) or bonuses
- vacation allowance
- details of a pension plan if appropriate
- any difficult or physically demanding aspects of the job (such as heavy lifting).

Immediately before the interview, arrange the seating and lighting. This will be affected by the sort of atmosphere you want to create. For a friendly, informal atmosphere, use a meeting table or coffee table rather than your desk; these are neutral locations so that you and the applicant are on a more equal footing. Ensure that your chairs are the same height, and that the lighting is not dazzling for either party. For a more formal atmosphere, you could use your office or a meeting table, and sit opposite the applicant; keep the lighting at a comfortable level – the goal is not to intimidate. Ensure that tea or coffee is available, and that you have a pen and paper to make notes.

THE INTERVIEW

When conducting an interview, the usual simple courtesies apply, such as rising to your feet to greet the applicant as he or she approaches.

DOS AND DON'TS OF INTERVIEWING

✓ Do put the applicant at ease.
✓ Do treat them with respect.
✓ Do offer them tea or coffee.
✓ Do sit at a similar height.
✓ Do get the applicant talking.
✓ Do ask open-ended questions.
✓ Do listen.
✓ Do take notes.

✗ Don't have any interruptions.
✗ Don't be influenced by first impressions.
✗ Don't sit behind a desk.
✗ Don't sit with a bright light behind you.
✗ Don't avoid awkward questions.
✗ Don't forget to discuss pay, vacation, and other practicalities.

Welcome each interviewee with a smile and a warm handshake, offer to take their coat or jacket, and indicate which chair you wish them to use. Offer tea, coffee, or water to encourage them to relax. Use the applicant's first name only if you are prepared for them to call you by your first name too.

A common, and often unconscious, error when interviewing is to size up people in an instant based on their physical appearance, dress, and manner of speech. Try hard not to form an opinion until the end of the interview. There is a risk that candidates with physical characteristics or interests similar to the interviewer will be looked on too favorably; having a colleague present for all or just part of an interview can help to correct any bias.

Be forthcoming and enthusiastic about your business and about the available the job – your goal is to impress the applicant in the same way as they are trying to impress you. Ensure you ask all the questions you want to ask, and that you listen attentively to the applicant's answers. Ask supplementary questions as necessary following on from the applicant's answers, or to clarify any points that remain unclear to you.

Watch the candidate's reactions and body language carefully. Nervousness is natural in an interview situation and should not unduly color your opinion of a candidate – unless you are recruiting them for a job that specifically demands a confident manner with strangers. Signs of evasiveness, overconfidence, or an arrogant attitude are worth taking note of, however. Personality is also an important factor; although very different personalities can be valuable in a small business and bring new

perspectives, consider whether you and other staff are likely to be able to work well day to day with the applicant.

At the end of the interview ask the applicant if they have any questions they would like to ask. Give a full answer to each question. An applicant's questions can reveal how much research they have done into the job, and what their priorities are. Even if you think you have found the right applicant, consider all applications after completing the interviews and checking the references, rather than offering the job to one applicant on the spot. Note, too, that if you make a verbal promise during an interview, it could be legally binding.

INTERVIEWING A CANDIDATE

Interviewer leans forward to welcome interviewee

Open posture helps relax interviewee

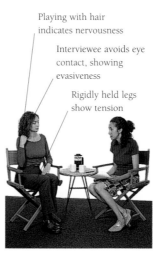

Playing with hair indicates nervousness

Interviewee avoids eye contact, showing evasiveness

Rigidly held legs show tension

Leaning forward indicates interest

Hand on chin indicated attentiveness

Hand gesture shows enthusiasm

1 STARTING AN INTERVIEW This interview for a sales clerk is set at a round table in a neutral space, to create a feeling of informality. After greeting the interviewee and offering her a drink, the interviewer starts by discussing neutral topics to put the interviewee at her ease.

2 ASKING PROBING QUESTIONS The interviewer has discovered some discrepancies in the interviewee's resumé, and asks a probing question. The interviewee reveals her discomfort by her body language. She is trying to evade the question.

3 ENCOURAGING DISCUSSION The interviewee responds to another question in a positive and eloquent manner. The interviewer listens thoughtfully, impressed at the enthusiasm and motivation that are shown in the language and posture of the interviewee.

SECOND INTERVIEWS

To help you select from two or more promising contenders, or in order to meet the most interesting applicant again, a second interview is worthwhile. It enables you to double-check the impression you received at the first interview, and to clarify any points that are still unclear on both sides. If you interviewed the candidates away from your premises the first time round, take them to see your business on the second interview – they are sure to want to see where they may be working.

COMPETENCE TESTS

For many jobs it is vital to check the skills of applicants. If you need fast and accurate typing

skills, for example, ask the applicant to type a letter on your computer. For an electronics technician, ask them to identify components on a printed circuit board. For a manual skill such as metalwork, carpentry, welding, and building skills, set practical tests. In all cases these competence tests should be similar to the work the applicant would have to do in the job being offered.

Where the competence being tested is more intellectual than manual, it is a good idea to ask the applicant to join you for a day when you are doing what the applicant would have to do if they got the job. For instance, if you were recruiting a sales manager, by visiting customers with the applicant you would get some idea of how they operate under real conditions. Depending on how easy the test is to set up, you could either use it at first interview, or use it as a deciding factor at a second interview.

Interviewer introduces candidate to partner

Partner shakes hand warmly to make candidate feel at ease

Direct gaze shows attention

Partner mirrors body language, indicating that both are relaxed

4 MEETING RELEVANT PEOPLE The interviewer introduces the interviewee to her business partner. The partner is more involved in the financial side of the business, and wishes to meet each interviewee briefly, since she is looking for different qualities in the interviewee.

5 ASKING DIFFERENT KINDS OF QUESTIONS The partner will not be working directly with the potential candidate, but takes the time to ask a few brief questions in order to formulate her own opinion, and to answer any extra questions the candidate may have.

Making a Job Offer

Before making a job offer, always check the references given. Often you obtain more information by phoning rather than writing to the referees, although some organizations will insist that you put your request in writing. References from previous employers are very important, since you want to know how the applicant performed at work and why they left. Where an employee is likely to handle cash, you might want to obtain his or her credit report. Private character referees can provide insights, but the candidate will have selected people who are likely to comment favorably. If an applicant hands you a copy of a reference, you still need to contact the writer directly to verify the information it contains.

JOB OFFER LETTER

Once you have found a suitable person and checked his or her references to your satisfaction, you can send a letter formally offering him or her the job. This job offer letter should ideally cover some of the key elements of the contract between yourself and the employee, such as: job title, job description, pay (in detail and including any overtime arrangements), hours of work, and holidays and vacation allowance. This may help to avoid any misunderstandings at a later date.

If the references have not yet been checked, the letter could state "this offer is conditional on satisfactory references being received." If you state the job is for a trial or probationary period, then add that this can be terminated by statutory notice, thus avoiding any possibility of a fixed-term contract.

As employment legislation continues to get ever more complex (see pp. 172–3), you would be wise to ask your attorney to check the wording of your job offer letter.

JOB REFUSAL LETTERS

It is a courtesy to write to all unsuccessful applicants, keeping your letters polite but short. Explaining why he or she has been rejected is unwise, since that may give them cause to sue you on discriminatory grounds. Until your preferred applicant has formally accepted your job offer, do not turn down your second or third choices.

Finally, consider paying interview expenses. Although many small businesses see this as an unnecessary cost, it is a good ethical practice, and the expenses paid can be modest, reflecting the applicant's likely travel costs.

Organizing Training for Staff

Providing thorough and relevant training is usually rewarded by having better motivated and more efficient staff. Where there is a safety aspect to the work, any failure to carry out proper training could prove very costly if there is an accident.

In a small business, staff training usually takes the form of either "learning on the job" or sending staff to a local college after work. The latter is generally appropriate where specific qualifications are required, including practical skills such as using computers or those required in certain vocational jobs. Occasionally there may also be specialized one- or two-day courses or seminars to which you can send

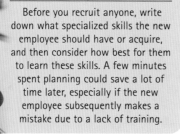

TIME SAVER

Before you recruit anyone, write down what specialized skills the new employee should have or acquire, and then consider how best for them to learn these skills. A few minutes spent planning could save a lot of time later, especially if the new employee subsequently makes a mistake due to a lack of training.

your staff, though these can be expensive. You can also bring in a qualified trainer to train your staff on the spot; this is also expensive.

Ideally the on-the-job training should be formalized and follow a set program. Doing your training on an ad hoc basis may be quick and cheap to set up but is unlikely to make the most of the new employee's skills. Try to do training on a one-to-one basis in short, regular sessions, at the start or the end of the working day, to minimize interruptions. Suggest that the employee takes notes. You may also be able to provide books on relevant subjects.

In appropriate cases you might link the acquisition of new skills to increased pay as an incentive for the employee. This would require you to set a standard or a simple test that the employee would have to pass to qualify for receiving the pay increase. The standard or test must be fair and achievable. After your new employee has been with you for several weeks, ask them if they feel they need additional skills or information to do their job better. If they do, then make arrangements to provide them.

Motivating Staff

Staff who are motivated will work better. One of the greatest ways to motivate staff is simply to make them feel needed and valued. People will endure difficult conditions and pressure if they feel their work is important and their contribution is acknowledged.

REWARDING STAFF

There are many ways of rewarding staff for good performance – from a simple "thank you" (much underused), to a letter of appreciation, promotion (and a change in job title), and financial rewards such as improved pay and bonuses. An incentive is where you reward your staff if they achieve preagreed targets; these should be attainable but require some effort on their part.

DOS AND DON'TS OF MOTIVATING STAFF

✓ Do show them respect.

✓ Do say thank you when thanks are due.

✓ Do give them real responsibilities.

✓ Do reward them, especially when they do well.

✓ Do keep their job varied.

✓ Do be fair in all your dealings with staff.

✓ Do lead by example.

✓ Do give a clear objective or target to achieve.

✗ Don't ask them to do something you wouldn't do yourself.

✗ Don't be ill-tempered.

✗ Don't show favoritism.

✗ Don't leave them in the dark.

DEALING WITH LOW MORALE

Where motivation is not present, you may find low morale in its place. Signs of low morale among staff include complaints, arriving late for work, absenteeism, poor standards of work, internal theft, and a high turnover of staff. If this situation exists it needs to be remedied without delay since it can be infectious and spread to other staff, it can reduce profitability, and it certainly makes the work environment unpleasant for everybody.

The best way to tackle low morale is by first finding the cause. It could be that someone thinks that they have been unfairly treated, or passed over for promotion, or perhaps an individual feels that they are not being paid enough, or have had their requests and suggestions ignored. A personality clash between two staff members can also be a factor, especially where one is giving orders to another. Usually, encouraging the staff members involved to speak out about their feelings in private will help to clear the air, provided that you then react to make the changes that are reasonable and necessary to ensure that the same conditions do not occur again.

STAYING in business

For your business to survive, you need to have a firm grasp of your financial situation and to know what action to take if things start to go awry. Responding positively to a changing marketplace and formulating your own long-term plan to guide your business will help to keep your venture thriving and on track.

CONTROLLING THE FINANCES

Business is all about money, and the proper management of that money is paramount to the success of any business. This chapter covers the operation of a business bank account, keeping records, how to keep a simple set of financial statements, how to do cash-flow management (based on the cash-flow forecast you did for your business plan), minimizing your overheads, solving cash-flow problems, and dealing with late payers.

The first principle to grasp is that it is vital to separate business money from personal money. In a business context this separation is achieved by opening a business bank account and keeping any petty cash from the business in its own container, which can be either a cash register or cash box clearly marked "Business."

Your Business Bank Account

To open a business bank account you will need to see your bank manager. The manager will want to know about the intended business, so take along a copy of your business plan. If you are also looking for financing, leave a copy of your business plan at the bank several days before your appointment, to give the manager time to read it. It is usual, but not essential, to have your business account with the bank that is lending you money. In addition

MONEY SAVER

To avoid bank charges on business checks, use your business or personal credit card to pay where possible. You can then pay off the business items on your card each month using just one business check.

to wanting to know all about you and your proposed venture, and assuming the bank is happy to open an account for your business, the manager will need you to supply information about the following:

■ **NAME OF THE ACCOUNT** If you are setting up a corporation, then the account name is normally the company title in full. If you are going to set up as a sole proprietor or partnership using the names of the partners, then the account name is usually the name of the proprietor(s) with the words "Business Account" (often abbreviated to "Business A/c") afterwards; for example, "John Smith Business A/c." Where a business name is going to be used for a sole proprietor or partnership, then the account would usually have the name of proprietor(s) plus the business name; for example, "Joan Smith T/A Simply Perfect."

■ **AUTHORIZED SIGNATORY** If the business is a partnership or there are two or more directors (in the case of a corporation), then the bank will want to know if one signature or more will be necessary on checks and other authorizations. Some businesses prefer to say that no check should be passed without more than one signature, or it may be more practical to instruct the bank not to pass any check that is over a specified amount, unless the check carries the authorized signatures.

CHOOSING SIGNATORIES
A bank will want to know who in the business will be able to authorize checks, and whether there are any authorization limits.

▪ **STATEMENTS** The bank will also want to know how often you would like to receive a bank statement (monthly is the most usual and is recommended), and to which address the statement should be sent.

▪ **DEPOSIT** To open the new account, the bank will normally request a deposit of money from your personal funds.

BANK CHARGES

Whereas you may have enjoyed free banking with your personal account, you will find that business accounts attract charges, and these can add up to a substantial amount over the year. In addition to any loan repayments and overdraft charges, you will usually pay for every check you write, every customer's check you

bank, any cash you withdraw or bank, standing orders and direct debits, and any nonroutine services. Shop around at different banks to compare their charges, and ensure you know exactly what you will be paying for. Investigate also whether internet or phone banking will reduce your charges.

KEEPING TRACK OF YOUR ACCOUNT

Once you have opened the business account, it is vital to keep track of the value of the checks you have written. If your check book has stubs, fill them in and then write on the next unused check stub the total amount left in the account after deducting the previous check. Thus you are always aware of the balance and are never in danger of inadvertently overdrawing the

CASE STUDY: Monitoring and Recording Cash Flow

JOHN HAD SET up his new shop selling bicycles. He was aware that, although retailing is a cash business, his overhead would be high – how he managed his cash flow would be crucial to his success. He chose a fairly sophisticated cash register that would produce a daily record of sales for tax purposes and so reduce the paperwork for his financial

statements. It would also give him some management information as to how many of each item or type of item he was selling, which would help with ordering and monitoring stock. John decided he would use computerized financial statements from the outset, due to his previous business experience. He also approached his suppliers to try to maximize his credit period for the first 12 months, to help his cash flow.

account. Watch out for direct debits and credits that will affect the balance. Using the internet or phone to access your account offers a flexible, convenient way to keep track of your money.

> *Keep receipts and financial documents even before you start in business*

HANDLING CASH

Many new businesses that handle cash create difficulties for themselves when cash received from customers is used partly for business purposes and partly for personal items, with no proper records being kept. A good habit is to pay all the money you receive (cash and checks) into your business bank account. When you need your wages, or drawings, you write a check to yourself. If you need to buy something for the business you would usually pay by check unless the item is very low in cost, in which case you could use petty cash or your personal cash. In the latter case you would then reimburse yourself from business funds each month. To operate petty cash, add funds to your petty cash box or drawer by cashing a check. As you buy the items you need out of petty cash, put the receipts into an envelope marked with the same check number as the cashed check. Alternatively, start a new envelope every week or month for receipts.

Keeping Records and Financial Statements

The two purposes of keeping financial records are: first, to meet the requirements of the tax authorities and, second, to allow you to control your business finances.

ORGANIZING INVOICES

Keep receipts and invoices for everything you buy in connection with your business. In this section, for simplicity, the word "invoice" will be used to mean both. The purpose of keeping invoices is so that you have proof of purchase and can justify all of your expenses to your accountant and any IRS agent. As you receive invoices, they need to be filed in a useful and accessible way.

For those invoices paid by check, you could file them in a loose-leaf binder, in check number sequence. Write the last three digits of the check number boldly in red ink on an outside corner of the invoice so that it can be easily cross-referred to your check book and financial statements. You can use a card divider in the file to separate paid from unpaid invoices. This should prevent you from forgetting to pay any bills, especially if you always put unpaid invoices into the file as soon as you receive them.

FILING INVOICES

From the outset it is essential to be organized about keeping track of your financial matters. File invoices you receive promptly, separated into paid and unpaid.

BASIC ACCOUNTING TERMINOLOGY

CREDIT NOTE Although this may look like an invoice, it is in fact a statement of money owed in the form of credit.

DELIVERY NOTE A contents slip included with goods that are delivered or collected (usually on credit).

INVOICE The bill you receive when you buy something, or the bill you issue to your customers for selling goods or providing services.

RECEIPT A slip confirming payment. This is not often issued if payment is made by check, but is useful when payment is by cash.

REMITTANCE ADVICE A slip (often sent with a statement to a customer) that the customer then returns with their check to indicate who is paying.

STATEMENT A summary of invoices issued and payments received. Normally issued monthly to a customer who is buying on credit.

TAX POINT This is the time of supply and is usually when the goods were supplied or a service was completed.

BASIC RECORDS

In every business you should have a record of your sales as proof for the IRS agent, and for your own information. In a shop, this record could be the cash register roll, while in other businesses it could be a duplicate copy of all the invoices you issue. In addition, you must retain your business bank statements, pay-in books, checkbook stubs, orders and delivery notes, relevant correspondence, import and export documents, copies of any credit or debit notes, and a list of goods taken from the business for personal use or supplied to someone else in exchange for goods or services. If you transfer any money between your business and personal bank accounts, then you must also retain those statements. Record, too, all purchases or sales of assets used in your business. Ask your accountant in advance what records he or she will want to see at the end of your tax year. If you employ staff, you will also need to keep records relating to PAYE.

BASIC BOOKKEEPING

You may be planning for your accountant to keep your financial statements for you. This is not ideal for two reasons. First, and most importantly, knowing your exact financial situation is the key to managing your business; if you do the books yourself, then you ought to know what is happening. Second, using an accountant to do your bookkeeping will be expensive.

There are many different ways of keeping financial statements, and any way is acceptable providing that you, your accountant, and the IRS can understand it. Understanding the system yourself is essential; some small businesses have failed partly because their bookkeeping system was so complex that the proprietor could not readily understand it. Unless you are familiar with bookkeeping, filling in the bookkeeping by hand will initially give you a better feel for your finances, especially in the critical first year of business. You could then consider switching to keeping your financial statements on computer.

Every business needs a financial statements book to record the funds received and payments being made, and these records should relate to the bank statements, and invoices from sales and purchases. When you start, you will probably only need to keep a single-entry financial statements book

SINGLE-ENTRY ACCOUNTING BOOK

The example here is for a cash business, and is a record of one week's transactions. In the single-entry system, each transaction is entered only once.

The week's transactions in cash, checks, postal orders, and credit cards are recorded here

This column records the week's business bank account transactions

In this column is the week's payments made by cash and check

The "start of week" figure is 0 for the first ever trading week; then it is the previous week's "end of week" figure

Here, the "start of week" figure is 0 for the first ever trading week; otherwise it is the previous week's "bank balance" figure

Write all daily sales here

This total should equal "cashed checks" in the next column

Record money from other sources here

It may be easier to record these when your bank statement arrives

Ensure that this figure is the same as "total bankings" in the next column

If there is a discrepancy between the balance and the money counted, record it here

Complete this only when your bank statement arrives; the bottom line should equal the balance on the bank statement

Add checks minus bankings that have not yet appeared on the bank statement

Enter this total in the "week's money balance" under "cash payments"

Enter this total in the "week's bank balance" under "check payments"

WEEK COMMENCING ....

MONEY RECORD

MONEY IN HAND AT START OF WEEK	$	
	178	23

DAILY TAKINGS		
Monday	63	12
Tuesday	39	73
Wednesday	127	32
Thursday	98	40
Friday	122	43
Saturday	163	82
Sunday		
TOTAL TAKINGS	614	82

OTHER MONEY, LOANS, ETC		
Cash from bank	50	00
From private a/c	1,000	00
TOTAL	1,050	00

WEEK'S MONEY BALANCE		
Money at start of week plus daily takings plus other money, loans etc	1,843	05
Less total bankings	1,571	71
Less cash payments	161	02
LEAVES: BALANCE	110	32

MONEY IN HAND AT END OF WEEK	110	22
DISCREPANCY +/–		10

BANK RECORD

BANK BALANCE AT START OF WEEK	$	
	841	27

DAILY BANKINGS		
Monday	158	23
Tuesday		
Wednesday	80	65
Thursday		
Friday	1,332	83
Saturday		
Sunday		
TOTAL BANKINGS	1,571	71

BANK DIRECT DEBITS, ETC		
Cashed checks (071)	50	00
Charges/interest	34	75
HP/lease/loan		
TOTAL	84	75

WEEK'S BANK BALANCE		
Bank balance at start of week plus daily bankings less bank direct debits plus bank credits	2,328	23
Less check payments	1,920	21
LEAVES: BALANCE	408	02

BANK STATEMENT CHECK		
Balance (from above)	408	02
Add total checks	1,509	00
Less total bankings	1,332	83
LEAVES	584	19

PAYMENTS RECORD

	PAID BY CASH		PAID BY CHEQUE	
	REF	$	REF	$
Stock/Raw Materials				
A. Jones	133	22 20		
A. Ali & Co			072	87 23
L. Armstrong	134	12 32		
Brown & Son			073	107 24
J. Smith Ltd			076	156 90
Stock/raw materials subtotals		34 52		351 37
Advertising/promotion				
Business insurance				
Cleaning				
Drawings/salaries/pension (Self)	140	80 00		
Electric/gas/heat (Elec)			074	23 79
Fees (e.g., accountant, lawyer)				
Car – Fuel			079	9 00
– Repairs/service				
– Tax/insurance				
Postage/parcels	136	1 12		
Rates				
Rent				
Repairs/maintenance				
Staff wages J. Walker			075	22 60
L. Woodall	139	40 00		
Employee benefits				
Stationery/printing	137	3 50		
Miscellaneous 135 56p 138 $1.32		1 88		
Telephone/fax				
Traveling				
Any other expenses				
Refund customer (by post)			077	13 45
CAPITAL EXPENDITURE				
Van (second-hand)			078	1,500 00
TOTAL CASH AND CHECK PAYMENTS		161 02		1,920 21

(sometimes called a "cash book"). You can buy a preprinted book (similar to that shown opposite) which comes with instructions. Alternatively, you could buy a blank "analysis book," which is merely ruled with lines and columns, has no headings or instructions (and therefore requires some knowledge of bookkeeping), but has the advantage of being more flexible. The headings used in a standard or a blank book need to relate to what is on tax forms; you can add your own subheadings relating to your own cash management systems if you wish. Cash businesses usually need to keep weekly records, while credit-based businesses usually keep monthly records.

Avoid letting your outgoings exceed your income – you will simply run out of cash

MORE COMPLEX BOOKKEEPING

As your business grows you may need to consider moving to more complex (and expensive) systems. As its name suggests, the double-entry system involves entering each transaction twice – once in the general ledger, and a second time in the appropriate ledger (such as a sales or purchase ledger). Usually the move to a double-entry multiledger system occurs not because your turnover has reached any particular level, but because you need more control of purchases and sales made on credit. The double-entry system enables you to keep track of credit transactions to come, as well as the current position. Not surprisingly, operating a multiledger system takes much more time and effort and its users usually computerize their accounts. Most computer accounting programs use a double-entry system; before using such a program it is essential to understand the concepts behind it.

PURCHASE AND SALES LEDGERS

A purchase ledger is essential for keeping track of a large volume of goods or services bought on credit. It is simply a lined book with columns to record your purchases from each supplier. Use one page per supplier and title your columns:

Order Date; Order Number; Description; Date Goods Received; Date Invoice Received; Debit; Credit; Balance; and Notes. When, for example, you buy $100 of goods, this is shown in the "Credit" column, and when you pay that supplier the payment is shown in the "Debit" column. Update the purchase ledger at least monthly.

If you are offering credit, you should have a record of who owes you, how much, and how long the bill has been unpaid. This record is called a sales ledger, and complements the purchase ledger. In a sales ledger, the columns would be: Order Date; Customer Order Number; Description; Date Goods Sent; Date Invoice Sent; Debit; Credit; Balance; and Notes. When you sell $150 of goods, for example, this

GOOD BOOKKEEPING

1 Always do weekly (or monthly) balances, since these will soon reveal any errors you may have made.

2 A good time to do your books is just after you receive your bank statement.

3 From the bank statement check off the transactions listed to reveal any checks not yet cashed or pay-ins not yet shown.

4 When balancing, if you are out by some amount, then first look for an entry of the same amount that might be in the wrong place or miscounted.

5 Remember that only expenditure that is wholly and exclusively for your business is normally tax-deductible and therefore worth recording.

6 Consult with an accountant at least once a year to determine whether you are compiling all the information necessary for your tax return.

7 Keep your bookkeeping up to date – it gets harder to do the longer you leave it.

is shown in the "Debit" column, and when the goods are paid for by the customer their payment is shown in the "Credit" column. Like the purchase ledger, this should also be updated at least monthly.

At Year End

At the end of the year (your financial or tax year, rather than the calendar year) there are important, but relatively simple, additional tasks to carry out. For instance, if you hold any stock, raw material, or partially completed work, you need to do a stocktake on the last day of your financial year. A stocktake involves counting all the different items you have and valuing them (normally at cost price). Another task is to list all your business creditors (people to whom you owe money) and debtors (people who owe you money) on that date.

From the financial records you keep and the additional figures you provide at the year end, your accountant will produce a tax return, an annual profit and loss account, and a balance sheet. Together, these describe and sum up your business's financial position.

Managing Your Cash Flow

Cash-flow management is a very simple but useful technique to help you forecast your future cash requirements. As applicable to small businesses as it is to large corporations, cash-flow management enables you to spot any problems early on and to do something about them in advance. Once you have mastered the technique, you will wonder how anyone could possibly run a business without it.

Reviewing Your Initial Forecast

You will already have produced a cash-flow

Keeping on Top of Cash Flow

1 Check that your cash-flow closing balances match your financial statement balances.

2 Review your cash flow regularly to stop your business from running out of cash.

3 Be pessimistic with your forecasts – assume lower sales and higher costs.

4 Never confuse cash flow with profitability.

5 Remember that the last line of the cash-flow forecast represents neither a profit nor a loss.

6 Write notes on your cash-flow forecast explaining assumptions you have made.

forecast for your business plan (see pp. 54–7). Use this forecast as the basis for reforecasting once you open your business. First you need to enter the actual figures. Make sure that your cash-flow headings are the same as those in your financial statement, so that you can readily extract the figures for your cash-flow forecast. Then, at the start of each month, simply replace the forecast figures with the actual figures for the previous month. As you enter the actual figures, give some thought to those figures that differ widely from the forecast. Is it possible to explain the differences? Will these differences have a significant impact on your cash flow in the longer term? Now make sure that as a result your "closing balance" line does not either go into the red or exceed your overdraft limit.

Make an extra totals column in the second year to compare the current with the previous year

Revising Your Forecast

Once you have entered the actual figures for the previous month, you can forecast the individual figures for the months ahead more accurately, and obtain a more realistic long-

REVIEWING A CASH-FLOW FORECAST

Below are the first two months of the cash-flow forecast for Simply Perfect's business plan (see pp. 42–57). You can see the actual sales for the month of May, which amounted to $783, are much lower than the forecast of $1,500 for that month. June sales are therefore also likely to be less than forecast and should be revised. The lower figure for May also has an impact on borrowings.

	MAY (Actual)	MAY	JUN (Forecast)	JUN (Revised)
CASH IN				
1 SALES	1,500	783	2,000	1,000
2 BANK OR OTHER LOANS	0	0	4,000	4,000
3 OWNER'S CAPITAL	10,000	10,000	0	0
4 OTHER MONEY IN	0	0	0	0
5 TOTAL CASH IN	11,500	10,783	6,000	5,000
CASH OUT				
6 ADVERTISING AND PROMOTION	300	284	0	0
7 BANK CHARGES/INTEREST	0	0	50	50
8 BUSINESS INSURANCE	500	490	0	0
9 BUSINESS RENT	1,000	1,000	0	0
10 CLEANING	0	0	0	0
11 DRAWINGS/SALARIES	0	0	500	400
12 ELECTRICITY/GAS/HEAT/WATER	0	0	150	150
13 FINANCE CHARGES	0	0	160	160
14 LEGAL AND PROFESSIONAL	450	435	0	0
15 CAR - FUEL	0	0	0	0
16 CAR - OTHER EXPENSES	0	0	0	0
17 OTHER EXPENSES	0	0	0	0
18 POSTAGE/PARCELS	0	0	0	0
19 REPAIRS AND MAINTENANCE	0	0	50	50
20 STAFF WAGES	0	0	0	0
21 EMPLOYEE BENEFITS	0	0	0	0
22 STATIONERY/PRINTING	50	55	10	10
23 STOCK/RAW MATERIALS	8,000	8,370	4,000	4,000
24 SUBSCRIPTIONS	0	0	0	0
25 MISCELLANEOUS	80	68	50	50
26 TAX PAYMENTS	0	0	0	0
27 TELEPHONE/FAX	100	100	50	50
28 TRAVEL AND SUBSISTENCE	0	0	0	0
29 CAPITAL EXPENDITURE	3,350	2,970	0	567
30 TOTAL CASH OUT	13,830	13,772	5,020	5,487
31 NET CASH FLOW	-2,330	-2,989	980	-487
32 OPENING BALANCE	0	0	-2,330	-2,989
33 CLOSING BALANCE	-2,330	-2,989	-1,350	-3,476

Actual sales figure significantly lower than forecast

June sales forecast figure revised downwards by $1,000

Cost of stock higher than expected

Stock purchases may need to be cut back

Closing balance dangerously near to agreed overdraft limit ($3,000)

Overdraft likely to exceed limit; need to talk to bank about temporarily increasing overdraft limit

term forecast. Whenever any major or unexpected financial event occurs, such as the need to make a large purchase, or the anticipation of a major customer defaulting on a payment, do a revised cash-flow forecast immediately. During especially busy periods, you may need to revise your cash-flow forecast every few days to keep a tight control on required stock levels; this will enable you to keep enough stock to meet demand.

Minimizing Overhead and Expenses

When you start any business, you purchase stock and equipment, maybe rent premises, and perhaps take on staff, all on the not unreasonable assumption that sales will be made, cash will flow in, and the overhead can be sustained. However, if sales are lower than expected you will soon run out of cash. The temptation is to try to increase sales, but the quickest way to solve the problem is to reduce the overhead since it is mostly under your control.

Reduce overheads rather than prices if sales are low

During the many months, or perhaps years, it takes for a business to become established, there is a natural tendency to acquire unnecessary practices and perhaps to have higher overhead than is wise. It is therefore good practice to review your overhead at least every year, and preferably more often – you will be amazed at how much you can save! This is an essential ongoing process, not just one to follow if your business is in crisis. Analysis of your profit and loss account (see p. 140), comparing the past year with previous ones, can reveal areas worth investigating.

Even relatively small amounts can add up in time. Let us assume your business bank account is being debited $15 each month, for something that you can save on or do without. At first glance you might think it hardly worth the trouble "just to save $15," but over the course of five years (which is no time at all in business terms) this will cost your business a total of $900. Would you willingly give away $900 of your hard-earned profit? There are numerous areas, covered below, where savings are usually possible.

Using Space Wisely
This shop combines studio space with a selling area. The shelves behind the counter are crammed with pots in progress, while the shop displays finished articles. This efficient use of space keeps overheads to a minimum.

STAFF

Only take on staff when you have to and minimize staffing needs by investing in automation (such as computers). It may be better sometimes to have one high-caliber employee who needs less supervision than several of lesser ability. More mature and experienced part-time staff can be particularly worthwhile. Alternatively, try contracting out parts of your work to other companies, or use freelancers. This gives you flexibility to suit a variable workload, but at a higher cost and possibly with less control.

Review work practices regularly, aiming to simplify processes and eliminate unnecessary work. Encourage your staff to suggest ways of improving systems. Try to increase productivity by tight control, comprehensive job descriptions, proper training, and realistic incentives. If you need to lay off staff, this is a costly and complex business, so seek professional advice first (see pp. 172–3).

VEHICLES

Choose your purchases carefully, as vehicles represent a major cost and can be more of a liability than an asset. Consider the best way to finance their purchase since there are big differences in costs, especially when maintenance prices are included. Try to buy nearly new, rather than new, so that someone else takes the initial massive depreciation.

BUSINESS PREMISES

This can be another major overhead, especially in retailing where a prime site is usually vital. In a shop, minimize on-site storage and maximize retail floorspace so that as much space as possible is devoted to selling. In all cases, rent as little space as you can squeeze into. In time, consider purchasing rather than renting, since the former is usually an investment (if you buy wisely), the latter merely an expense.

MONEY SAVER

If you are trying to save on vehicle overheads, remember that mileage costs money. To minimize the length of journeys, consider using software designed to help you plan your route. This has the bonus of saving valuable time too.

HEAT AND LIGHT

We insulate our homes and try to save on domestic energy costs, but seem less interested in doing this in our workplaces, which are often large and poorly insulated, so therefore wasteful. There could be major savings here, especially since the energy market is highly competitive. Consider consulting a specialist in ways of conserving energy – making a few changes at a reasonable cost could improve energy efficiency and reduce your bills over the long term.

INSURANCES

Check that you are neither under- nor overinsured, and get alternative quotes when your policy comes up for renewal. Major savings can often be made by using an insurer who is used to your particular business (and hence risk) and who can therefore quantify it better than a more general insurer.

PURCHASING

Approve all major purchases yourself. If you decide to delegate some aspects of purchasing, then do so under strict guidelines with definite limits and controls in place. Staff have different priorities from proprietors and this can be reflected in their purchasing decisions.

TRAVEL

If you have to use trains, planes, or hotels, research the different fare or tariff options, since considerable savings are always possible. Ensure your staff do so, too. Investigate deals that offer savings to regular travelers.

FINANCE

If you are borrowing, look at the interest rates you are paying. Investigate the best way to fund your venture. Generally an overdraft is the cheapest way. Excessive stock levels are one cause of high borrowings, so check your stock control. In the long term, aim to be financially self-sufficient with no need for borrowing.

ADVERTISING AND PROMOTION

Assess if this expenditure is generating sufficient sales to cover its costs – do not be surprised if it is not. Ads are often placed in response to salespeople who persuade proprietors into thinking they must advertise. Many small businesses will receive a better response from promotional work rather than straight advertising.

PHONE BILLS

These are almost always larger than necessary. Try to reduce the number of long, chatty calls by using faxes or email. These can also be transmitted at cheaper phone times. Investigate alternative phone companies since this is a competitive area.

Make evolutionary rather than revolutionary changes

SUNDRIES

Expenses lumped together under this general heading, which often includes petty cash purchases, can cover a multitude of areas, analysis of which often causes a few surprises (and further savings).

Solving Cash-flow Problems

Many small businesses are confronted with cash-flow problems. The term "cash-flow problem" can cover a variety of ailments, but the net effect is that the business runs out of money so that bills cannot be paid. New or recently started businesses are particularly vulnerable, with their upfront launch costs and low initial sales. If the problems are not handled correctly they might lead to the premature demise of the venture. In general, cash-flow problems occur due to either one or, worse, a combination of the following factors:

▉ Overhead too high
▉ Sales levels too low
▉ Unexpectedly great trading levels
▉ Profit margins too small
▉ Debtor payments too slow.

DETECTING THE PROBLEM

First of all, you have to be aware that there is a problem. This may not be so obvious in its early stages, particularly if the financial statements are not fully up to date. One of the best early indicators is if your cash flow is continually failing to meet its forecasts. If you did a "break-even" cash-flow forecast (where predicted sales just match outgoings) and then found that the actual transactions were falling below these forecasts, you would know that the business was heading toward a major cash-flow problem. For how to do a cash-flow forecast, see pp. 54–7, and for cash-flow management, see pp. 140–42.

In any business, sales go through peaks and troughs, which may be seasonal in character or may be signs of something more serious; with a properly prepared cash-flow forecast, it will be possible to spot a problem as distinct from the usual fluctuations. If nothing is done, the situation will deteriorate and classic warning signals may become evident. These are:

▉ A rising overdraft level (without any specific reason)
▉ Increasing difficulties in paying creditors
▉ Falling behind in the monthly PAYE and Social Security payments.

These are all very serious signs of impending disaster and they demand immediate action.

A SURVIVAL STRATEGY

Once a looming cash-flow problem is detected, you must move fast since the business will be growing weaker and there will be less time to make changes and fewer options available.

People tend to react to this situation in two ways, either completely ignoring the problem because they simply cannot face up to it (and they may be unsure about what to do) or overreacting and instituting panic measures, which may be ill-considered and potentially damaging. In most people's minds questions fly around. Should they advertise more? Should they cut their prices? Should they lay off their staff?

The only sensible course of action is to approach the problem methodically (see the box, right). To do this, you need to work out how to give yourself some time. When a business is not going smoothly the demands on you can increase, making it very difficult to find "thinking time." But if the business is facing a crisis you must simply make time. A practical suggestion is to set aside half an hour before the start of work each day to concentrate your full energy on the problem (since most people are more alert in the morning and the day's dramas have not yet intruded).

LOOKING AGAIN AT OVERHEAD

Reviewing your overhead costs should be a routine task (see pp. 142–4), though the action you choose to take if your business is in difficulty may be more radical than is usual. In some businesses the overhead is simply too high for the level of business. Possibly the proprietors or directors are drawing too much cash from the business – perhaps forgetting to make provision for taxes and so on.

TACKLING LOW SALES

Having sales levels that are too low is probably the most common cause of cash-flow problems, especially with new small businesses (under two or three years old), and there are several reasons for this. Many new businesses are set

FOUR STEPS TO SOLVING CASH-FLOW PROBLEMS

When business is going badly, it is helpful to have a plan to follow. Try to approach cash-flow problems with a clear mind, concentrating on the crisis at hand, but with an eye on the long term, too.

1 FIND OUT HOW BAD IT IS The problem needs facing up to. Obtain a complete and up-to-date financial picture by quickly putting together a cash-flow forecast, with lists of all outstanding creditors and debtors, and a further note or list of orders or sales that are likely to materialize over the next few weeks or months.

2 REDUCE YOUR OUTGOINGS The business is running out of cash so the next step is to reduce the outgoings until they match the income. This might require drastic action. It may involve reducing staffing levels, getting out of expensive rented premises, and generally cutting back wherever possible.

3 CONSIDER THE OPTIONS Now you know where you are, start to look at the possibilities for improving the situation, and getting the business back on track.

4 TACKLE THE ROOT CAUSE You can now turn your attention to tackling the root cause of the problem. It is important to identify clearly which factor or factors are relevant in your own case – it may be fairly self-evident – and to try and prevent more damage.

up with a lot of optimism, but insufficient knowledge of the market and too little capital. Another major factor is that it takes time, often a great deal of time (years, not months), to become established, and this period is normally much longer than most initial business plans allow for. The problem is, of course, that sales during this early period can be lower than that required to support the business (and give you a reasonable wage). Take heart in knowing that there is hardly a business in existence that, at one time or another, has not presented its proprietors or directors with the task of how to increase sales to rectify a cash-flow problem. The first task is to identify the main reason why sales levels are low. A low turnover means that you have too few customers and/or each customer is spending too little. If you are faced with either or both situations, you have a number of options to try:

▪ **IMPROVE YOUR SALES AND MARKETING**
This is the interface between you and the customer. Making improvements in this area is relatively straightforward and inexpensive, and should be the first option you consider to resolve cash-flow problems. See the box below for details. If all the steps in the selling process are genuinely being done reasonably well (and there is little point in kidding yourself if this is not the case), then the truth may be that there is insufficient demand for your product or service as it currently stands.

▪ **MODIFY YOUR BUSINESS** In many cases your analysis of the problem of low sales will reveal a number of areas that need

REVIEWING SALES AND MARKETING PROCEDURES

Look at all the steps in the selling process in turn to see whether there are any mistakes or omissions you can identify – there are bound to be a few. If any of them are not being done right, this is where to concentrate your efforts.

1 FINDING CUSTOMERS Ask yourself how you expect people to hear about your new business and then try asking some how they actually heard about you. Modify your actions accordingly. Also, work out roughly how many people need to hear about you to produce sufficient inquiries to lead, in turn, to enough sales to support your business.

Many small businesses promote themselves inadequately due to lack of time, money, and possibly expertise. But simply deciding to spend more money on advertising is unlikely to be the right answer, and, in any event, your business may not be able to afford much advertising in its present condition. It is better to listen to your existing customers so that you can improve this fertile area. As a simple guide, if your customers are other businesses, then a direct approach by phone or letter followed up by a meeting is likely to give the best results. With the general public, the task is a little more difficult (unless you are a retail business), and the precise approach will require careful thought. For example, if you have a grass-cutting and gardening business, you might put leaflets through mailboxes and then follow up in person. If you have tried this before, you may need to increase the size of your target area or concentrate more effort on higher-income neighborhoods.

improving, but it may also show that you need to modify what you are offering to make it more sellable. Due to your cash-flow predicament there may be a temptation to do something really drastic in terms of changing the product or service offered, but it is probably much safer to stick to what you are doing, to make a number of fine adjustments, and then to check the response to each of those. These small changes can be implemented much more quickly, at a much lower cost, and involve considerably lower risks than a more radical move. In deciding which changes you could make, think back over the questions, criticisms, suggestions, or shortcomings that have been voiced by would-be customers. Ideally, this is where the inspiration for your modifications should come from initially.

▪ **DIVERSIFY** It may be that your initial market research was not quite accurate, and that the market is really looking for a different product or service, or a major adaptation of what you are currently offering. This is not an unusual situation. However, calm consideration needs to be given to this option, as change or diversification on a large scale must be thought of as akin to an entirely new project, almost like setting up a new venture from

---

SALES TECHNIQUE

When reviewing sales techniques, be aware that intrusive or pushy techniques discourage purchasers who walk away from the sale to avoid being put under pressure to buy.

2 STIMULATING CUSTOMER INTEREST It may be that sufficient customers are aware of you, but their interest has not been caught. Your company or its products or services may not look up-to-date enough, or they may look too upmarket or too downmarket for most of your potential customers. Your leaflet, display window, or ads may be confusing to potential customers, or people may simply not realize what you can offer (this is a surprisingly common problem). If you are in retail, try speaking to some of the people who are not making a purchase, perhaps to ask what they are looking for in your shop – their answers could be highly illuminating.

Something else you can do is to look at the competition. What are they doing successfully that you are not? Although your market research investigated competitors, it is useful to look again once you are in business, with the benefit of experience. Also, business conditions change, and your competitors may have realized this before you.

3 SATISFYING CUSTOMER NEEDS Compare your products or services carefully with those of your competitors. Maybe you include a feature which is putting off potential buyers, or are missing a feature that your competitors are offering, and which makes all the difference. Your business may be projecting one image, but the bulk of your stock may be more suitable for a different image, so you may attract customers but cannot satisfy their needs.

Price is often of crucial importance, so ensure your pricing is correct. Just reducing the price is not necessarily a good idea, since a low price may send the wrong message (that what you are offering is cheap or of low quality). Again, talking to potential customers will shed more light on this.

4 MAKING THE SALE Sometimes the product or service is right, the customer is ready to make the purchase, but the sales technique being used is simply inadequate or even off-putting. Not everyone is a good, natural salesperson, and selling does require its own persuasive skills, knowledge, and enthusiasm, even when the product or service is itself excellent. New or refresher courses in sales techniques may be needed.

scratch. Thus it will take time and money to establish, and may mean venturing into uncharted waters. Diversification should not be seen as a panacea to your current problems, but it can be very successful if carried out with due market research and especially if it is allied to what the business is currently doing, building on the contacts and business knowledge that have already been acquired. It is often difficult to look for a change in direction if all your efforts have been focused on making one plan work. Brainstorming is a good way to enable you to think along new and creative paths, to come up with possibilities for diversification.

UNEXPECTEDLY HIGH TRADING LEVELS

Another situation in which a cash-flow problem can appear is when a business is expanding more rapidly than its available working capital

BRAINSTORMING

To come up with new ideas for a diversified product or service, hold a brainstorming session with your fellow partners, directors, key staff, and other confidant(e)s.

■ **VENUE** Hold the session away from the work environment. You could probably use the living room in one of your homes, provided it is large enough and peaceful, or, if that is not suitable, rent a small function room in a local hotel. Ensure that lots of drinks and sandwiches are on hand and that there are absolutely no interruptions.

■ **TIMING** The session should start in the morning when everyone is fresh, and may last until mid- or even late afternoon.

■ **RULES** The rules of the session are that people come up with as many ideas as they can. These ideas are never criticized or ridiculed by the others, however wild they may seem at first. This tends to encourage people to come up with more unusual ideas and to do some lateral thinking.

■ **EQUIPMENT** If there are more than three or four people in the group, it might also be useful to have a large piece of paper, a writing board, or a flipchart, which everyone can see and on which all the ideas are written.

■ **SELECTING IDEAS** After a few hours the group can switch from generating fresh ideas to looking in more detail at those already thrown out, and by the end of the session there should be a number of ideas to be followed up as "possibles." All these should be recorded, in brief, for any future sessions or discussions.

BRAINSTORMING
The point of a brainstorming session is to generate as many ideas as possible, no matter how outlandish they may seem at first. This freedom can throw out unexpected and innovative suggestions.

allows. Called "overtrading", this situation affects businesses that could otherwise be regarded as successful. There are two options: either the business slows down by turning down business or staggering jobs, or they have more capital injected.

LOW PROFIT MARGINS

Cash-flow problems can also be caused by margins that are lower than anticipated for a variety of reasons. These can include:

- The need to discount heavily, possibly due to competition or demands by a large customer.
- Rises in raw material or stock costs which cannot be passed on immediately to customers.
- Exchange-rate fluctuations when you import or export.

Another cause of low profit margins is that, even though you may be making sales at your full normal price, these prices may themselves be too low, allowing an inadequate margin to sustain the business.

Many businesses offer a variety of products and services which have different profit margins. This gives them the opportunity to switch slowly from low-margin work to higher-margin work. This simple and gentle change in marketing strategy may mean a temporary decrease in turnover, but an increase in overall profitability of the business, especially if overhead is reduced to match the initial lower level of business.

Another point to note is that, even if your margins are typical for your industry, you should always work at increasing them by a few percentage points here and there, wherever possible; cumulatively this can add up to a useful increase in profit.

SLOW DEBTOR PAYMENTS

New, small businesses are particularly vulnerable to the effects of bad payers. This is for several reasons: often the new business is undercapitalized; a second factor might be inexperience in sensing a poor credit risk;

finally, in their eagerness to get a sale or win a contract, the new business might turn a blind eye to the creditworthiness of a buyer. It is better to walk away from doing business with a risky customer if you feel uncomfortable about it; learn to trust your instincts on matters of payment. Since bad payers affect almost all businesses, large or small, the subject is covered in more depth below.

Dealing with Late Payments

Late payment by customers (or, worse still, nonpayment) is a business problem most ventures have to deal with. Almost every business needs to spend time pursuing bad payers. Whereas private consumers do not usually expect credit, other business customers invariably expect 30 days minimum. Three tips to encourage prompt payment are:

- On your invoice, state the date by which the payment is due, rather than a general "Please pay by 30 days."
- Highlight (in color) this date on your invoices.
- Offer a discount (2.5 percent is a typical figure) for payment made within 30 days (this is more common in some sectors than others, so be guided by what is normal in your industry).

The important point is to minimize future exposure to such risks. Proper credit checks should be carried out on all customers requiring credit over a threshold you feel is relevant to your business.

CREDIT CHECKS

The first step is to ask a potential customer for their bank details and the names and addresses of two suppliers to whom you should write. Whereas the bank can give an indication of the ability of the company to pay, the other suppliers will give a clue as to their willingness to pay, which might be a different matter entirely. If the customer is a limited company, you can obtain a copy of their annual financial statements. Some internet sites also offer on-line credit checks for a fee. In addition to doing your own credit checks, you might also choose to employ a credit checking agency, particularly if the potential order is significant financially.

A DEBT RECOVERY STRATEGY

On completing the job, send an invoice promptly, specifying payment due date

⬇

At the end of the month, send a statement

⬇

Two weeks after payment is due, phone the customer's accounting department (taking the contact's name)

⬇

One to two weeks later, phone the same contact asking why there is a delay

⬇

One to two weeks later, send a polite letter requesting payment

⬇

One week later, phone the boss asking if there is a problem

⬇

Within a week or two, if possible, visit in person, or send a sharper letter, maybe reminding them of your right as a small business to claim interest on late payments

⬇

If this does not work, consider taking them to court (take legal advice first)

RISK REDUCTION

Other ways to reduce your exposure to bad debt include spreading the risk by having more small customers rather than several big ones (though your administration time rises dramatically); requesting payment by proforma invoice (payment in advance); taking a deposit; splitting larger orders into several smaller deliveries (each of which has to be paid before the next part of the order is despatched); and, finally, where appropriate, by the use of factoring (see opposite).

Refinancing a Business

Sometimes businesses need to refinance. This may be due to an expansion of the business, but is more often caused by other problems, which must also be tackled. Refinancing is not an easy task – there may be few assets, the business may already be up to its maximum overdraft limit, and its creditors may be pressing for their money. The first step is to decide on a preferred course of action and its cost. A contingency factor should be allowed for: if the funds raised are insufficient it is most unlikely that you could refinance again while the business is still in trouble.

As the business is still active, there is one important thing in its favor – its main creditors will normally want to see your business continuing to operate and get over its problems, since they will then be more likely to get their money back. On the other hand, if they believe there is little hope of saving the situation, they will probably just cut their losses and close you down.

Many people put off telling their creditors that their business is running into problems. This reluctance is quite natural, but unfortunately, this silence may cause the creditors to panic and to withdraw their support altogether. So it is essential to talk, albeit guardedly, to them all.

A RESCUE PLAN

A letter can outline your plan. It should confidently and clearly explain how you intend to correct the situation with their support. The letter should be brief, though your banker (who knows your finances anyway) will probably need more details. Any promises of repayments should be on modest timescales, as creditors will lose confidence if any subsequent repayment is missed or late. Two precautions must be stressed:

■ Divulge as few of your business details as absolutely necessary.

■ Assume that your creditors will take whatever action is in their best interest, not yours – so proceed with caution and first take impartial and professional advice.

Treat your creditors with care – they can be your best bankers

SHARED RISK

Banks will often refuse to inject further cash (in the form of a loan or larger overdraft) unless new capital, possibly equal to the bank's increased risk, is introduced into the business. This cash may come from the sale of some personal effects, finding a new partner or shareholder, or a loan from a friend.

If your product or service is unique and vital to the smooth operation of a larger business that is a major customer of yours, that business may be prepared to make a loan (with interest) to keep you going, or to purchase a shareholding in your business.

FACTORING

For those nonretail businesses with a cash-flow problem caused by rapid expansion, and where the turnover is already $100,000 plus, one option to consider is factoring (also called sales-linked funding, invoice finance, or cash-flow financing). In this method, when you invoice your customer you send a copy to the factor, who then pays you typically 75 percent of the invoice total almost immediately. The factor then takes the responsibility for chasing the debt, issuing statements and reminders. Your invoice states that payment should be made to the factor and not yourself. When your customer pays, you receive the balance from the factor (minus their charges). Factoring costs are broadly comparable with the cost of a bank overdraft, but with the advantages of faster payment, and the factor has the problem of chasing the debt.

FACT FILE

A key reason why a bank (or another creditor) will pull the plug on a business in financial difficulty is a lack of confidence in that venture. Hence, any steps to refinance your venture need to be presented positively, and include confidence-building measures, such as using an impartial accountant to help prepare figures.

KEEPING AHEAD

Starting a business is relatively easy – it is staying in business that is the real challenge. Simply working long hours and expending a huge amount of effort does not necessarily achieve results. Success comes after a combination of thought, preparation, application, and perhaps some good luck too. Whether you want to grow your business or simply keep it running successfully, you need to keep on top of how you are performing, avoid complacency, and adapt to the changing competition and market place. You also need to consider the long-term future of your business and build this into your plans.

What are the likely problems your new business will face as it grows? An early challenge will be finding good, capable staff to help cope with increasing sales. Related to this is the need to delegate for the first time, which some people find hard to do. Your business may also need increased funding to support the greater turnover, although ideally it will fund its own growth organically. It may outgrow its initial premises, and the resulting relocation is likely to be a time-consuming task, occurring at the very time when you are stretched anyway. An increase in business also brings with it an increase in day-to-day problems that need solving, and this can be wearing and stressful until new procedures, and possibly extra staff, are in place. So by making more sales the whole business may have to be transformed, which can be quite an upheaval.

Analyzing Your Business Performance

If you want to keep ahead and make progress, then you need to know how well your business is doing. From the start, every business should evolve procedures that monitor its performance. These procedures need to be simple, quick to carry out, and easy to understand. The results need to be useful to you and free of any ambiguity.

ANALYSIS OF SALES DATA

This vital process requires some form of record-keeping, which needs to be reviewed every year or so to ensure you are still recording the right sort of information. Every business will have its own priorities in terms of what information is

CASE STUDY: Looking to the Future

DIANA AND BILL had both taken early retirement and sold their home so that they would be able to purchase a small hotel. In their first year of business they had attracted sufficient visitors to meet their financial targets, helped by the website they had created to promote their hotel. They had also attended various trade shows and seminars to keep up with the fast-moving trends of the tourist industry, and had implemented some new ideas and made refinements as a result. They decided to extend their business plan, which currently looked only at the first year of business, to look at between five and 10 years ahead. This would enable them to keep tabs on the success of their business, while at the same time working towards their ultimate goal of getting the business in shape for a profitable sale and their full retirement.

CUMULATIVE
SALES TOTAL

CHARTING YOUR
PERFORMANCE
By transferring your performance figures into a graph, you can see the direction of the general trend. This graph compares actual sales to forecast sales. You could also use it to compare sales in one year with those in another. A spreadsheet program will usually be able to create a graph of your figures.

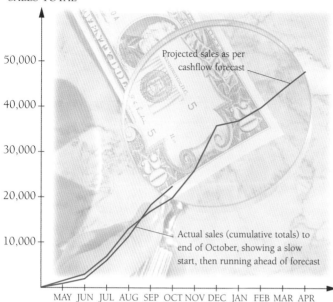

50,000

40,000

30,000

20,000

10,000

Projected sales as per cashflow forecast

Actual sales (cumulative totals) to end of October, showing a slow start, then running ahead of forecast

MAY JUN JUL AUG SEP OCT NOV DEC JAN FEB MAR APR

TIME (MONTHS)

needed, and priorities may change. However, the information you record should answer the following questions, which are fundamental to most businesses:

■ Are my sales rising, steady, or falling?
■ Are sales to each of my biggest customers rising, steady, or falling?
■ Which products or services are my best sellers and which are the poorest?

Your cash-flow records will show your sales on a monthly basis. It is not ideal to compare one month with the same month a year ago since there may be some onetime or seasonal factors that distort the overall picture. Instead, aim to look at a longer time period, such as a quarter. This can be a rolling quarter, consisting of the month in question together with the month on either side. Even better is to chart the

Allow for inflation in your analysis of business performance

performance over a year or so to reveal the direction of the trend. Service businesses might want to work out the amount earned per hour to see the direction of the earning trend. To do this, divide the annual profit by the hours worked (not hours invoiced) in the year. This will show how the actual rate compares with the invoicing rate.

Retailers and mail-order businesses might want to calculate the value of their average sale by dividing the total value of sales by the number of purchases made. Another useful measure for retailers is the RST (Rate of Stock Turn), which is the turnover divided by stock value at retail prices. This is easiest to do at year end, when you will know your total sales and stock figures. To interpret this, you need to know the norms for your trade sector.

MAKING TIME FOR REFLECTION
In the first few years of a new business, it is easy to get bogged down in paperwork. For long-term success, it is essential to make time to gain a broader perspective.

Some questions you may have will probably require the assistance of an accountant, such as:
■ How profitable is the business?
■ What is the return on my capital investment?
Your annual accounts provide the all-important profit and loss account and a balance sheet. Both may require your accountant to explain the significant aspects of each.

Keeping Up to Date with Developments

The whole world and your own market is constantly changing, and you need to make a major effort just to keep up with events. Look at the checklist opposite to see if you are really keeping up or slipping behind. In running your own business there is a danger that you can become isolated and less aware of changes in the wider world. To overcome this, you need to create a support and information network. This can be formal, such as membership in a trade or small-business organization, or quite informal. In addition, make an effort to keep in touch with former work colleagues.

CHANGE BY EVOLUTION
To survive, almost every business needs to keep evolving. Evolution can be anything from a minor improvement, such as sourcing better paper that does not jam your computer's printer, to a major change, such as the launch of a new product or service. Often small changes added together can make a large positive impact. Your evolutionary changes all have one or more of the following objectives:
■ **INCREASING PROFITS** This is not simply about making more sales, but about making more profit from your present endeavours – which may mean changing your prices, charging for services that you currently offer for free, or changing the balance from low-margin work to higher-margin work.

ASSESSING HOW UP TO DATE YOU ARE

Look at each question and then decide which answer best matches your situation. Score 4 points for each A answer, 2 points for each B, and 0 points for each C. Add up your scores and then look at the score assessments at the bottom.

Do you use the internet?
A I have a website. ☐
B I use the internet for my business. ☐
C I do not use the internet for my business. ☐

Do you visit trade shows?
A I visit a relevant trade show at least once a year. ☐
B I visit a trade show occasionally. ☐
C I tend not to visit trade shows. ☐

Do you read a trade publication?
A I subscribe to a trade publication. ☐
B I occasionally read a trade publication. ☐
C I don't read any trade publications. ☐

Do you meet others in your industry?
A I meet others regularly and exchange information. ☐
B I meet others only on occasion. ☐
C I rarely meet anyone else in my industry. ☐

Are you a member of your trade association?
A I am an active member of my trade association. ☐
B I am a passive member of my trade association. ☐
C I am not a member of my trade association. ☐

Do you read the financial press?
A I read several financial publications regularly. ☐
B I sometimes read a financial publication. ☐
C I do not read financial publications. ☐

Do you attend seminars or conferences?
A I usually attend one or two per year. ☐
B I have attended them on occasion. ☐
C I do not go to these events. ☐

Are you a member of your chamber of commerce?
A I am a member of our local chamber of commerce. ☐
B I am not a member, but occasionally meet members. ☐
C I am not a member. ☐

Are you aware of changes in relevant laws?
A I think I am aware of what is coming. ☐
B I have a hazy idea of what legislation is coming. ☐
C I do not know what legislation, if any, is in the pipeline. ☐

Do you attend training courses?
A I attend a training course every year or so. ☐
B I attend a training course on rare occasions. ☐
C I do not attend any training courses. ☐

RESULTS

0–10 points
You are probably not keeping up with what is happening in your industry. Set aside time to network and inform yourself.

12–20 points
Although you are keeping up to some extent, there are gaps. Look at the questions where you scored B or C and improve on these areas.

22–30 points
You are keeping up with many of the developments in your industry, but a little more effort could be beneficial.

32–40 points
You are obviously trying very hard to keep up to date. Well done. Aim to keep your knowledge at the same level, or even higher.

■ **MAKING MORE SALES** No matter how successful you are, you might lose a major customer at any time, so you should always be aware of options for improving sales. Look at ways of increasing your market share, offering new products or services, or moving into other markets, possibly further afield.

■ **MAKING THE BUSINESS RUN MORE SMOOTHLY** Often, the people who start a business are not the best ones to run it. This is partly because they may not be very interested in arranging administrative matters. However, time spent on these important details helps the business run more efficiently and is good for staff morale and customer confidence.

■ **IMPROVING THE PRODUCT OR SERVICE** Think hard about how you can improve the product you sell or service you offer. The improvements themselves may be modest, but cumulatively they will be significant and the process of continual improvement will keep you ahead of the competition.

■ **REDUCING THE OPERATING COSTS** A winning characteristic of almost every successful entrepreneur is that they are very careful with their money and ensure there is little waste and no unnecessary expenditure. You can learn from them by keeping a tight control on the business finances, especially operating costs. This is one activity that should not be readily delegated.

Avoiding Common Pitfalls

Businesses are most vulnerable in their first few years of existence. If you can survive them, your chances of keeping going are much greater and you can consider your business as having become established. One way to help you get through those first tricky years is to learn from the mistakes of others. Look at the checklist on the right to see how well placed you are to avoid various problem areas.

Spare a few minutes to read through this checklist to see how well prepared you are to avoid some of the most common pitfalls of running a business. Give each question some thought and indicate your answers with a check, an "X," or a question mark (if you are unsure). This checklist is intended to provoke thought and suggest aspects of your business, all of equal importance, that you need to look into further; there is no "perfect score" to achieve.

Competitors
Some competitors can be benign, others distinctly less so.

A Do you monitor your main competitors' prices, promotions, expansion, etc? ☐Y ☐N

B Do you subscribe to any trade information source? ☐Y ☐N

C Do you think you are gaining on your competitors? ☐Y ☐N

Suppliers
Your business may be dependent on one or more critical suppliers.

A Do you have a "dual-sourcing" policy or designated alternative suppliers? ☐Y ☐N

B Do you keep in close touch with critical suppliers? ☐Y ☐N

Staff
Your business may be vulnerable if it relies on one or more key staff members.

A Do you have someone to take over should a key worker be ill or leave? ☐Y ☐N

B Are you paying a good wage to discourage staff from leaving? ☐Y ☐N

C Do you have an incentive program to encourage key staff to stay with you? ☐Y ☐N

Customers
The loss of a major customer or a bad debt could be disastrous.

A Do you have any customer that accounts for more than 25 per cent of your turnover? ☐Y ☐N

CHECKLIST OF PREVENTATIVE MEASURES

B Do you know the potential effects of losing your largest customer? ☐Y ☐N

C Is there any noticeable shift in your customer base or their buying habits? ☐Y ☐N

D Do you have a procedure for checking the creditworthiness of all new credit customers? ☐Y ☐N

E Do you have a procedure for ensuring customers keep within their credit limits? ☐Y ☐N

F Do you have a procedure for chasing late payers? ☐Y ☐N

Financial Control
Lack of financial control is one of the commonest reasons why businesses fail.

A Do you write up your accounts at least weekly? ☐Y ☐N

B Do you do a cash-flow forecast monthly? ☐Y ☐N

C Are you keeping well within any overdraft limit you have? ☐Y ☐N

D Is there a written plan to reduce or end your borrowings? ☐Y ☐N

Pricing
There is a temptation to set a price and stick to it even when things change.

A Have you done a price comparison with rivals in the last six months? ☐Y ☐N

B Are your prices keeping up with inflation? ☐Y ☐N

C Have you changed your prices during the last 12 months? ☐Y ☐N

D Do you know what your profit margin is? ☐Y ☐N

Products
Most products (including services) become dated as time goes on and sales ultimately suffer.

A Are your present "products" in midlife or older? ☐Y ☐N

B Have you new "products" in the pipeline? ☐Y ☐N

C Are these new "products" properly funded and scheduled? ☐Y ☐N

Overhead
Rising running costs can soon overwhelm the profitability of a business.

A Have you reviewed your overhead in the last six months? ☐Y ☐N

B Is your overhead the same as or less than at the same time last year? ☐Y ☐N

C Do you know which overhead you plan to reduce? ☐Y ☐N

Performance Indicators
It is important to have indicators to give you advance notice of a problem.

A Do you have a business plan that you can follow? ☐Y ☐N

B Do you tabulate or chart key indicators, such as monthly sales? ☐Y ☐N

C Do you analyze your sales to spot significant changes? ☐Y ☐N

D Does your accountant produce an annual profit and loss account for you? ☐Y ☐N

Insurance Cover
A fire, flood, or major theft could wreck your business. Proper insurance coverage may cushion the blow.

A In the last 12 months have you reassessed all likely risks? ☐Y ☐N

B Do you have insurance coverage for the main insurable risks you have identified? ☐Y ☐N

C Are you complying with all stipulations made by your insurers? ☐Y ☐N

D Do you have any contingency plans, however simple? ☐Y ☐N

E Do you have any procedure to monitor internal or external theft? ☐Y ☐N

RESULTS

If you had a majority of checks, you are already aware of common pitfalls and taking action to avoid them. If you had more Xs and question marks than checks, there is still plenty of scope for you to look further at your business and systems to take preventative action.

Two very common reasons for failure are lack of financial controls and insufficient trade (low sales). You should focus most of your attention on avoiding those two key areas. A lack of financial control normally means a business has problems because it runs out of cash and is unable to pay its bills. The best way to avoid these cash-flow problems is to practice cash-flow management (see pp. 140–42); this will also identify a situation where there is insufficient trade (which is usually obvious anyway). For suggestions of corrective actions, see pp. 145–8.

LEARNING FROM YOUR MISTAKES

Finally, do not be scared of making the odd mistake. Many successful large companies make mistakes and some of their ventures are disastrous – the difference between them and you is that they can usually afford the mistakes.

If you do make a mistake, large or small, take the time to look at what led up to it, and how you could have acted to avoid it. In this way you will avoid making the same mistake twice, and perhaps learn how to spot when things are going awry earlier and have the time to take corrective action.

Planning for the Future

Once your business is established and has been running for a couple of years, it is useful for you to begin to create a long-term business plan. The process may take many months, or even years, while you ponder the different options open to you. As it becomes clear in which direction you should be heading,

CHOOSING FUTURE OPTIONS

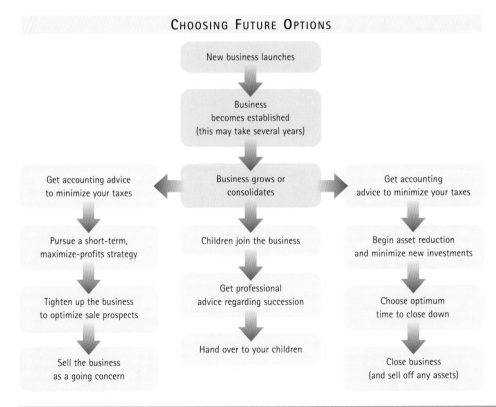

New business launches

Business becomes established
(this may take several years)

Business grows or consolidates

Get accounting advice to minimize your taxes

Get accounting advice to minimize your taxes

Pursue a short-term, maximize-profits strategy

Children join the business

Begin asset reduction and minimize new investments

Tighten up the business to optimize sale prospects

Get professional advice regarding succession

Choose optimum time to close down

Sell the business as a going concern

Hand over to your children

Close business (and sell off any assets)

then start to structure your thoughts to form the basis of a plan. The format of your plan can be similar to your original business plan, but the objectives are different – the viability of the business is not an issue, and you are not trying to raise finance. What you are trying to do is to create a five- or 10-year plan with a clear objective. You need to allow for unexpected changes as circumstances change, and plans do have a habit of going astray. When you are ready, show the draft to your accountant.

CHOOSING THE WAY FORWARD

Many people assume that a business needs to grow to be considered successful. In fact, many very successful businesses do not grow beyond a certain point, and the people behind those businesses have consciously chosen not to grow their businesses further. There may be many reasons for this, but often it is because the business suits them and is generating sufficient profit for their needs. Instead of striving to grow the business, they will endeavour to consolidate it by making it more efficient and ensuring they keep existing customers and attract sufficient new customers to replace those lost through natural wastage.

Ultimately you may choose to sell or hand over your business, or to close it altogether. These options all need long-term planning:

▓ **SELLING A BUSINESS** While you are running a business, you minimize your taxes by offsetting operating costs against profits to reduce the net profit figure. However, the selling price of a business is a function of its profitability, so it is useful to maximize your profits for the final year (or more) before a possible sale. To do this, first restrict all expenses and, second, as you approach year end, invoice all possible sales. In addition, you should physically spruce up the business and redecorate the premises to make them as attractive as possible.

▓ **FAMILY BUSINESS SUCCESSION** This requires specialist professional advice; it is important that you bring all family members into the decision-making process at an early stage.

▓ **CLOSE THE BUSINESS** The optimum time to close down depends on the nature of the business, the tax position of the proprietors, and many other factors, so this requires good accounting advice to get the most (taxes paid) money for your business.

PLANNING FOR RETIREMENT

Whatever your age, you need to think about your retirement arrangements. The sooner you start, the easier it is to make provisions for retirement. The decision has various tax implications and so needs to be discussed with your accountant.

.69   2.10   4.40
.44   1.59   1.94
.83   4.46   1.82   2.11
.13   2.28   3.72   2.04
.09   5.00   1.89   2.10
.09   2.86   4.15   2.02   20.00
       2.54   1.75   2.87   12.98
              2.14   15.22
                      28.37   17.43
                              0.07

1.4

1.2

1.0

0.8

0.6

USEFUL
information

*T*his section covers the important
aspects of the law and tax as they
apply to business, providing a
straightforward, basic grounding in
the numerous and complex regulations
that are likely to affect you. The
Glossary explains key business terms,
while the Useful Contacts and
Suggested Reading sections point you
towards other sources of information.

LEGAL MATTERS

There are an increasing number of laws and regulations with which businesses, including small businesses, must comply in the U.S. This chapter provides general guidance, but should not be regarded as a complete or authoritative statement of the law. For more information, consult an attorney or the relevant authorities.

Choosing Your Business Status

An early decision you need to make is what legal form your business should take. If you are going to be a one-person business, you could be a sole proprietor (that is, self-employed). If several people are involved on an equal basis, you need to be a partnership or a corporation.

SOLE PROPRIETORSHIP

This is probably the most common legal status for starting a business. You can trade under your own name or a business name. You can also employ staff. Should the business fail,

---

DRAWING UP A PARTNERSHIP AGREEMENT

These are suggestions of clauses to consider in a partnership agreement. You may not need all those listed here, and you may wish to include others; this is a starting point:

■ **DESCRIPTION OF THE PROPOSED BUSINESS** This should not limit future developments.

■ **LOCATION** Initial location of the business.

■ **DATE OF COMMENCEMENT** Some agreements also state the duration for which the agreement is to last, though this can be extended by arrangement between partners.

■ **CAPITAL** The initial capital each partner will provide at the commencement. If, due to personal circumstances, the partners contribute different amounts of capital, then they might choose either to: a) apportion the profits in the same ratio as the amounts invested; or b) allow time, say six or 12 months, for the partners to equalize their investments to allow the profits to be shared equally. In both cases voting rights and personal drawings (wages) should be equal.

■ **ROLE OF EACH PARTNER** Definition of the role, adding that the partners will not undertake other employment or self-employment during the period of the agreement. Where one partner is a sleeping partner, this would obviously need to be taken into account.

■ **DECISIONS** The particular circumstances where decisions need to be unanimous to guard against reckless acts by individual partners. For example: agreeing or terminating contracts; offering or terminating employment; entering into or terminating property lease arrangements; lending, borrowing, or removing any property or assets of the business.

■ **VOTING** The voting rights and who might arbitrate should there be disagreement.

■ **OPERATION OF THE BANK ACCOUNT** For example, how many signatures are required on cheques (often only one signature for amounts less than some specified figure).

■ **DIVISION OF PROFITS AND LOSSES** This includes the nomination of an accountant.

■ **LEVEL OF DRAWINGS AND EXPENSES** The latter could have an upper limit per annum.

■ **HOLIDAYS** The length of holidays that can

owing money, then you are personally liable, and your creditors can seize your personal possessions to recover their losses. Many businesses start with sole trader status, but as they grow they usually change to a corporation status for three reasons:

■ It provides limited liability protection of their personal possessions.

■ It is easier for them to raise larger sums of money for expansion.

■ It permits other people to take a stake in the business.

PARTNERSHIP

If two or more people work together and none is an employee of the other(s), then the law regards the arrangement as a partnership. A partnership can take on employees. Unless there is an agreement to the contrary, profits in a partnership have to be shared equally between partners. Likewise, each partner will be regarded by law as "jointly and severally liable" for any debts that the business may run up. What this means in practice is that if the first partner buys a car, for example, using a business check that subsequently bounces, the car dealer can pursue the second partner for the entire amount.

It is therefore essential to start off with a good written partnership agreement. Start by drafting your own agreement, get advice from an accountant, and then see an attorney who can draw up the final document. There are many complex issues involved and you will need professional advice.

A silent partner is someone who invests in a business, but does not work in it. His or her

---

be taken. Also, who needs to agree to proposed holiday dates, and any restrictions as to duration or to not taking holidays during prescribed busy times of the year.

■ **ILLNESS OR INCAPACITY** The procedure in the event of illness or incapacity of a partner.

■ **ADMISSION OF ANY NEW PARTNER** The procedures for admitting a new partner. This might also include a clause that allows the expulsion of one partner under certain specified circumstances.

■ **RETIREMENT OF AN EXISTING PARTNER** Usually the retiring partner is entitled to an equal share of the business assets, excluding goodwill, as valued by the firm's accountants at the date of retirement. The key issue here is that the payment to the retiring partner must be made in instalments that are fair to the outgoing partner and yet affordable by the business. The tax implications for both parties need consideration too. Goodwill should probably be excluded as: a) any goodwill the business has built up has already been enjoyed by the outgoing partner by way of shared profits; b) the departure of the partner might alter any goodwill significantly; and c) it is a very difficult aspect to quantify.

■ **DEATH OF A PARTNER** Usually an agreement will state that the partnership will continue and the estate of the deceased partner will be entitled to a proportion of the business assets, excluding goodwill, with phased payments made to the estate.

■ **TAX CONSIDERATIONS** A clause for tax reasons where the partners (and their executors) elect under the Income and Corporation Taxes Act to have the profits of the business assessed to income tax on a continuation basis as if no change in the partnership had taken place.

■ **DISSOLUTION** The dissolution of the partnership by mutual agreement as to what should happen to the assets.

■ **UNFAIR COMPETITION** It may be wise to incorporate an unfair competition clause if you are concerned that a partner may leave the business at some time in the future and set up in competition with you. The wording can be tricky and must not attempt to prevent a person from earning a livelihood.

role within the partnership should be spelled out clearly in the agreement, but they are usually jointly and severally liable in the same way as a full partner.

Choose your partners carefully. They could lead to your personal bankruptcy just as easily as helping you to make your fortune. Partners, even within the same family, commonly fall out. It may be better for them to be your employees rather than partners.

Corporation

Unlike a sole proprietorship, a corporation is a legal entity in its own right. Its shareholders and directors may change, but the company itself will continue to exist until it is wound up. Corporations have many laws to regulate them and no one should consider setting up a corporation without having taken professional advice, and fully understanding the implications.

A private corporation requires a minimum of one shareholder and one director. The company must also have a company secretary who could be a second director, another shareholder, or your accountant or solicitor. A sole director cannot also be the company secretary.

Directors derive benefits by being paid a salary or fees, while shareholders get paid "dividends" out of the profits. To register a new company, it is usual to contact a company registration agent (usually listed in the Yellow Pages or similar directories).

Choosing Your Business Name

As a sole proprietor you can trade under your own surname (with or without first names or initials), for example: Smith, William Smith, W. Smith, Wm. Smith, or William David Smith. You can also trade under a business name, such as William David Smith T/A Smith's Gifts ("T/A" stands for "trading as"). A partnership can trade under the names of all the partners or under a business name. A corporation registers its proper company name automatically at the time of incorporation.

If a business name is to be used, whatever the business status, then the requirements of the Business Names Act 1985 apply. The Act prevents you from using certain words in a business name and regulates the disclosure of business ownership.

Should You Form a Corporation?

Advantages of a Corporation	Disadvantages of a Corporation
▓ Limited liability of shareholders: should the company fail, in most cases all you would lose is your share capital (unless you have signed personal guarantees or are guilty of some misdemeanor)	▓ Higher annual accountancy charges
▓ Easier to raise larger sums of money	▓ Public disclosure of some key data
▓ Easier format to cope with investors who do not want to work in the business	▓ Cannot offset losses against your previous income tax
▓ Greater credibility with some customers	▓ Cannot easily move personal funds in and out of your business bank account
▓ Possibility of advantageous tax rates (although this can vary)	▓ Onerous legal responsibilities on all directors

TRADEMARKS AND SERVICE MARKS

Before choosing a name or symbol that will identify your business, it is important to review the laws regarding trademarks and service marks. According to the United States Patent and Trademark Office, a trademark is a word, phrase, symbol or design, or combination of words, phrases, symbols or designs, which identifies and distinguishes the source of the goods or services of one party from those of others. A service mark is the same as a trademark except that it identifies and distinguishes the source of a service rather than a product.

It is important at this point to distinguish trademarks and service marks from patents and copyrights. A copyright is the legal protection of an original artistic or literary work. A patent provides similar protection for an invention. Patents and copyrights are intended to protect the ownership interests of the creator of an original idea. They restrict the production, sale, and distribution of products to which the creator retains legal rights.

The primary purpose of trademark law is to protect the good will and reputation of established businesses. It is meant to prevent businesses from exploiting another business's standing with the public by fraudulently using that business's name in connection with goods or services.

Trademark rights arise from either using the mark, or filing an application to register a mark in the Patent and Trademark Office stating that the applicant has a bona fide intention to use the mark in commerce regulated by the U.S. Congress.

Federal registration is not required to establish rights in a mark. It is also not required to begin use of a mark. Federal registration, however, can secure benefits beyond the rights acquired by merely using a mark. The owner of a federal registration is presumed to be the owner of the mark for the goods and services specified in the registration. Once a mark is registered, the registrant is entitled to use the mark nationwide.

The owner of a trademark or service mark retains two distinct rights. He or she has the right to use the mark and the right to register it. In general, the first party who either uses a mark in commerce or files an application with the Patent and Trademark Office has the ultimate right to register that mark.

The Patent and Trademark Office's authority is limited to determining the right to register a trademark or service mark. The right to use a mark can be more complicated. When two businesses have begun use of the same or similar marks without knowledge of one another and neither has a federal registration, it will be up to the courts to decide which business has the right to use the mark.

FINANCING AND GUIDANCE

The U.S. Small Business Administration (SBA), a division of the U.S. Department of Commerce, offers several programs providing financing for new businesses, with a particular emphasis on exporting. SBA loans are made by commercial lenders, who are willing to make the loans because most of the principal is guaranteed by the federal government. The critical element in these loans, as well as most loans to new businesses, is the creditworthiness of the business owner, as well as the business plan. The SBA also offers a mentoring program of particular interest to new businesses, the Service Corps of Retired Executives (SCORE). These volunteers have a lifetime of experience in business, credit, finance, or marketing, and can help new businesses develop business and marketing plans, loan applications, and grant proposals, at no charge. SBA staffers and SCORE volunteers can also help new businesses take advantage of other guaranteed and reduced-rate loan programs, industrial development programs, grants, and opportunities for exporting, and for doing business with the government and large corporations.

Remedies for trademark infringement include issuing an injunction preventing the infringing business from using the mark, or awarding the owner of the trademark damages for infringement. Because the mere use of a mark can be disputed in a trademark infringement action, federal registration can provide significant advantages to a party involved in a court proceeding.

Unlike copyrights or patents, trademark rights can last indefinitely if the owner continues to use the mark to identify its goods or services. The term of a federal trademark registration is 10 years, with 10-year renewal terms. To keep a registration alive, however, the registrant must file an affidavit between the fifth and sixth year after the date of initial registration. If no affidavit is filed, the registration is canceled.

Any business claiming the rights to a trademark or service mark may attach the commonly accepted TM (trademark) or SM (service mark) designations to the mark in order to alert the public to the claim. Neither registration nor a pending application is required to use these designations. While the TM and SM designations indicate a claim to the mark, they do not ensure a claim's validity.

The Patent and Trademark Office's registration symbol, ®, may be used only after federal registration is filed. It is not legal to use this symbol at any point before federal registration is complete. When filing an application with the Patent and Trademark Office, all symbols should be omitted as they are not considered part of the mark.

If a federal application reveals a conflict between two marks, the Patent and Trademark Office determines whether any similarities between the mark in the application and an existing mark would present a likelihood of confusion. The standard the Patent and Trademark Office uses to decide a conflict is whether relevant consumers would be likely to associate the goods or services of one party with those of the other party as a result of the use of the marks at issue by both parties. In reaching its determination, the Patent and Trademark Office considers the similarity of the marks and the commercial relationship between the goods and services identified by the marks. When determining that a conflict between trademark exists, the Patent and Trademark Office considers only whether a likelihood of confusion would result. The marks need not be identical, nor do the goods and service have to be the same.

It is possible for the protection of trademarks and/or service marks to cease if the owner does not take certain precautions. In order to retain protection, a trademark of service mark must not lapse from disuse. Furthermore, it is important that you ensure your trademark or service mark be specifically associated with your business and its products or services. If a trademark or service mark becomes so widely used that it is accepted by the public as a generic term, it will lose its protected status. Former trademarks that have become so commonly used that they have lost their protected status include cellophane, aspirin, and thermos.

While it is recommended that you register your trademark with the Patent and Trademark Office in order to avoid potential conflicts, as stated above, it is not necessary. If you decide to rely solely on use of the mark to establish ownership, however, it is essential that you perform a search to determine whether the mark you intend to use might present a conflict with an existing mark.

Except when acting upon an application, the Patent and Trademark Office will not conduct a search to determine if a conflicting mark is registered or the subject of a pending application. There are several ways which you may obtain this information, however.

The Patent and Trademark Office has a public search library in which information on all registered trademarks and pending applications are listed. The search library is located on the second floor of the South Tower Building, 2900 Crystal Drive, Arlington, Virginia 22202.

It is also possible to perform a search at one of several patent and trademark depository libraries around the country. These libraries have CD-ROMS containing the trademark database of registered and pending marks. You may consult your local phone book or an attorney to discover the trademark depository library nearest you.

If, however, you do decide to forgo the federal registration process, it is essential that you consult with an attorney before using your mark. The Patent and Trademark Office will not provide advice on conflicting marks. In order to determine whether a conflict exists, an attorney will be best suited to advise you on the nuances of whether a likelihood of confusion will exist between your mark and an existing mark. It is suggested you consult your phone book or the an internet search engine to find a local attorney who specializes in intellectual property, the area of law concerning trademarks, copyrights, and patents.

Licenses and Registration

You can start most businesses right away as there is usually no need for registration or licensing, but there are important exceptions, some examples being: selling tobacco or alcohol; providing driving instruction; operating an employment agency; childminding; scrap-metal dealing or processing; providing public entertainment; owning a nightclub; providing massage; dealing in second-hand goods; operating as a street trader or mobile shop; driving a taxi or private hire car; operating certain goods and passenger vehicles; cleaning windows; hairdressing; selling door to door; running residential care and nursing homes; betting and gaming; most activities relating to pets or animals; providing credit services (and debt collecting, hiring, leasing, and so on).

The sale of financial services is highly regulated, by federal or state authorities, or both. In general, the sale of insurance products requires a state license, and the sale of investment products requires licensing by a federally authorized organization, such as the National Association of Security Dealers. Selling other investment-related products, such as real estate and mortgages, generally require state licenses.

Business Insurances

If you have a vehicle, employ anyone, or have plant and machinery, it is a legal requirement to have insurance cover for these risks. It is prudent to be adequately insured for other risks, and for specialist risks associated with your business, so you should discuss your proposed venture with a registered insurance broker. It is a balancing act to a certain extent to take out as much insurance as you need, no more and no less. In any event, you should review the position at least once a year to take into account changes in your business.

WHEN STARTING UP

The following are insurances that you might want to consider before you start trading, as you acquire a vehicle, premises, and so on:
- **VEHICLES**
  You must, of course, carry auto insurance, but if you intend to use your car in the business, check that your insurance covers you and any other driver for the commercial purpose you propose. Car insurance is

INSURANCE BROKERS
Always use a registered insurance agent. Their services are generally free as they are paid commission by the insurance companies. A good agent will not try to sell you insurance you do not require, but will take care that you do not under-insure.

normally for social, domestic, and pleasure purposes only, unless specified otherwise, and generally there will be an additional premium for using your car in connection with your business.

■ **Engineering**

If the business has plant or machinery that must have a periodic statutory inspection, then it is usual to arrange for this to be done by a specialist engineering insurer.

■ **Public Liability**

This provides you with protection against claims for which you may be legally liable brought by anyone other than employees for bodily injury or loss, or damage to property, arising in the course of your business. It also covers the legal costs that may be incurred when defending such claims.

■ **Product Liability**

This provides protection for legal liability of claims arising from injury, loss, or damage due to products you have sold, supplied, repaired, serviced, or tested. It can be expensive but is usually unavoidable.

■ **Professional Indemnity**

This is for consultants (legal, technical, management, marketing, financial, and so on). The insurance protects you against your legal liability to compensate third parties who have sustained some injury, loss, or damage due to your own professional negligence or that of your employees.

■ **Goods in Transit**

As a rule, motor insurance policies do not cover goods being carried in the vehicle, so if you intend to carry goods you may need this additional insurance cover.

■ **Premises**

If you are buying premises or it is a condition of the lease that you should insure the premises, then you should be covered against fire and other perils (such as burst pipes, storms, malicious damage). Check too that any plate-glass windows are covered. Your insurance broker will advise you if you need to be covered for Property Owners'

Liability as this risk may already be covered by the Public Liability Policy. If you plan to work from home or store business goods at your home, your normal domestic policy is unlikely to cover your business risks. Furthermore it may invalidate your existing policy; discuss this with your insurer.

■ **Stock, Fixtures and Fittings, Plant, and Machinery**

Be careful not to underestimate the value of these. Note that if your cover is for "reinstatement value" it provides for the full replacement cost, while "indemnity value" is the current market value less depreciation (which can be significant). Insurance should cover losses due to theft, vandalism, fire, flood, and so on. Accidental damage or all-risks cover can be arranged, but is expensive.

■ **Money**

If your business involves handling cash in significant amounts, then insurance cover against theft would be prudent. Policies normally cover loss of money on the premises and also money in transit to or from the bank. If covered for cash in transit, be sure to comply with any stipulations by the insurers.

■ **Cross Insurance**

This is a life assurance policy payable to the other partners in the event of a partner dying. The insurance enables the surviving partners to purchase the deceased partner's share of the business from the estate and to continue trading.

Once Established

As your business becomes established, you may want to consider the following types of policy:

■ **Employment Protection**

When you are employing people, particularly a large number, the complex employment legislation which covers employee's rights, unfair dismissal, redundancies, and so on can cripple a small company both financially and in terms of management time if a personnel problem occurs. This insurance covers not only legal fees but can also cover personnel advisory services that you may need.

■ **FIDELITY GUARANTEE AND INTERNAL THEFT**
This provides protection against dishonesty or theft by members of your own staff.

■ **CONSEQUENTIAL LOSS**
If your premises are put out of commission due to fire or any other insured peril, then this insurance will maintain the financial position of the company as if the calamity had not occurred. Such insurance can be expensive, but failure to have it may close down a business should such a disaster occur.

■ **PERSONAL HEALTH**
It is wise to consider personal health insurance cover for yourself to provide you with an income should you be unable to work. Similarly, if the company is very dependent upon one or two other key people, it may be wise to insure them against death, accident, or sickness, for the business may suffer financially in the event of their prolonged absence from work.

A final caution – should you ever need to make an insurance claim, the insurers will scrutinize your policy to see if you have not declared some material matter or not complied with one of their stipulations, as this would give them a reason to not pay out. So make a full declaration, read the small print of the policy, and comply with any stipulations the insurers make.

Business Legislation

There are many laws and regulations that may affect you when you run a business. Here is a brief guide to just some of the more important ones. Other laws are mentioned elsewhere in this book. Be sure to consult an attorney to find out all the laws and regulations that may apply to your own business.

■ **THE SHERMAN ACT (1890)**
Outlaws monopolization, attempted monopolization, or any other business activity that would result in the "restraint of trade." Courts apply the "rule of reason" to any challenged activity. If the activity is found to have an adverse impact on competition, criminal penalties and/or civil suits may result. Most "restraint of trade" activity will be found lawful if it is connected to a legitimate business purpose and is deemed economically efficient by a court.

■ **THE CLAYTON ACT (1914)**
Provides a much stricter standard to determine restraint of trade. Violations include acts that have a probable adverse impact on competition. Included among these violations are exclusive dealing arrangements and mergers that would result in a monopoly.

■ **THE ROBINSON-PATMAN ACT (1936)**
Prevents sellers from charging different prices to separate buyers for the same, or similar-grade commodities. Actions may be brought by the Federal Trade Commission or individual plaintiffs.

■ **THE FEDERAL TRADE COMMISSION ACT (1914)**
Outlaws unfair or deceptive business practices. Factors considered by the Federal Trade Commission are whether the business actions are against public policy, unethical, or harmful to consumers.

■ **THE CLEAN WATER ACT (1972)**
This Act charges the federal Environmental Protection Agency (EPA) with establishing a criteria regulating the amount of pollutants that may be permissibly discharged into the navigable waters in of the United States. The Act requires that businesses obtain permits from the federal Environmental Protection Agency (EPA) before they discharge pollutants into navigable waters.

■ **THE RESOURCE CONSERVATION AND RECOVERY ACT (1976)**
This Act requires handlers of hazardous wastes to follow strict instructions for their

discharge. Hazardous wastes are those that would endanger human health when they are improperly handled. The criteria used to determine whether a waste is hazardous includes its proclivity for corrosiveness, its toxicity, and whether there is a potential for it to become ignited.

Advertising and Sales Promotion

Much of the regulation of advertising and promotion is self-regulation, with industry groups largely policing themselves. These groups are usually very influential, because their membership is composed of the largest and most prominent companies in the particular industry, and the group's ethical standards become the industry's code. There are few regulations governing advertising and sales promotion as such in United States. Although federal and state laws do not regulate advertising, they do prohibit the use of false and misleading statements to sell goods.

On a national basis, the Federal Trade Commission administers laws and regulations that prohibit the use of fraudulent, deceptive and unfair business practices in all manner of trade involving interstate commerce, and state and local laws often supplement the federal rules and regulations.

Enforcement actions can be brought by both federal, and by state or local, authorities for violations of different laws involving the same deceptive scheme. In general, these laws prohibit false advertising, and regulate the use of comparative statements in marketing materials.

Consumer Protection

The Federal Trade Commission, as well as state and local agencies, regulates many aspects of consumer protection. Federal and state regulations prohibit deceptive business practices in the sale of franchises, network marketing and business opportunity plans, and work-from-home schemes. Similar regulations prohibit the use of unfounded claims to promote the sale of diet, health and fitness products.

Federal regulations prohibit the fraudulent use of "Made in the U.S.A." labels on products, and prohibit deceptive product labeling.

Both federal and state authorities are gearing up to stop the growing problem of identity theft, and the fraudulent use of the identification and credit profile of unsuspecting victims. The Federal Trade Commission publishes several booklets to educate businesses about the applicable rules, and to encourage compliance, including: *A Business Guide to the Federal Trade Commission's Mail Order Rule, A Businessperson's Guide to Federal Warranty Law, Complying with the 900-Number Rule: A Business Guide for Pay-per-Call Services, Complying with the Telemarketing Sakes Rule, Guides Against Bait Advertising, Guides Against Deceptive Advertising of Guaranties, Guides Against Deceptive Pricing, Guides Concerning Use of Endorsements and Testimonials in Advertising, Guides Concerning the Use of the Word "Free" and Similar Representations, Guides for the Use of Environmental Marketing Claims,* and *How to Advertise Consumer Credit: Complying with the Law.*

Data Privacy

Many states are enacting or considering laws to grant individuals greater control over the use and dissemination of their private data, especially credit and medical information. This area may become subject to greater federal and state regulation, especially with the increasing ability to identify and create databases of genetic or heritable medical conditions.

Franchise and Network Marketing

Many states are enacting or considering laws to provide greater protection for purchasers of franchises and multilevel marketing plans.

Price Marking

State laws require goods offered for sale to be clearly marked as to price, but these laws differ markedly as to the specifics, and as to how they are interpreted. Some states require each item to be clearly marked as to the price of that unit.

Other states merely require the per-unit price be displayed reasonably near the item. Local ordinances may offer consumers greater protection.

WEIGHTS AND MEASURES

The regulation of weights and measures in the sale of food, beverages, household supplies, etc., is generally regulated by state law and administered by local authorities. Enforcement is typically through the use of spot- and random testing, especially during holidays and other peak buying periods.

Workplace Legalities

There are a number of legal requirements and guidelines to be aware of when looking for premises and then equipping them.

PLANNING PERMISSION

Before buying or renting any workplace, check your local zoning regulations to determine if you may conduct a buinsess in the area. If not, you need to apply for a change of use: this can take a month or more to be granted. Classes of use include: residential, retail (several classes), offices, light industrial, and mixed use. Permission will also be required for proposed extensions, changes to frontages, and external signs or advertisements. If structural alterations are required, these need formal approval. If you are hoping to sell direct to the public from your workshop or industrial unit, or work on cars, you may face problems with planning permission. Manufacturing businesses, in contrast, are seen as desirable by government development agencies and concessions may be negotiated. Be wary of buildings of special architectural merit, particularly listed buildings; insurance cover and repair work could be extremely costly. Finally, contact your local Health and Safety Executive officer (see the phone book) to find out what regulations are relevant to your proposed business.

WORKING FROM HOME

If you own your home it may be an infringement of local planning regulations or bylaws to work there, and it may also breach a condition of your ownership of the house. If you have a mortgage, the mortgage lender may not like it. Conducting business from a privately rented or council-owned house will almost certainly breach your tenancy agreement. If you are a council tenant, ask a friend to make discreet enquiries at the local government offices to let you know where you stand. In most cases, if your neighbours object to your business activities, you could have a problem, so it is essential to get proper legal advice. If you are working from home, inform your insurers – there are special policies for home-based businesses.

ENTERPRISE ZONES

Worth considering when you are looking for premises, these zones have been created by the government to encourage enterprise. They can be quite small, often consisting of a specific industrial estate. Usually, incentives to use the zones include exemption from business rates, and 100 per cent tax allowances for any capital expenditure on industrial and commercial buildings. Planning permission is also simplified.

FIRE SAFETY

If you employ anyone, you need to ensure they have a means of escape in the event of fire, and to provide a means of fighting a fire (such as a suitable fire extinguisher). If you employ more than a certain number of people, then you will need a Fire Certificate. Contact your local Fire Department for more information.

BUSINESSES SELLING FOOD

If your proposed business involves the making or selling of food, consult the local Department of Health to ascertain what regulations are currently in force. Converting non-food premises for food may be very costly. If you plan to sell alcohol, check on local licensing laws and opening hours.

Employment Law

Many laws and regulations apply when you employ someone, and these are constantly evolving. A surprising number of the laws are relevant even if you only intend to employ one part-timer. For more information, consult an attorney or the relevant authorities.

EMPLOYEE RELATIONS

■ **THE FAIR LABOR STANDARDS ACT (1938)**
Establishes a minimum wage which is periodically changed by Congress. Mandates increased overtime wages and compensation for activities paid by employees that are related to their jobs. Forbids employment of anyone under 14 years of age, limits employment of 14- and 15-year-olds to non-school hours, and prohibits employment of persons under 18-years-old in hazardous occupations.

■ **WORKERS' COMPENSATION**
Statutes found in every state giving employees the right to receive financial compensation from their employers for accidental death, injury, or disease arising in the course of their employment. While the statutes do not take into consideration whether the employers are at fault in relation to the injuries, they prohibit employees from suing their employers in civil suits regarding such damages.

■ **OCCUPATIONAL SAFETY AND HEALTH ACT (1970)**
This act requires all businesses involved in interstate commerce to have workplaces that are free from recognized hazards that may cause death or injury. Employers are required to keep records of employees' illnesses, accidental deaths, or injuries arising from their employment. The Act allows the Occupational Safety and Health Administration conducts investigations into workplaces.

■ **FAMILY AND MEDICAL LEAVE ACT (1993)**
Requires government agencies and private employers with 50 or more workers to provide up to 12 weeks of unpaid leave for serious illness, childbirth, or the serious illness of a close relative. Workers must give reasonable notice and must have worked for the employer for at least one year.

■ **UNEMPLOYMENT COMPENSATION**
Requires employers to contribute to unemployment insurance plans that compensates workers who were laid-off or terminated without cause. Applies to employers who have a payroll of at least $1,500 per quarter, or who have at least one employee working one or more days per week for 20 or more weeks per year.

■ **THE SOCIAL SECURITY ACT (1935)**
This Act provides compensation to employees whose incomes from employment are reduced because of death, permanent injury, or retirement. It requires employers to withhold a specified percentage of their employees to be deposited in the Social Security Trust Fund. Employers are then required to provide the Trust Fund with contributions matching the amount they withhold from their employees.

■ **EMPLOYEMENT RETIREMENT INCOME SECURITY ACT (1974)**
This Act regulates the private retirement plans of employers. It sets standards for the funding of private pensions, governs eligibility for pension plan earnings.

ANTI-DISCRIMINATION LEGISLATION

■ **TITLE VII OF THE CIVIL RIGHTS ACT (1964)**
This Act prohibits discrimination based on a person's race, color, religion, sex, or national origin. Employers may not engage in such discrimination when hiring or firing employees, or on deciding their compensation.

■ **THE EQUAL PAY ACT (1963)**
Makes illegal differences in pay between the

sexes for jobs that involve the same skill, effort, responsibility, and other working conditions. Other factors, such as seniority, quantity of production, or shift differential may be used to determine differences in pay.

■ **THE AGE DISCRIMINATION IN EMPLOYMENT ACT (1967)**

This Act prohibits discrimination by employers against employees who have reached the age of 40. Employers must have at least 20 employers before coming under the jurisdiction of the Act.

■ **THE AMERICANS WITH DISABILITIES ACT (1990)**

Employers are prohibited from discriminating against qualified individuals who have mental or physical impairments. A "reasonable accommodation" must be made by the employer. An employer is not required to make such accommodations if they would result in an undue hardship. The act covers employers who retain a minimum of 15 employees.

■ **THE PREGNANCY DISCRIMINATION ACT (1978)**

Requires employers to treat pregnancy and childbirth as they would treat any other medical condition affecting an employees ability to work. Employers may not force a pregnant woman to take leave if she can still perform her duties. The workplace must be monitored for toxins and dangers that would affect their employees, and employers may not fire or refuse to hire a woman of childbearing age because of fear of exposure to workplace hazards or toxins.

CONFIDENTIALITY

If your work involves trade secrets you may be able to get your employees to sign a non-disclosure agreement. Such a contract can prevent them from passing on information about your secret processes or the names of your customers. It can also prevent them competing directly against you, but it cannot prevent them using their technical skill or trade

knowledge to earn a living. This is a tricky area of law, so requires expert professional advice.

UNFAIR DISMISSAL

Before dismissing anyone, do take professional advice. It is a tricky legal area. Grounds for fair dismissal include incompetence, misconduct, some other substantial reason, or redundancy, but must be both fair and reasonable. In the case of misconduct, unless the employee is found guilty of gross misconduct, such as stealing or assault, it is good management practice to allow the employee adequate opportunity to improve their conduct. They should have had a verbal warning, then at least one (possibly two) written warnings, which should spell out: what they are doing wrong; what they must do to correct their behaviour; the consequences should they ignore the warnings; the fact that the warning constitutes the first formal stage of the disciplinary procedure. The second or final written warning should clearly state that no improvement or any recurrence will lead to dismissal. In addition, you should have fully and fairly investigated the situation, allowed the employee to have their say, and told them how they can appeal.

An employee cannot normally claim unfair dismissal until he or she has worked for you for a year. However, there is no qualifying period if a complaint of unfair dismissal is made due to dismissal for any of the following reasons, all automatically deemed to be unfair: trade union membership; seeking in good faith to assert a statutory employment right; taking certain specified types of action on health and safety grounds; pregnancy; refusing (in certain circumstances) to do shop work on a Sunday; dismissal in relation to the Working Time Regulations or national minimum wage.

After one year's service, a dismissed employee is entitled, at their request, to receive a letter within 14 days explaining why they are being dismissed. A woman dismissed while pregnant or on maternity leave must always receive a letter.

Letterheads and Invoices

Your letter and invoices should state the
name, address (including Zip code), and
telephone number. If your business has a
license that must be displayed, such as for a
home-improvement contractor, include the
license number.

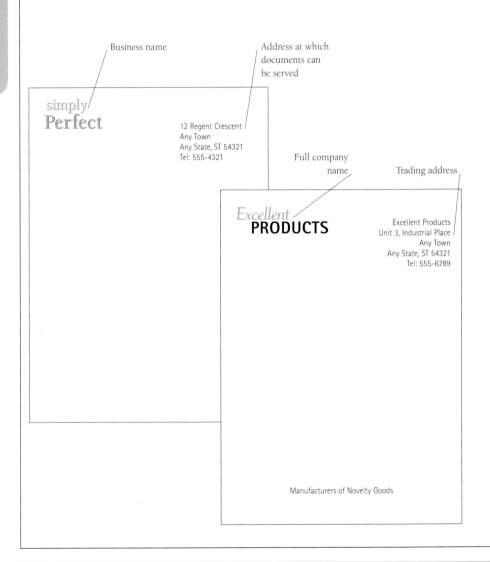

Business name

Address at which
documents can
be served

simply
Perfect

12 Regent Crescent
Any Town
Any State, ST 54321
Tel: 555-4321

Full company
name

Trading address

Excellent
PRODUCTS

Excellent Products
Unit 3, Industrial Place
Any Town
Any State, ST 54321
Tel: 555-6789

Manufacturers of Novelty Goods

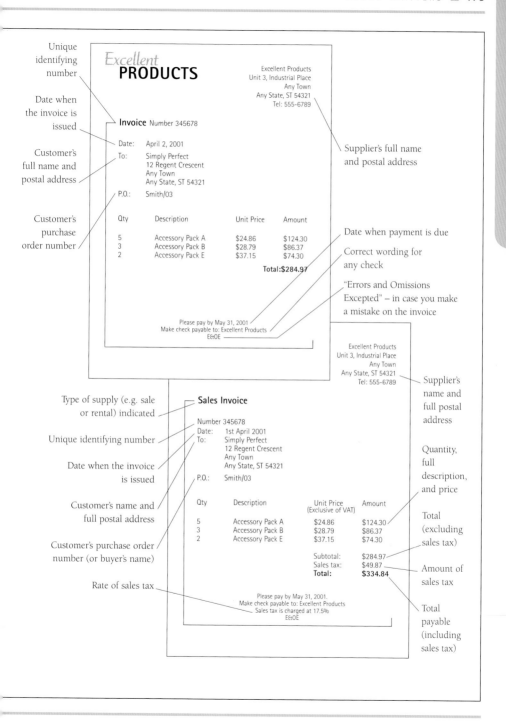

Unique identifying number

Date when the invoice is issued

Customer's full name and postal address

Customer's purchase order number

Excellent
PRODUCTS

Excellent Products
Unit 3, Industrial Place
Any Town
Any State, ST 54321
Tel: 555-6789

Invoice Number 345678

Date: April 2, 2001
To: Simply Perfect
  12 Regent Crescent
  Any Town
  Any State, ST 54321
P.O.: Smith/03

Qty	Description	Unit Price	Amount
5	Accessory Pack A	$24.86	$124.30
3	Accessory Pack B	$28.79	$86.37
2	Accessory Pack E	$37.15	$74.30
		Total:$284.97	

Please pay by May 31, 2001
Make check payable to: Excellent Products
E&OE

Supplier's full name and postal address

Date when payment is due

Correct wording for any check

"Errors and Omissions Excepted" – in case you make a mistake on the invoice

Excellent Products
Unit 3, Industrial Place
Any Town
Any State, ST 54321
Tel: 555-6789

Type of supply (e.g. sale or rental) indicated

Unique identifying number

Date when the invoice is issued

Customer's name and full postal address

Customer's purchase order number (or buyer's name)

Rate of sales tax

Sales Invoice

Number 345678
Date: 1st April 2001
To: Simply Perfect
  12 Regent Crescent
  Any Town
  Any State, ST 54321
P.O.: Smith/03

Qty	Description	Unit Price (Exclusive of VAT)	Amount
5	Accessory Pack A	$24.86	$124.30
3	Accessory Pack B	$28.79	$86.37
2	Accessory Pack E	$37.15	$74.30
		Subtotal:	$284.97
		Sales tax:	$49.87
		Total:	**$334.84**

Please pay by May 31, 2001.
Make check payable to: Excellent Products
Sales tax is charged at 17.5%
E&OE

Supplier's name and full postal address

Quantity, full description, and price

Total (excluding sales tax)

Amount of sales tax

Total payable (including sales tax)

FINANCIAL MATTERS

This chapter is an introduction to income tax, corporation tax, and capital gains tax. The information is for general guidance only and should not be regarded as a complete or authoritative statement on taxation. For more information, please consult an accountant or the Internal Revenue Service (IRS).

In general, sole proprietorships require no special formalities in their formation. With the exception of a written partnership agreement, the same can be said about the formation of a partnership. For both forms of businesses, there are usually no organizational fees, annual licencing fees, nor annual reporting requirements. It is helpful, however, to discuss the formation of a sole proprietorship or a partnership with an attorney in order to ensure no legal matter tangentially related to the formation is ignored.

Corporations, considered distinct legal entities, must meet strict statutory requirements before they can be formed. In order to form a corporation, a certificate of incorporation must be filed, usually with the secretary of state of the state in which incorporation is desired. Included in the certificate must be the name of the corporation, the purpose for incorporation. Once a certificate of incorporation is properly filed, the person charged with incorporating appoints the first board of directors and approves its bylaws. At its first meeting, the board of directors perform duties such as opening a bank account in the name of the corporation and issuing shares.

AN EMPLOYER'S TAX OBLIGATIONS

Employers are responsible for withholding certain income from their employees' paychecks that must be used to pay income taxes to the IRS, Social Security taxes, and Medicare taxes. Employers may also be required to withhold unemployment taxes.

Employers must have their employees complete a W-4 form when hired. On this form, the employee must list the number of dependents she or he will claim, and his or her filing status. This information will let the employer know how much money should be withheld. Employers are also under the duty to make known to employees the amount they are taking from each paycheck. For more information contact the Internal Revenue Service.

Income Tax

Income for both sole proprietorships and partnerships is not taxed separately. A sole proprietor's profits are reported on his or her federal personal income tax return. For a partnership, each partner is personally taxed on his or her share of the profits derived.

Because corporations are considered separate and distinct legal entities, a "double taxation" exists. The corporation itself pays income tax on net profits, while each stockholder's dividends are taxed as part of his or her personal income.

INCOME TAX FOR SOLE PROPRIETORSHIPS AND PARTNERSHIPS

In the case of sole proprietorships or partnerships, income tax is based on the business profits as declared in the annual personal tax return. In the case of partnerships, the profits of the business are divided equally between the partners unless the partnership agreement says to the contrary. Each partner is liable only for the tax due on his or her share of the partnership's profits.

But what is meant by profits? Consider this example: your total annual sales (turnover) are $50,000, but you had to spend $40,000 on stock, part-time staff wages, and other overheads. Your profit is $10,000. That amount is declared in your tax return.

Note that your liability to income tax is dependent upon the profitability of your business. It makes no difference how much money you actually draw from the business, be it $25 or $250 per week! Hence the "wages" a sole proprietor or partner takes from the business are more correctly called profits.

Deductible Expenses

What types of expenditure and overheads are you allowed to deduct from your annual sales figure to calculate your taxable profits? An important distinction is made between ordinary and necessary business expenses and capital expenditure.

■ **Ordinary and Necessary Business Expenses** Broadly speaking, ordinary and necessary business expenses covers the purchase of stock or raw materials, staff wages, business rent and rates, phone bills, electricity and heating charges, advertising, stationery, business insurances, professional fees, the replacement of worn-out tools by similar tools, necessary repairs and maintenance, interest on business loans, and most vehicle expenses that relate to the business. Only an expenditure which is "wholly and exclusively" for your business can be deducted (or is "allowable") for income tax purposes. Items that are not allowable for income tax purposes include: your own drawings (wages), household food or other domestic expenditure, income tax, and business entertainment.

■ **Capital Expenditure** This covers one-off purchases of tangible assets, such as business equipment, tools, and vehicles. Only certain categories are allowable.

There are frequently situations in small businesses where expenditure is partly for business and partly for domestic purposes. Examples include the use of a car, the use of a telephone at your home, and heat and lighting used in an "office" in your home. In the case of a car, you could keep a vehicle log book in which you record every business trip (with date, destination, mileage, and purpose of journey). In the case of a telephone, you could also keep a simple log of all business calls you make to back up an itemized phone bill (if available). In this way you will have the necessary proof to claim the correct proportion of the charges against tax. Before you start to log anything, speak to your accountant as you may be giving yourself an unnecessary burden.

Provided you keep accounts, as suggested in Controlling the Finances (see pp. 134–51), and you use an accountant to advise you, then you should be able to cope with income tax. Always keep money aside to pay your tax bills.

Typical Tax Deductions and Accounting

The deductions discussed in this subsection represent the most common types taken by employers. It also provides information on the process of withholding employee taxes from an employee's pay. While the Internal Revenue Service permits deductions for each of the business expenses listed below, it is recommended that you consult with an accountant before filing your tax return in order to ensure the expenses you want to deduct meet the criteria required by the Tax Code.

Salaries

The Internal Revenue Service permits deductions of most salaries, wages, and other compensation provided the payments were reasonable and paid in exchange for an employee's service. It is important to understand that the Internal Revenue Service has strict rules concerning business owners who try to avoid taxation by paying themselves, their friends, or their relatives wages for services that were not actually performed. Trying to get around the tax rules in such a way could lead to severe penalties.

In order to ensure proper accounting, the Internal Revenue Service requires employers to withhold certain amounts from each paycheck issued to an employee. These include sums for the employees' income taxes, Social Security, and Medicare expenses. An employer's determination of the amount he or she should withhold from an individual employee's paycheck is based on the information that employee submits on his or her W-4 form.

A W-4 form should be issued to every employee upon his or her hire. It establishes the number of dependents an employee may declare on his or her individual income tax return. It also establishes the employees filing status as single, married, or one of the other acceptable filing statuses.

In addition to determining how much income tax wages an employer must withhold, the W-4 form helps the employer establish the amounts to be withheld for Social Security and Medicare contributions. Employers are required to contribute a matching amount for each employees Social Security and Medicare withholdings. *Circular E, Employer's Tax Guide* is a booklet distributed by the Internal Revenue Service in which employers may determine the appropriate amounts to withhold based on an employee's paycheck and W-4 information.

Employers are also required to pay federal unemployment taxes. These payments are not derived from withholdings, but from direct payments by the employer to the Internal Revenue Service. The amount you will pay will be based on the number of employees you have, their average salaries, and your history of lay-offs. Sole proprietors and partners will not be required to pay the tax for their contribution to the business as an owner.

Annually, an employer is required to provide each employee with a W-2 form. W-2 forms state the amount the employee earned in the previous year and the amounts withheld by the employer for tax purposes.

If you choose to hire independent contractors to work for you, you will not be required to meet any of the above requirements. It is not necessary for the employer of an independent contractor to contribute to Social Security, Medicare, or any other federal insurance fund. If an independent contractor is paid more than $600 for the job performed, however, the employer must complete a Form 1099-MISC. A copy of this form must then be provided to the independent contractor and the Internal Revenue Service. Independent contractor are required to provide the employer with a W-9 form.

The Internal Revenue Service has strict guidelines establishing the criteria for who qualifies as an independent contractor. Mis-classification of an employee as an independent contractor can lead to severe fines or even imprisonment. It is essential that you consult an accountant and become well-versed in the Internal Revenue Service's requirements for independent contractors before you declare such a classification.

BONUSES

If an employer rewards an employee with bonus incentives as a form of additional compensation, the employer may deduct these funds on his or her tax form. If the additional compensation takes the form of cash or similar monetary payments, the employer is required to withhold taxes from the employee's paycheck as described above.

Generally, if an employer gives a non-monetary item or a gift as additional compensation, the gift may be excluded from the employee's income and the employer will not be required to withhold the value from the employee's paycheck. If you intend to provide such non-monetary items to your employees it is crucial that you discuss the tax ramifications with an accountant as the Internal Revenue Service rules stated above concerning gifts apply only to those of "nominal" value.

MEALS AND LODGINGS

The Internal Revenue Service allows an employer to deduct certain meals he or she provides to his or her employees so long as the meals are reasonably related to doing business. In general, employers will be permitted to deduct 50 percent of the cost of these meals. The value of the meals will be excluded from the employee's taxable income if they are provided at the employers premises and for the benefit of the employer.

Business owners are also entitled to deduct the cost of lodging employees if that cost is a reasonable part of doing business. These deductions can arise from the acts of allowing employees to live on the business premises, or from the cost of travel lodging expenses that are reasonably related to business operations. Again, it is essential that you discuss such deductions with an accountant before taking them.

FRINGE BENEFITS

Depending on the form and size of your business, you may be permitted to deduct various fringe benefits on your tax returns. These deductions may include expenses for health insurance, tuition reimbursement programs, and stock or profit-sharing plans. Because these benefits are not considered part of an employee's taxable income, it is not required to withhold any funds from an employee's paycheck in relation to them. It is important to understand that any fringe-benefit program must be provided to all employees in order to be considered equitable by the Internal Revenue Service. Fringe benefit plans that favor only the business owner or other top employees will be considered inequitable by

the Internal Revenue Service and may result in the plan being considered taxable or other penalties.

SALES AND USE TAXES

Sales and use taxes are set by state, county or local law, and the rates, exemptions and items subject to tax vary from one locality to another. Also, regulations differ as to whether mail, telephone and Internet sales are subject to taxation. In most cases, the business owner is liable for tax whether or not it has been collected from the customers. Local authorities should be consulted as to the applicability of these laws as soon as the business begins operations.

Corporation Tax

Corporation tax is a tax on the profits of a business. It applies only to corporations, and is normally paid nine months after the end of the company's accounting year.

Capital Gains Tax

If you dispose of any asset for more than you paid for it, you have made a gain, which may be liable to capital gains tax (CGT). A sole proprietor or partner has an allowance before CGT becomes due. The tax rules are complex, as the initial value of the asset can be adjusted by "indexation" to reflect inflation, and there may be "roll-over relief" if the proceeds are used to buy another "qualifying" asset within a set time. If you work from home, and set aside part of the property exclusively for your business, you may have to pay CGT on that part when you come to sell the house; seek professional advice.

GLOSSARY

Allowable Expenses
Expenditure that is allowed (by the Inland Revenue) to be deducted from annual sales to calculate the taxable profits.

Balance Sheet
A statement of what a business owns (its assets) and what it owes (its liabilities) on a particular date. Usually prepared as part of the annual accounts at the end of the financial year.

Brainstorming
A creative technique used for generating new ideas. Individuals suggest ideas, which are recorded but not judged. At a later stage the ideas are then evaluated and developed.

Break-even Point
The point at which a business's gross margin from its sales is sufficient to cover its overheads. At this point, the business is just trading viably.

Business Plan
A written report setting out details of a proposed business. Often used to raise finance to start a business, or to raise finance to expand or take an existing business into a new direction.

Capital Expenditure
An outlay on one-off, tangible business assets, such as equipment, computers, tools, and vehicles. For tax purposes, the whole amount is not usually deductible in the year of purchase, but over the projected lifetime of the asset through capital allowances.

Cash Flow
The movement of money in and out of a business.

Cash-flow Forecast
A prediction of the money that will flow into and out of a business. Often prepared as part of a business plan. Also an ongoing business planning tool.

Depreciation
The loss in value of an item over time. The life of an item for tax purposes is set by the Inland Revenue.

Double-entry Accounts
A method of bookkeeping in which each transaction is entered twice – once as a debit and once as a credit.

E-commerce
The carrying out of business transactions over the internet.

Equity Finance
Financing of a limited company by the purchase of its shares, usually by an outside investor.

Estimate
The approximate price given to a customer in advance for doing a job. See also **Quotation**.

Floating Charges
A form of security taken by a bank over the assets of a limited company. This asset value may "float" up and down.

Franchising
The right, under licence, to copy the successful business format of another business, including its name, its products, and its image.

Goodwill
The value of a business when the physical business assets have been deducted – usually a highly negotiable figure.

Guarantor
An individual who guarantees to pay the bank in the case of a named person defaulting on loan repayments.

Invoice
A list of goods purchased (or services provided), with particulars of quantity and price. Sent or given to the customer. Less formally called a "bill".

Liquidity
The amount of funds or assets that can be readily changed into cash to meet immediate debts.

Margin
The profit made on selling goods or services. Usually expressed as a percentage.

Market Share
The portion of the total market taken by a business or its products or services.

Mark-up
The difference between the cost price and the selling price – mark-ups tend to be broadly standard within a trade. Usually expressed as a percentage.

Network Marketing
A term used in direct selling to describe a multi-level system in which a salesperson receives bonuses based on the performance of those they recruit as salespeople.

Overgearing
A term decribing the situation when the ratio of loans to share capital in a business is such that the profits cannot support the interest payments on the loans, and the business slowly sinks.

Overheads (Fixed Costs)
The regular (often monthly) expenses of keeping a business running – includes electricity, telephone, insurance, and most wages.

Overtrading
Trading beyond the financial resources of a business. Overtrading can cause cash-flow problems.

Profit and Loss Account
A summary of the profits and the outgoings of a business. Usually prepared as part of the annual accounts at the end of the financial year.

Prospect
A sales term; abbreviation for "prospective customer". Used of someone to whom a salesperson is pitching a sale.

Public Relations
The interaction of a business with the public. Often used to refer to the communication of a message via the media.

Purchase Ledger
An accounts book in which all the purchases made by a business are recorded.

Quotation
The fixed price quoted to a customer in advance for doing a job. If agreed, the quotation is normally binding on the seller and the customer. See also **Estimate**.

Re-financing
The process of raising additional finance for an existing business, either to fund expansion or to see it through financial problems.

Sales Ledger
An accounts book in which all the sales made by a business are recorded.

Single-entry Accounts
A method of bookkeeping in which each transaction is entered once only into an accounts book.

Start-up Capital Expenditure
The one-off costs of purchasing equipment in order to start up a business.

Statement
A summary of financial transactions, usually sent by a business to a customer at the end of the calendar month. May act as a reminder of unpaid invoices.

Target Market
The section of the population that could potentially use a product or service.

Turnover
Total sales made in a specified period of time.

Unique Selling Proposition
The singular factor that differentiates a product or service from others in the marketplace.

Variable Costs (Direct Costs)
The irregular and changing costs of keeping a business running. These usually vary directly in relation to the level of business.

Venture Capital
Finance for a limited company invested by an outside party with the aim of getting a good return on the investment. Venture capitalists are either individuals, or companies set up for the purpose.

Working Capital
The amount of short-term funds a business needs to carry out its normal work.

Useful Contacts

Arts and Crafts

The National Council for the Traditional Arts
1320 Fenwick Lane, Suite 200
Silver Spring, MD 20910
Tel: (301) 565-0654
Fax: (301) 565-0472
www.ncta.net

The National Endowment for the Arts
1100 Pennsylvania Avenue, N.W.
Washington D.C. 20506
Tel: (202) 682-5400
www.arts.endow.gov

Business Advocacy

National Association of Manufacturers
1331 Pennsylvania Avenue, N.W.
Washington, D.C. 20004
Tel: (202) 637-3000
www.nam.org

Business Information

American Business Information
1717 Pennsylvania Avenue Northwest
Washington, D.C. 20006
Tel: (202) 887-8001

Business Management and Consulting Group Corporation
1201 Pennsylvania Avenue Northwest
Washington, D.C. 20004
Tel: (202) 661-4625

Corporate Information

US Securities and Exchange Commission
450 Fifth Street, N.W.
Washington, D.C. 20549
Tel: (202) 942-2950
www.sec.gov

Direct Marketing and Selling

Direct Marketing Association
1120 Avenue of the Americas
New York, NY 10036
Tel: (212) 768-7277
www.the-dma.org

Direct Selling Association
1275 Pennsylvania Ave NW
Suite 800
Washington, D.C. 20004
Tel: (202) 347-8866
Fax: (202) 347-0055

Employment Law

U.S. Equal Employment Opportunity Commission
1801 L Street, N.W.
Washington, D.C. 20507
Tel: (202) 663-4900

Exporting

American Management Association
1061 Broadway
New York, NY 10019
Tel: (212) 586-6100
www.amanet.org

Export Administration Bureau of the Department of Commerce
Washington, D.C. 20001
Tel: (202) 482-4811

Finance

National Venture Capital Association
1655 North Fort Myer Drive
Suite 850
Arlington, Virginia 22209
Tel: (703) 524-2549
Fax: (703) 524-3940
www.nvca.org

FRANCHISING
American Association of Franchisees and Dealers
P.O. Box 81887
San Diego, CA 92138-1887
Tel: 1-(800) 733-9858
Fax: (619) 209-3777

American Franchisee Association
53 W. Jackson Blvd.
Suite 205
Chicago, IL, 60604
Tel: (312) 431-0545
Fax: (312) 431-1469
E-Mail: afa@infonews.com
www.infonews.com/afa

GOVERNMENT OFFICES
Board of Trade
1129 20th Street Northwest
Washington, D.C. 20036
Tel: (202) 857-5900

Copyright Royalty Tribunal
1111 20th Street Northwest
Washington, D.C. 20526
Tel: (202) 653-5175

Financial Management Service
401 14th Street Northwest
Washington, D.C. 20227
Tel: (202) 874-7050

Internal Revenue Service
1111 Constitution Ave NW
Washington, D.C. 20224
Tel: (202) 622-2000

National Black Chamber of Commerce
2000 L Street Northwest
Washington, D.C. 20036
Tel: (202) 416-1622

United States Business and Industrial Council
220 National Press Building
Washington, D.C. 20090
Tel: (202) 662-8744

United States Chamber of Commerce
1615 H. Street Northwest
Washington, D.C. 20062
Tel: (202) 463-5869
www.uschamber.com

LABOR ORGANIZATIONS
AFL-CIO
815 16th Street, NW
Washington, D.C. 20006
Tel: (202) 637-5000
Fax: (202) 637-5058

SMALL BUSINESS ORGANIZATIONS
Association of Small Business Development Centers
3108 Columbia Pike
Suite 300
Arlington, VA 22204
Tel: (703) 271-8700
Fax: (703) 271-8701

YOUNG ENTREPRENEURS
Edward Lowe Foundation
P.O. Box 8
Cassopolis, MI 49031
Tel: (800) 232-5693
www.lowe.org

Initiative for a Competitive Inner City
727 Atlantic Avenue, Suite 600
Boston, MA 02111
Tel: (617) 292-2363
www.icic.org

Suggested Reading

101 Best Home-Based Businesses for Women
Priscilla Y. Huff (Prima Communications, Inc., 1998)
For every woman who wants to work at home, maintain a flexible schedule, and be her own boss. This book provides readers with everything they need to know about different businesses, from start-up costs and financing sources to the potential income the business can generate. Actual businesswomen share their stories of success and financial reward and give advice on what works and what does not.

199 Great Home Businesses You Can Start (and Succeed in) for Under $1,000
Tyler Gregory Hicks (Prima Communications, Inc., 1999)
Home-based business guru Tyler Hicks shows you how to achieve your work-at-home dream. Contains information on how to choose the home-based business that's right for you, getting started with minimal cost, running a business from home while keeping your day job, and using the internet to advertise and promote your home-based business.

1101 Businesses You Can Start from Home
Daryl Allen Hall (Wiley, John & Sons, Inc., 1994)
This book contains expert information on start-up enterprises. The majority of businesses discussed have low start-up costs and are suited for communities of any size. It includes a cost rating system for beginning a business along with a chapter discussing why people start-up and run their own home-based businesses.

The Adams Businesses You Can Start Almanac
Katina Jones (Adams Media Corporation, 1996)
Features hundreds of interviews and success stories from people who have started their own businesses. Each one of the business ideas presented is a realistic, professional enterprise.

The Complete Idiot's Guide to Starting Your Own Business
Ed Paulson, Marcia Layton (Macmillan General Reference, 1998)
This book offers valuable advice about financing, business planning, legal issues, technology, and more. It contains the latest information about financing, business planning, legal issues, and technology.

Entrepreneur Magazine's Start Your Own Business
(Entrepreneur Media, 1998)
A step-by-step guide that includes expert advice regarding market research, business structure, creating a winning business plan, financing, bookkeeping, and taxes.

Free Help from Uncle Sam to Start Your Own Business: Or Expand the One You Have
Gus Berle (Puma Publishing Company, 1997)
The author tells the inside story on how to generate a business plan that commands attention. The book provides advice on how to avoid wasting your time and energy on complicated business plan preparation schemes, and how to optimize your efforts to drive profits up.

High Tech Start Up: The Complete Handbook for Creating Successful New High Tech Companies
John L. Nesheim (The Free Press, 2000)
This Silicon Valley bestseller incorporates 23 case studies of successful start-ups, including tables of wealth showing how much money founders and investors realized from each venture. It is filled with hard-to-find information and guidance covering every key phase of a start-up.

If You're Clueless about Starting Your Own Business and Want to Know More
Seth Godin (Dearborn Financial Publishing, Inc., 1997)
This addition to the popular "Clueless" series is aimed at people who want to know what it takes to get a small business up and running. Well known entrepreneur Seth Godin provides readers with everything they need to know to jump-start a new enterprise.

The Legal Guide for Starting and Running a Small Business
Fred S. Steingold, Mary Randolph, Ralph E. Warner (Nolo, 1999)
This "nuts-and-bolts" guide to starting and running a small business provides clear explanations of the laws that affect businesses. It includes the latest tax law changes that affect home-based business, as well as advice on how to select a business name in the age of the internet.

Mancuso's Small Business Basics
Jospeh R. Mancuso (Sourcebooks, Inc., 1997)
In this book, Joseph Mancuso draws on his more than 20 years' experience helping entrepreneurs build business enterprises. It assists readers in how to start an enterprise, how to buy an existing enterprise and how to open a franchise.

Mother's Work: How a Young Mother Started a Business on a Shoestring and Built It into a Multimillion-Dollar Company
Rebecca Matthias (Doubleday & Company, Inc., 1999)
With a new baby, little money, but lots of determination and drive, Rebecca Matthias started a business from scratch out of her home. Today her company, Mothers Work – which includes the retail outlets Mimi Maternity, Motherhood, and A Pea in the Pod – has grown to become a multimillion-dollar maternity clothing empire. This book describes how Matthias got her company off the ground,

offering specific lessons for other entrepreneurs and would-be entrepreneurs on the nuts and bolts of building and growing a business.

Nobody's Business but Your Own: A Business Start-up Guide with Advice from Today's Most Successful Young Entrepreneurs
Carolyn M. Brown, (Hyperion, 1999)
This guide includes essential information for budding entrepreneurs, including how to carve out a niche for your business, how to write a business plan, how to choose a location, and how to run a nonprofit organization.

The Restaurant Start-Up Guide
Peter Rainsford, David H. Bangs (Upstart Publishing Co., Inc., 1997)
A book written by internationally known restaurant consultant Peter Rainsford and business planning guru David "Andy" Bangs. It provides advice on what type of restaurant to start, what focus to bring to your restaurant, what market to target for your restaurant, how to find the best location, and how to develop your menu.

Retail in Detail: How to Start and Manage a Small Retail Business
Ronald L. Bond (The Oasis Press, 1996)
Covers all the steps of planning, opening, and managing a retail store, beginning with an honest assessment of whether the reader is really suited to running a business. Contains practical information on planning a store opening, from selecting a product line and hiring employees to buying an initial inventory and obtaining the required permits, licenses, and tax numbers.

Small Business Formation Handbook
Robert E. Cooke (Wiley, Johns & Sons, 1999)
A complete guide to formations for the new business owner. This comprehensive book describes the different types of business formations. The book offers examples of tax

consequences as well as liability scenarios. Also included are sample legal forms, such as articles of incorporation and stockholder's agreements, and relevant IRS forms.

The Small Business Handbook: A Comprehensive Guide to Starting and Running Your Own Business
Irving Burstiner (Simon & Schuster, 1997)
This instructional handbook offers practical advice on finding the right business for you, targeting customers, getting financing, choosing a location, hiring and managing employees, marketing your products and services, pricing for profit, distribution, managing the company's finances, planning for growth and expansion, and much more.

Start up: An Entrepreneur's Guide to Launching and Managing a New Business
William J. Stolze (Career Press, Inc., 1999)
Provides advice to those who want to embark on a new venture, have started a new business in the past few years, or who are seasoned pros. It addresses key problems that are crucial to the success of any new business, including information on how to write a successful business plan, what is most important to your business's success, how to pick a mentor, and the benefits of small companies.

Start Your Own Business in Thirty Days
Gary Joseph Grappo (Berkley Publishing Group, 1998)
This book offers 30 key concepts that will help you launch your own successful venture. With helpful charts and problem-solving tips, this guide covers discovering the business that's right for you, preparing a game plan, developing leads and networking, generating sales and following up, staffing your company, and using the internet for marketing and promotion.

Starting and Building Your Own Accounting Business
Jack Fox (Wiley, John & Sons, 1999)
This book details the advantages and disadvantages of setting up and running your own accounting operation. It explains how to establish and develop a business plan, how to prospect for new clients, the types of advertising and sales promotion techniques that are successful, the fee to charge and how to collect, how to plan for growth, and how to buy a business or sell your own business.

Starting and Running a Nonprofit Organization
John M. Hummel (University of Minnesota Press, 1996)
A book for people who are forming new nonprofits; thinking about converting an informal, grassroots group to tax-exempt status; reorganizing an existing agency; or currently managing a nonprofit. The book describes, step-by-step, all of the phases of creating and operating a new nonprofit, including incorporation, establishing a board of directors, writing bylaws, obtaining tax-exempt status, creating a strategic plan, budgeting and grant seeking, understanding accounting principles, managing human resources, and creating a community relations plan.

Success for Less: 100 Low-Cost Businesses You Can Start Today
Rob Adams, Terry Adams (Entrepreneur Media, 1999)
This easy-to-use guide is packed with the latest, up-to-date expert information on current small-business trends and opportunities. It reveals 100 low-cost, in-demand businesses you can start with little or no money down. Profiles of successful entrepreneurs who started businesses give an insider's look at the world of entrepreneurship and offer practical advice you can use to get your own business off the ground.

The Unofficial Guide to Starting a Business Online
Jason R. Rich (IDG Books Worldwide, 1999)
A guide for the cyber-entrepreneur concerning every aspect of conducting business over the World Wide Web. Information includes advice on setting up websites, advertising, and marketing. Also includes addresses for hundreds of websites that can be used as start-up references.

Winning Strategies for Capital Formation: Secrets of Funding Start-Ups and Emerging Growth Firms without Losing Control of Your Idea, Project or Company
Linda Chandler (McGraw-Hill Companies, 1996)
This book focuses on the thought processes involved in planning financing and obtaining capital. It considers the determining factors in which businesses form and which sources of financing are appropriate, as well as preparing an appropriate business plan and financial statements, and a representation for investors that focuses on their needs. Included among its topics are: mental strengthening and preparation for "the money hunt"; building credibility with investors; structuring your business to meet your needs as well as your partners'; understanding the options; and attacking myths that block your path to success.

The Young Entrepreneur's Guide to Starting and Running a Business
Steve Mariotti, Tony Towle, Debra Desalvo (Crown Publishing Group, 1999)
This book contains real, inspirational stories of young people finding success in the business world. It includes the stories of Microsoft's Bill Gates, Motown Records' founder Berry Gordy, and young people who are just starting out. It provides a practical, step-by-step pathway, including everything you need to know to start your own business, from creating financial statements to developing marketing techniques.

INDEX

ACKNOWLEDGMENTS

AUTHOR'S ACKNOWLEDGMENTS

I would like to thank Charlotte Hingston for reading my manuscript and for her many useful suggestions. I would also like to thank my hard-working editors and designer and, finally Julie Servante and Stuart Ramsden for their kind assistance.

PUBLISHER'S ACKNOWLEDGMENTS

Grant Laing Partnership would like to thank the following for their help and participation in producting this book:
Photographer: Mark Hamilton
Proofreader: Nikky Twyman
Indexer: Kay Ollerenshaw
Models: Rhoda Dakar, Augustin Luneau, Katja Mazzei, Francis Ritter, Raffaella Somma.
Thanks also to Blue Island Publishing for kindly allowing us to use their premises.

The illustration on page 103 is used courtesy of amazon.com
The accounts book illustration on page 138 is reproduced with kind permission of Hingston Publishing Co.

PICTURE CREDITS

5 centre and below: gettyone stone; 16: gettyone stone; 23: The Stock Market; 26: Wolfgang Kaehler/Corbis; 36: Richard Olivier/Corbis; 40: gettyone stone; 62: gettyone stone; 63: Robert Harding Picture Library; 64: Paul Thompson/Eye Ubiquitous/Corbis; 68: RW Jones/Corbis; 79: Charles O'Rear/ Corbis; 82–3: gettyone stone; 85: gettyone stone; 88: gettyone stone; 92: Garden Picture Library/Ron Sutherland; 98: gettyone stone; 101: gettyone stone; 110: The Image Bank/Stephen Derr; 120: gettyone stone; 123: gettyone stone; 132–3: gettyone stone; 135: gettyone stone; 142: gettyone stone; 146: gettyone stone; 148: gettyone stone; 160–61: gettyone stone.

AUTHOR'S BIOGRAPHY

After serving in the RAF, Peter Hingston started his first business in 1979, working with cars near Oxford. He sold this, and later started an electronics manufacturing business in Barbados. Then, with his wife, he launched a fashion shop in Edinburgh, a national trade magazine, and a book publishing business. All traded profitably and were eventually sold, apart from the publishing business, which he runs today. He has written six books on running a small business, some of which have been bestsellers and translated into several languages. Peter is also a non-executive director of a large retail business in Barbados.